BLESSED

The Watchers Trilogy
Book 2

By

International
Bestselling Author

S.J. West

CONTENTS

COPYRIGHTS

Cover Design: coversbyjuan.com, all rights reserved.
Interior Design & Formatting by Stephany Wallace, all rights reserved.
Proof Read: Kimberly Huther.

Published by Watchers Publishing: October, 2012.
www.Sjwest.com

BOOKS IN THE WATCHER SERIES

The Watchers Trilogy
Cursed

Blessed

Forgiven

The Watcher Chronicles
Broken

Kindred

Oblivion

Ascension

Caylin's Story
Timeless

Devoted

Aiden's Story

The Alternate Earth Series
Cataclysm

Uprising

Judgment

The Redemption Series

Malcolm

Anna

Lucifer

Redemption

The Dominion Series

Awakening

Reckoning

Enduring

The Everlasting Fire Series

War Angel

Between Worlds

Shattered Souls

OTHER BOOKS BY S.J. WEST

The Harvester of Light Trilogy

Harvester

Hope

Dawn

The Vankara Saga

Vankara

Dragon Alliance

War of Atonement

Vampire Conclave Series

Moonshade

Sentinel

Conclave

Requiem

Circle of the Rose Chronicles

Cin D'Rella and the Water of Life

Cin D'Rella and the Golden Apple

Cin D'Rella and the Lonely Tower.

(Coming Spring 2019.)

ACKNOWLEDGMENTS

I would like to express my gratitude to the many people who were with me throughout this creative process; to all those who provided support, talked things over, read, wrote, offered comments, allowed me to quote their remarks and assisted in the editing, proofreading and design.

I would like to thank Lisa Fejeran, Liana Arus, Karen Healy-Friday, Misti Monen, and Erica Croyle, my beta readers for helping me in the process with invaluable feedback.
Thanks to Kimberly Huther my proofreader for helping me find typos, correct commas and tweak the little details that have help this book become my perfect vision. Thank you to Stephany Wallace for creating the Interior Design of the books and formatting them.

Last and not least: I want to thank my family, who supported and encouraged me in this journey.

I apologize to those who have been with me over the course of the years and whose names I have failed to mention.

CHAPTER 1

My life is blessed. Everyone should be woken up with kisses at least once in their lifetime. I could feel Brand's warm lips gently coaxing me to leave the world of dreams and join him in our reality. I opened my eyes, only to be mesmerized by the pale beauty of the man, my angel, lying next to me on my pillow.

"Good morning," he murmured in between kisses, which felt like the gentle flutter of butterfly wings against my skin.

We lay there, basking in the joy of being close to one another. How had I ever doubted Brand was the love I'd been waiting for all my life? I realized the feelings I once harbored for Will were just a glimmer of what true love was meant to feel like.

"You seemed to sleep well," Brand said, brushing his fingertips against the side of my face, instantly making me feel cherished.

"I must have been exhausted. I don't even think I had a dream."

But if I didn't dream...

"You didn't sleep last night?" I asked. I knew if Brand had slept and dreamt, I would have experienced his fantasy world; just one of the peculiarities about myself I had discovered in the last few days.

"I didn't have any reason to dream," he said. "I already had you in my arms."

I couldn't help but smile, even though his words sounded like they were a direct quote from a sappy romance novel.

"How do you do that?"

"Do what?" he asked, perplexed.

"Make my heart melt with just a few words."

He smiled, obviously pleased. "My words only affect you because you know I mean them."

After a long while of enjoying each other's company, we decided it was time to get out of bed and face the day we had ahead of us.

I knew we had promised my best friend Tara that we would explain everything to her about my abduction, and why Malcolm had lied to the police saying we had spent the six days I was missing vacationing together in Las Vegas. I wasn't looking forward to the talk with her. Telling her everything would just make the events of the past few days even more real for me. She was my only ground in an insane world. I knew after she understood everything, nothing would be the same again. I wouldn't be able to go back to the way my life had been before.

But, was that a bad thing? Trading in my ordinary existence for a chance at an extraordinary life with Brand seemed like a fair exchange.

Brand went down to cook some breakfast while I hopped into his bathtub for a quick shower. When I was done, I turned off the water and slid the curtain aside to step out.

"I can't *believe* he left you alone."

I quickly grabbed the shower curtain to hide behind, almost yanking it off its rail. Through the steam collected in the bathroom, I could see Malcolm leaning casually with his back against the door, facing me. Of course, he wore his red silk shirt open to expose his model-perfect chest and a pair of tight black jeans which left little to the imagination.

"Malcolm! What are you doing?" I hissed.

I felt my cheeks flush hotly. How much had he been able to see through the fog in the room? From the leering grin and pleased look on his face, I assumed he had seen a lot more of me than anyone else in the world had, except for maybe Utha Mae and my mom.

"I came to make sure you were all right, dearest. I did promise Tara I would stop by and check in on you. Anyway, it's a good thing I did. You shouldn't be left alone!"

"You need to leave. If Brand finds you in here there's going to be trouble, and that's the last thing I need right now."

"I could take him in a fight." Malcolm shrugged his shoulders, like it wasn't a big deal.

"Please, Malcolm," I pleaded. "For my benefit, he's trying to accept you. I don't want to ruin that. You're my friend. I don't want there to be any more tension than there already is between the two of you."

With a sigh of resignation, Malcolm said, "Oh, all right. But can I at least gloat that I've seen you naked before he has?"

Malcolm grinned, wiggling his eyebrows suggestively.

I tried to hold my temper in check. I didn't need to start yelling at my friend for his inappropriate behavior, even though I desperately wanted to.

"You know the answer to that," I told him through clenched teeth, feeling like I was scolding a teenage boy instead of an angel more ancient than time itself. "Now, get out. And don't forget about going to my apartment later for our talk with Tara. I'll call you when we're ready."

Malcolm made an extravagant bow in my direction.

"As you command, dearest."

Malcolm phased out of the bathroom to points unknown. I just hoped it wasn't anywhere near Brand.

After he left, I stood motionless for a good minute, just to make sure he wasn't planning to phase back in, uninvited. When it seemed the coast was clear, I grabbed a towel and went back into Brand's bedroom.

I really didn't want to put the T-shirt and jeans I'd been wearing for the last six days back on, but didn't have much of a choice. Although, maybe I could phase back into my apartment long enough to grab some fresh clothes. I closed my eyes and concentrated on my bedroom. I really didn't have a clue how I had phased out of my prison cell the night before, right as I was supposed to meet the person who wanted me dead. I just remembered thinking about Brand and wanting to be with him. Maybe if I just thought hard enough about where I wanted to go, it would work again.

I'm not sure how long I stood there trying to phase back into my apartment, but I eventually gave up and just put my old jeans back on. I rummaged through Brand's chest of drawers and found a plain white T-shirt to wear.

I made my way back downstairs and found Brand setting the table. I must have been trying to phase into my apartment a lot longer than I thought; at least long enough for Brand to make omelets, chocolate waffles, scones, bacon, sausage, and what looked like freshly-squeezed orange juice.

"Are we expecting guests?" I asked, surveying the feast.

"No. I just wanted to give you plenty to choose from. I wasn't sure how hungry you would be. Did they feed you?"

"Yes."

I didn't want to talk about that aspect of my time away. I didn't feel like reliving any of Robert's visits or what happened before I was able to escape. I knew I would have to tell Brand about my experiences eventually, but I didn't want to do it just yet. I wasn't ready.

When I looked up from the table into Brand's eyes, I could tell he knew I wasn't telling him the whole truth with my simple yes, but he didn't push me to tell him anything more.

"Lilly?"

I turned to the front door at the gentle whisper of my name from a friendly, familiar voice. Abby stood there, wearing a sherbet-orange-and-pink wig and a white eyelet summer dress. She walked to me quickly, embracing me in a tight hug.

"Are you all right, love?" She pulled away slightly to look up at me with her hazel eyes. "I've been worried sick about you. What happened?"

Brand and I gave Abby the condensed version of the events after my capture by Justin, not really wanting to dwell on the specifics. The pain of our forced separation was still too fresh. We invited Abby to have breakfast with us. She, of course, jumped at the opportunity, since she hated to cook for herself. Rose Marie usually did all of her cooking, but Abby told me she and Carl would be gone for a while.

"Their mother is sick, so they needed to go home to be with her," Abby told us.

"I didn't realize they were brother and sister," I said.

"They probably won't be back for a month or more."

I couldn't honestly say I would miss Rose Marie. She always made me feel uncomfortable when I was around her. She didn't seem to like me for some reason. I barely knew Carl, so his absence wasn't particularly troubling to me either.

Out of the corner of my eye, I noticed Brand sitting back in his chair, watching Abby and me talk with one another. I got the distinct feeling he wanted to say something but wasn't sure if he should. Finally he cleared his throat, gaining our full attention.

"I'm not sure if this is the right time to tell you this," Brand said to me hesitantly. "But I feel funny having you both sit here and you not know who Abby really is. I don't want there to be any secrets between us."

What was he talking about? Abby was his cousin, wasn't she? Oh, but how could that be if he was an angel?

"Is Abby an angel too?" I asked.

"No."

The worried look in Brand's eyes told me he was concerned about how I would react to his next words.

"She's my daughter."

I looked back at Abby, completely dumbstruck by this announcement.

"Well, about bloody time that was out in the open," Abby said, pouring a liberal amount of syrup onto her waffles. "I really hate lying to people I like."

"Daughter?" I turned to Brand, still trying to wrap my brain around what he'd just said.

"You remember when Tara asked me if I'd ever been in love, that day on the Commons terrace?"

I nodded.

"Abby's mother was that woman."

"But I thought that was a long time ago. Abby looks like she's in her twenties."

"Our children age, but at an incredibly slow rate," Brand answered.

Which brought up an interesting question...

"You don't age, do you?" I asked.

"No," he said, almost as if he was apologizing for his immortality.

It was all he had to say. There was no way we would be able to grow old together and have a normal life, even though he wanted that just as much as I did. It was a detail that would have to take a number in the line of my worries. I didn't really care what people might think about us later in life when I was eighty and he still looked like he did now. Why should I fret about what people thought, as long as I was able to spend my life with him? But what worried me most was Brand. How would he feel being left behind after I died?

It was a concern that would have to be pushed back for now, too far in the future to be classified as a real problem at the moment. Right now we needed to focus on the present. Like finding out what Lucifer's plan was for me, who ordered Justin to kidnap and murder me, and why I possessed the power to phase like an angel.

"You're not upset about it, are you?" Abby asked me, mistaking the reason for my silence.

I put my hand over Abby's resting beside me on the table.

"No," I squeezed her hand lightly before letting it go. "It doesn't bother me. I'm just glad to know the truth."

"Good," she said, relieved. "I always thought you'd under-stand. Now I don't have to wear these wigs around you anymore."

Abby pulled the sherbet-colored wig off, revealing the most beautiful head of white hair I've ever seen. It shimmered in the light as she ran her fingers through the strands, as if they were made from diamond dust.

"Why do you cover that up?" I asked, experiencing an uncontrollable urge to run my own fingers through her white mane.

"It draws a lot of attention," she answered. "I've tried dyeing it, but it doesn't stick. So, I wear the wigs when I have to go out."

"Are the contacts used to hide something, too?" I asked.

"No, I just like them," she confessed with a guilty smile. "They look like Dad's, naturally."

I wanted to ask Brand if there was any way he and I would ever be able to have children of our own. I felt confident I already knew the answer to that from what Malcolm told me not so long ago. He said the mothers of the children of the Watchers lost their lives early in the pregnancy, because their bodies were taken over by the babies, leaving the mother's body an empty shell, simply kept alive until the child was ready to be born. I can't say it didn't make me a bit sad to realize I would never give birth to a child of my own, but having children had never been a high priority for me.

After we ate breakfast and cleaned up, I called Tara to let her know we were on our way to the apartment.

"I'll be waiting," was all she said.

I knew then that she was definitely not going to make this easy on us.

I called Will and Malcolm to let them know we were heading over to talk with Tara. I knew it was going to be hard to explain everything to her, and I needed the back-up of my small troupe of angels to face the challenge.

"Maybe it won't be so bad, love," Abby said to me before we left Brand's house.

"No, Tara knows we've all been lying to her," I replied, an uncomfortable knot forming in the pit of my stomach. "She won't let that go easily. I can't say I blame her. I'd be mad, too."

"She'll understand," Brand said, putting a comforting arm around my waist. "She was devastated when we couldn't find you. I've never seen a human grieve the way she did. I think, once she gets the answers she needs, everything will be fine."

When we arrived at the apartment, Will and Malcolm were already in the parking lot, sitting in their cars, waiting for our arrival. I could only assume they didn't want to go in and be met by Tara's questions before I got there. I hugged them both and thanked them for coming to help.

When I stepped into the apartment, I definitely noticed a tension in the air that I had never felt before.

Tara was sitting in a chair at the kitchen table with her hands clasped tightly together in front of her, watching us all file in one by one. I felt like an errant schoolgirl about to be disciplined by her teacher. I sat across from her while everyone else found a place to stand or sit in the small living room.

"Start explaining," was all she said to me.

"What do you want to know first?"

"Where were you? And why did Malcolm lie to the police?"

"I was being held captive by someone. Malcolm lied because there wasn't any reason to tell the police where I'd been or who had me. There isn't anything they can do to him and, more than likely, they would have just thought I'd gone insane if I'd tried to tell them the truth."

"Who had you? Why wouldn't the police believe the truth?"

I took in a deep breath and explained what I knew to Tara: everything about Brand, Will, and Malcolm being fallen angels; everything about the strange accidents that had happened in my life, including the loss of the real Will that night at the lake and the fact the Will we knew had been sent by Lucifer to protect me from them, and almost everything that happened to me while I was being held captive by Justin. I tried to be as concise as I could be.

"That's all I know," I finished. "If you need to know anything else, you'll have to ask one of the guys."

Tara sat through my explanation without saying a word, hardly moving, just staring at me.

She looked to the roomful of angels behind me and then looked back at me.

"Lilly, have you lost your mind? Did somebody brainwash you while you were gone?"

"No, Tara. You wanted the truth. I just told you the truth. I know it sounds crazy, but it's the way things are."

"What did y'all do to her?" Tara stood up and walked closer to the guys. "Lilly ain't never lied to me before now, and I want to know what's going on!"

"It's not a lie, Tara," Will said. "Everything she just told you is the truth."

"Oh yeah? Prove it." She crossed her arms over her chest and dared them to do something to show her that what I had said was true.

One by one, they all disappeared and then reappeared.

Tara became a blur of motion as she dashed into her bedroom and slammed the door shut behind her.

I glared at the guys as I stood and went to her door. "You could have given her some warning."

Malcolm grinned and shrugged. Brand looked worried and came to stand with me at her door and Will responded with, "She said she wanted proof, Lilly. It was the simplest way."

"Oh, Lord Jesus," I could Tara praying fervently behind her door. "What the hell's going on?"

"Tara, are you all right? I know it wasn't the most subtle way to show you I wasn't lying, but you can't deny what you just saw either."

"Oh, yes, I can!"

I looked to Brand, at a complete loss as to what we should do.

"Tara?" Brand said through the door. "You have nothing to fear from us. Come back out so we can all talk."

"Y'all just need to stay away from me!"

"Tarajinka Shovanda Jenkins," Will said as he came to join Brand and me by the door. "If you don't open this door, I'm coming in there!"

"You just stay where you are, Will Allen! Or whatever the hell you are!"

"This is absurd," Will said, and vanished.

I heard Tara scream as if she'd just been stabbed.

"Stop that, Tara," I heard Will admonish her on the other side of the door. "You're being ridiculous. You've known me all your life. Have I ever tried to harm you in any way in all that time?"

I could tell Tara was thinking about what he said, because she was quiet.

"Well, there was that time you put that spider in my bed," she said. "I never forgave you for that, Will Allen."

"We were nine years old, for goodness' sake, Tara. It was a prank."

"Well, it sure enough seemed *evil* to me. How do I know the devil didn't put you up to it?"

"Tara, you're being silly," he told her. "We're best friends. Lilly is standing outside that door right now, and you're sitting in here, cowering. I know how much you missed her when she was gone. She needs you to be strong for her now. We all need to help her figure out what's going on."

Tara whispered something, but I couldn't make it out from where I stood.

"It'll be ok," Will said to her kindly, as if he was speaking to a frightened child. "You just need to trust us, Tara."

After another minute, the lock on Tara's door was finally unlatched, and she came out with Will standing close behind her.

"You know I love you more than anything, girl," she said, standing there with her shoulders hunched over. "And I don't intend to let the devil himself take you away from me again."

She wrapped her arms around me, and I knew then that everything would be all right.

Once Tara was calm enough to talk rationally, we all sat in the living room to discuss what needed to be done next. Brand and I sat on the futon. Malcolm sat in the rocking chair, and Will and Tara brought in two kitchen chairs.

"So," Tara said sitting down in her chair, "none of you angels knows what the devil wants with Lilly?"

"He won't tell me," Will answered, sitting down in his chair. "I ask him every time I see him, but he just tells me it's better if I don't know."

"Well, you know it can't be good. I don't remember hearing about anything good coming from something he did, right?"

"Not that any of us have ever seen," Brand acknowledged.

"While Lilly was missing, Will and I talked about doing something," Malcolm said. "We'd like to test Lilly's blood."

"Test it?" I asked. "What for?"

"Well, we know you're different in some way. Especially now that we know you can phase," Will said.

"Yeah," I hesitated to tell them what I found out that morning. "I know I can do it, but I'm not sure how to trigger it. I tried to phase back to the apartment to pick up some fresh clothes this morning, but it didn't work."

"You probably just need to practice," Will said. "I know when I take over a new body, it takes me a while to get it accustomed to phasing."

"I honestly don't know how I did it last night to escape," I confessed.

"Fight or flight instinct," Malcolm said. "You knew you were going to die if you didn't do something, dearest. Your mind and body worked together to get you where you would be the safest."

"I can help you practice phasing, if you want," Will offered. "You need to be able to do it whenever you need to. That way, no one can just grab you like they did last time."

"So what do you think testing my blood will tell us?" I asked Will.

"We're mostly interested in looking at your genetic profile to see if your DNA is different in some way from a normal human's. We know you can phase, which indicates you must have some characteristics similar to angels, and we know your blood doesn't interest the Watchers who are vampires. I'm just not sure who we can trust to do the tests."

"I know of someone," Brand said. "He's a fellow Watcher. He has a private lab where we can run the necessary tests."

"Good," Will said. "If there's something different about Lilly, genetically, it might give us the information we need to figure out what's going on. We need to know why Lucifer wants her. Once we know that, maybe we can come up with a list of suspects who would want to stop him from using her."

"Well," Tara said, "I'll let y'all handle all this business. We need to figure out what we're gonna tell Utha Mae and Lilly's mom about where she's been."

Malcolm looked confused. "Why not tell them the Las Vegas story I made up? The police seemed to accept it readily enough."

"Obviously, you haven't met my grandma," Tara said, crossing her arms in front of her chest as she leaned back in her chair. "She can smell bullshit a mile away. She's not going believe Lilly went anywhere without telling me first. And I ain't about to tell her the truth. She'd have a heart attack on the spot. Y'all need to figure something out. I told her last night I would call her this morning to explain things. She's going to want to know where Lilly's been."

"I'll handle it," I said, looking to Brand. "I should go see them today. Would you come with me?"

"Of course," he said, squeezing my hand reassuringly.

"So what are you going tell her?" Tara asked, skeptic that I could come up with something that would satisfy Utha Mae. "It's going to have to be good."

"I'll figure it out before I get there."

"Give me a call when you get back," Will said to me. "We need to practice your phasing. It has to take top priority. It's your best self-defense."

Tara called Utha Mae and told her Brand and I would be coming to her house to explain things.

On the drive over, I wracked my brain trying to think of something to tell Utha Mae that wouldn't be a lie.

"Couldn't we tell her the truth?" Brand asked. "Or do you think it would upset her as much as Tara seems to believe?"

"Honestly, I don't know. Utha Mae's always been religious, but I'm just not sure how she would respond to actually coming face to face with the reality of her beliefs."

"I think she's stronger than you or Tara gives her credit for."

"Maybe, but I just can't take that risk. If anything happened to her because of me..."

I couldn't finish the sentence. I knew I would have to lose Utha Mae one day. Like all kids, you grow up knowing your parents will eventually die, but it's so far in the future you just don't worry about it until you see age write the history of their lives on their faces and notice they don't move quite like they used to when you were younger. However, just the thought of losing Utha Mae brought me close to tears. She'd been my friend, my advisor, my source of comfort all my life. I couldn't lose her. I needed her, especially now.

I felt Brand take my left hand and kiss it gently, forcing me out of my sad reverie.

"Don't worry. Everything will work out," he promised.

I looked at him, my heart breaking all over again at his perfection.

"How do you know that?" I whispered.

"Because I believe God brought us together for a reason, Lilly. I'm not sure what His plan is for us, but I don't believe our meeting was merely by chance. We were meant for each other, and I'm not going to let anyone or anything take you away from me again."

It made me think of what I'd realized that morning.

"But you *will* lose me," I gently reminded him. "I'm human. I'll grow old and die one day."

"I know. It's not like the thought hasn't already crossed my mind a million times."

He was silent for a while, obviously thinking about something. I could tell he wasn't sure if he should say what was on his mind.

"Tell me what you're thinking," I urged, not wanting him to feel like he needed to keep his thoughts hidden from me.

"You don't know how much I wish I could become human," he finally admitted. "I'd give anything to have a normal life with you, but I just don't know of any way to do that, barring some sort of miracle."

"We'll never be able to have children, will we?"

At least with a child, he would have some small reminder of me after I was gone.

"No," he looked at me. "Do you remember the game we played when I asked if you wanted to have kids?"

"Yes," I replied, remembering the game of questions and answers. I won the right to ask Brand to show me as many of his favorite things as we could fit into a 24-hour period.

"We would have to adopt if you wanted a child. I swore when Abby's mother died the way she did I would never put another human through that. I didn't think I would love anyone else again until I saw you. I never imagined I could love someone as deeply as I do you. If you were ever killed because of something I did, it would break me, Lilly. There's no way I could recover, because I just wouldn't have the will."

His words broke my heart. How had I earned the right to have someone love me the way he did? It made me wish we could hide from the problems in our lives and simply concentrate on us. It was a romantic notion I knew would never have a chance of coming true unless we figured out why Lucifer needed me.

"So, will normal birth control be enough to prevent me from getting pregnant?"

"I think so. I need to consult with someone about that before we ever make love, but I'm pretty sure it's all we need."

"How long has it been since you... you know...did that with someone?"

The flush of color that covered Brand's otherwise-porcelain white face told me what I needed to know even before he confirmed it verbally.

"Abby's mother is the only one I've ever shared a physical relationship with."

"Why?" I couldn't help but ask.

"Because I can't do that with someone I don't love, and I'm not one to fall in love easily."

"Were you married to Abby's mother?"

"Yes."

"Do you see us getting married one day?"

"Of course," he took his eyes off the road for a split second to look at me. "Don't you?"

"Yes, but I'd really like to graduate college first. Would you mind waiting that long?"

Brand smiled. "Lilly, I can wait as long as you need me to. I'm in no rush. As long as I can be with you every day in between, I really don't care how long you want to wait to get married."

"And are you ok with waiting to make love until then?"

"You're worth waiting for," he said, kissing my hand. "But do I have your permission to dream about that moment while I'm waiting?"

"Only if you share it with me every so often."

He chuckled softly, "Deal."

CHAPTER 2

When we arrived at Utha Mae's, I was surprised to see my mother come out of her trailer and greet us before we even stepped out of the car. I swear I think Cora still thinks she's seventeen and a go-go dancer. She was wearing a tight denim mini-skirt, white halter top and three-inch blood-red stilettos. Apparently, she was trying something different with her brown hair, because it looked permed and teased into a bird's nest on top of her head.

"Hey, sweetie," she said, giving me a quick hug. I saw her eyes quickly take in Brand's Porsche and Brand himself as he got out of the car.

"Hi, Brand. I'm surprised to see you here." She looked down at me, confused. "I thought you might be bringing your new boyfriend over, sweetie."

"New boyfriend?"

What was she talking about?

"Yeah, that man they showed on the news, big handsome guy with long black hair. They had a picture of him getting out of this red and black car at your apartment. I swear I think he looks like a Chippendale dancer I've seen before."

I could feel my body start to tremble.

"What did you hear on the news?" I asked my mom as Brand came to stand by me to place a comforting hand against the small of my back.

"They said you hadn't been missing at all. That you'd just been on vacation with that guy in Las Vegas and forgot to tell anyone. I told people you probably just needed to get out of town after all that business with the crazy girl trying to kill you. I asked Tara not to involve the police, but she wouldn't listen to me. Who was that guy, sweetie?"

"Just a friend. He's not my boyfriend. Brand is."

I could tell by my mother's expression that she had surmised that fact already.

"Well, you better go talk to Utha Mae. She was awfully upset when we didn't know where you were last week. Come on over to my place when you get through talking to her. I'd like to ask you about something."

Cora gave me a kiss on the cheek and went back into her trailer.

I couldn't move. Why had my mother just accepted Malcolm's lie so easily? It was just another piece of proof that she didn't know me at all. It wasn't in my character just to leave town without telling someone where I was going. I didn't live as she had all her life, doing what she wanted whenever she wanted, no matter how selfish it was.

"Are you all right?"

The worry in Brand's voice made me snap out of my reverie.

"Everyone's going to think I'm some kind of floozy now," I said, completely despondent. "How am I going to face people at school? Dr. Barry's going to think I'm a complete flake."

I felt like crying. Brand pulled me into his arms, instantly making me feel a little bit better - comforted and loved at least.

"Don't worry about what other people think," he told me. "The ones who matter the most know the truth. Don't let the rest of the world bother you."

"But what if Utha Mae believes it, too? I couldn't stand it if she were disappointed in me."

"Come on. Let's go talk with her."

Brand took my hand and walked me up to Utha Mae's front door. After he knocked, we heard her tell us to come in.

She was sitting at her kitchen table, shelling purple hull peas into a glass bowl on her lap.

"Hey, child," she said, looking up at me and smiling. "Come have a seat. I think we need to have a talk."

Brand sat beside me, holding my hand, trying to provide me the strength I needed to talk to Utha Mae.

"Now," she said, setting the bowl half full of peas onto the table, giving me her full attention. "Can you tell me where you've been this past week? 'Cause I know that story they told on the TV isn't true. I didn't raise you to run wild in Sin City with a stranger."

The relief I felt from her words untied the knot in my stomach.

"Thank you for not believing that," I said.

"Can you tell me what's really going on?"

"I can't tell you everything; at least not right now. I just need you to trust me, Utha Mae."

She leaned forward and put her hand on my knee. "Are you in trouble, baby? Can I help you somehow?"

"I am in trouble," I said, unable to lie to her. "And there really isn't anything you can do to help me, but I have people who can.

We just need time to figure out some things. Maybe after everything is over we can talk about it, but right now I just need you to believe in me. As long as you do, I won't worry about what anybody else thinks about me."

"I'll always believe in you, baby."

I got up from my seat and hugged Utha Mae. I fought back my tears of relief. I don't know what I would have done if Utha Mae had believed the lie Malcolm concocted for the benefit of the police, to explain my sudden disappearance. It hadn't even occurred to me that the story would reach the news media.

"Now then," Utha Mae said when I finally let her go. "I hope y'all came hungry 'cause I made a ham, chicken and dumplings, and I'm gonna boil these peas up and make some biscuits, too."

"You know I can't pass up your chicken and dumplings," I kissed her on the cheek, feeling lighter of heart than I had all day.

"Why don't y'all go get your mom, baby? I bet she hasn't eaten anything yet."

"Ok, we'll go get her."

"If it's all right," Brand said. "I think I'll stay here and help Ms. Jenkins finish cooking."

"Sure," I said heading for the door. "I'll be back in a bit. I got the feeling Mom wanted to talk to me in private about something anyway."

As I closed the door, I heard Brand say, "I'd like to ask you something, Ms. Jenkins."

I made a mental note to ask what that was all about later.

When I went inside my mom's trailer, I found her sitting on the couch in the living room, thumbing through the latest issue of *Vanity Fair*.

"Hey, Mom. What did you want to talk to me about?" I asked, sitting down beside her.

"Are you using birth control?"

The bluntness of her question caught me off-guard, but I quickly recovered. I had nothing to hide.

"Why should I? I'm still a virgin."

"Well, you don't have to tell me the truth." She gave me a business card. It was for a gynecologist in Lakewood, named Dr. Laura Spencer. "She's a good doctor."

"I'm not lying to you, Mom. I *am* a virgin. Why's that so hard to believe?"

"Well, honey, no one spends a week with a man like what I saw on TV and comes back a virgin."

"Well, I'm not like some people. I know how to keep my legs together." I tried to contain my temper, but my words couldn't hide how I was feeling. My mom had always said my thoughts were mirrored on my face anyway. I was sure she could see what I thought about her insinuation.

"All right, maybe you still are," she conceded, "but you're getting older now, and I'm sure if you haven't already had sex, it'll be in your near future; especially if you and Brand stay together this time. Guys like him don't stick around with a girl who isn't giving something out."

Never in my life had I felt like slapping my mother more than in that moment.

"You don't know anything about Brand. He's not like the guys you go out with. He actually *respects* me. He doesn't mind waiting until we're married before we make love. He's not hanging around me because he thinks I'll spread my legs for him whenever he wants. He actually loves me, Mom! As odd as that concept might seem to someone like you, he loves me for who I am, not for what I give him!"

I knew I was yelling by the end of my tirade, but I didn't care. How dare she talk about Brand as if he was someone who would leave a girl just because she wouldn't have sex with him!

"Well, I hope you're right, sweetie," my mother said, changing her tune quickly after my outburst. "Maybe I've just been looking for someone to replace your father for so long, I've become cynical about falling in love. I just don't want you to get pregnant too young. It can be a hard life, especially if the father isn't around to help out."

My anger was deflated slightly by her words. I knew how hard she had struggled to put food on our plates and keep a roof over our heads.

"I know, Mom. I wish you could find someone to love, too. Now that I know what it really feels like, I can't say I blame you for trying so hard to find it. You just need to start going out with a better class of men. Honestly, the guys you've brought home just aren't good enough."

"I know," she said with a sigh. "I've been thinking that, too."

"Listen, I do appreciate you trying to look after me. And I promise you, if Brand and I decide to have sex, I'll be on birth control."

It was either that or death anyway. At least now I knew a doctor who could help me when the time came.

I put the card in my back pocket.

"Come on," I said, holding out my hand to my mother. "Utha Mae's fixed lunch for us. You know you can't pass up her chicken and dumplings any more than I can."

When we stepped into Utha Mae's kitchen, I heard her

humming a happy tune while she cut up some bacon and tossed it into the boiling pot of peas on the stove. Brand was rolling up the last of the dough for biscuits, a bright smile lighting his handsome face.

"What's got you two so happy?" I asked, immediately suspicious something was going on.

They both just shrugged and gave each other what looked like a conspiratorial glance.

After we ate, Utha Mae made us take the leftovers home for Will and Tara.

When we got back on the road, I pressed Brand a little harder for an answer.

"What did you and Utha Mae talk about while I was over at my mom's?"

He just smiled and shook his head. "Nothing you need to know about yet."

"I thought you said we weren't going to have any more secrets between us."

"Let me have this little one for a while. You'll know soon enough."

"Is it at least something good?"

"I think so," he said, refusing to say anything else.

I decided to let it pass. If I were being honest, I had a secret of my own that I had no intention of ever telling Brand about: Malcolm's unexpected visit while I was showering. Brand could have his little secret, and I would keep mine for as long as I could.

"I've got a question for you," he said. "Where's the most romantic place you can think of?"

"Gosh, I don't know. Paris was nice. There were a lot of couples there who seemed to really enjoy it."

Brand's brow creased. "When were you in Paris?"

"Do you remember that Sunday I spent with Malcolm?"

"He took you to Paris?"

"Well, he took me to Venice first, but I told him I didn't like the water. Then he took me to the Eiffel Tower and gave me a tour of Paris."

"Where else did he take you?"

"He took me to see a pyramid he said he helped build. And then he took me to his house in Hawaii."

"Is that all?" Brand asked in a tense voice.

"Yes, that's all."

The frown on Brand's face almost made me laugh. I could tell he was disappointed he hadn't been the first one to take me on a whirlwind date. I didn't like seeing him upset, though. I took his free hand off his lap and held it tight.

"Don't look like that. You know there's nowhere in the world I'd rather be than with you."

"I know, Lilly. It's just that I wanted to be the first one who showed you those things."

"We'll have plenty of other firsts to share with each other," I promised him.

He couldn't help but smile at my subtle reminder.

"True. At least he won't be the first one to see you with all your clothes off."

I involuntarily tensed.

"Lilly?" I could hear the disbelief clearly in Brand's voice, and cursed myself for being so easy to read. "He hasn't seen you naked, has he?"

I couldn't lie. I just couldn't. I desperately *wanted* to. Why couldn't I just say no and try to mean it? But I knew he would see right through a lie.

"He was in the bathroom this morning when I was about to step out of the shower." I said it so fast I wasn't sure if he'd heard it clearly.

Apparently he did. Brand took his hand out of mine and gripped the steering wheel so tight I thought he was going to break it in two.

"Please don't be mad," I begged.

He looked over at me, and I could see it was too late. He was already mad.

"I'm not mad at you. I'm mad at that overstuffed imbecile you insist on keeping as a friend."

"Please, don't do anything to him. He's just a big kid some-times. I swear he's worse than some of the teenage boys I went to high school with, but he does care about me."

"I'm fully aware of the fact that he cares for you, Lilly," Brand said, trying to keep his temper under control. "But he's not getting off the hook as easily as you want."

"What are you going to do?"

"He won't be hurt permanently, if that's what you're concerned about."

"What is that supposed to mean?" I asked, Brand's words not reassuring me at all.

"Malcolm and I are just going to have a little talk. But, you need to know if he does anything like that again after we talk, he won't be welcomed into my home again. I've been trying my best to be civil to him for your sake, but disrespecting you like that in my own home is something I cannot let slide by unpunished."

I wasn't sure what type of punishment he was talking about. For all I knew, angels couldn't be killed, but I honestly didn't know. And now wasn't the time to ask just how angels could be hurt. I didn't want to give Brand any more ideas than what he was already thinking.

The rest of the ride was mostly in silence. I just kept worrying about what Brand was going to do, and I think he was mentally running through his plans for Malcolm. When we got back into town, Brand pulled out his cell phone to call someone.

"Hey, are you still at Lilly's apartment?" I assumed he was talking to Will. "Can you go back there and look after her for me? I need to have a private talk with Malcolm." Brand looked over at me. "Lilly can tell you why if she wants. We'll be there in a few minutes."

He ended the call and put his phone back in his pocket.

"Please don't make me regret telling you the truth," I begged, wishing I had been able to keep this morning's events a secret. "I need you both."

"Don't worry so much about Malcolm, Lilly. He can take care of himself. He doesn't need you to defend him."

"It's my fault you found out."

"Did he tell you to keep it from me?"

If it were possible, I think the mere idea of that made Brand even angrier.

"No. In fact, he wanted to gloat about it to you."

Brand snorted. "That certainly sounds more like him."

We pulled into my apartment complex's parking lot. By the time we got all the food in that Utha Mae made us bring back, I saw Will's Honda Civic park right beside Brand's car.

Brand leaned down and gave me a quick kiss.

"I'll be back as soon as I can. Stay close to Will." And he phased.

"What's going on?" Will asked, coming to stand by me.

"Can angels kill each other?"

"Not exactly. Why?"

"What does 'not exactly' mean?"

"Well, it depends on which angels you're talking about. Watchers can rip each other apart, but that doesn't kill them. They can reattach the pieces or regenerate new ones. Fallen angels like me can have the body die, but then all we have to do is take over another one. What's going on?"

"They can rip each other's limbs off?" I asked in disbelief.

"Sure. What's going on, Lilly?"

"I think Brand's going to rip something off of Malcolm," I said, resigned to the fate of my friend. "He said it wouldn't be permanent."

"What did Malcolm do?"

"Saw me get out of the shower naked this morning." I regretted telling Will this small bit of information as soon as the words left my mouth.

"He *what?*"

"He was just checking up on me is all," I tried to defend, but knew Malcolm's voyeurism wasn't defendable.

"Listen, I know you like Malcolm and, from all my talks with him this past week, I agree he's not as bad as I originally thought he was. However, he wants you, Lilly. If you give him even the slightest show of interest, he'll take it as you wanting him, too."

"Malcolm knows I love Brand. I think I've made it pretty clear."

"Yeah, I guess you have."

When I saw the look of hurt on Will's face, I instantly regretted proclaiming my love for Brand without considering how Will would be affected by it.

"I'm sorry," I said, remembering the declaration of love Will had made to me, only a couple of weeks ago.

"No, don't be sorry because you found someone who can love you the way you deserve to be. He may not be my first choice for you but you could have done worse, I guess."

"Well, thanks, I think." It seemed like a backwards compliment but that was better than resentment.

"At least he was smarter than me, and didn't try to keep himself distanced from you the way I did." The look of regret and loss on Will's face made me feel sad for him. I'd seen that same look on my own face a hundred times when I was pining for Will to return my love for him. To see it on his face brought back the memories of my own heartache.

"Why did you do that, Will? Would it have been so bad for us to be together?"

"I was scared, Lilly," he admitted. "I didn't feel like you should settle for something like me. You deserved better."

It made me wonder how my life would have turned out if Will had found the courage to tell me he loved me after that first kiss. Would we still be together? Would we be engaged, or possibly even married by now?

Then Brand's sweet words came back to me about how he thought our meeting wasn't just by chance. That God had planned for us to meet and love one another for a purpose. I hoped he was right. I prayed God had a hand in our finding each other because, if He did, then our love was meant to be and blessed by someone we desperately needed on our side right now. But whether God brought us together or not, I was thankful Brand hadn't decided to follow the same path as Will and stayed away from me because he thought it was the right thing to do for my sake. At least Brand had the courage to fight for our love.

"Utha Mae sent some leftovers from lunch. You better get in the apartment before Tara eats them all up," I told him, breaking the serious turn our conversation had taken.

After Tara and Will ate, Tara went to her bedroom for a nap and Will sat me down in the living room to begin my first lesson in phasing.

"Ok, you need to clear your mind of everything around you. Phasing is more of a psychic ability than a physical one. Once you clear your mind, think of where you want to go, like your bedroom. But don't just picture it. You have to convince yourself that you can feel the room around you. You're folding the molecules of space between where you are and where you want to go. You'll need to start thinking of the world as being fluid and bendable."

I tried to clear my mind. Once I had it cleared, I did what Will said and tried to visualize myself in my bedroom. I'm not sure how long I sat there trying to phase two feet behind me to the other side of the wall, but I finally just gave up.

"I can't do this," I said, feeling defeated. "Maybe it was just a fluke that I did it the first time."

"No, you can do it. It's just going to take some practice to stop thinking of the world as structured and start thinking of it as pliable."

"Why do you think I can phase? Do you think I'm part angel?"

"I'm not sure. That's why we want to do those tests."

"Can all offspring of angels phase?"

"No, that's what's odd. None of the Watcher children have

any of the abilities their fathers do. And angels like me can't get a human woman pregnant."

"Why? You're inside a regular human body."

"When we take over a body, we mutate the DNA slightly. It's enough to cause a significant enough difference and make mating with a human impossible."

I looked at the clock on the cable box below the TV, and saw it was already 5:00PM. Brand had been gone for at least an hour.

"What could be taking him so long?" I asked worriedly. "You're positive they can't kill each other?"

"Don't worry about Brand. He can take care of himself. Trust me."

As if he heard us talking about him, Brand suddenly appeared in the living room, startling me.

"I'm sorry, Lilly," he said, seeing me jump slightly. "I wasn't thinking."

I stood up and went to Brand. He quickly enveloped me inside his warm embrace. As far as I could tell, he was still in one piece.

"Did you give that jerk what he deserved?" Will asked, still sitting on the futon.

"He won't be appearing unannounced inside my house or Lilly's apartment anymore," Brand replied. "I told him if he needed to see her, he could knock on the front door like everyone else."

"You didn't tear any of his limbs off, did you?" I asked, looking up at my over- protective angel.

"Nothing he'll miss," Brand said cryptically.

I didn't want to know what that meant. As long as he was willing to let Malcolm continue to be a part of my life, I wasn't going to worry too much about it.

Tara came out of her bedroom, yawning loudly.

"So, you give the big guy an ass-whoopin'?" she asked Brand.

I had to tell her why Brand wasn't with me earlier. She wasn't exactly pleased with Malcolm either. I was sure she'd make her feelings known clearly, the next time she saw him.

"He won't be seeing Lilly in a compromising position again," Brand promised. "I think he understands the consequences of doing that now. If you two don't mind," Brand said to my friends, "I'd like some alone time with Lilly. It's been a busy day for both of us."

"Just have her back at a decent hour. We've got school tomorrow, and Lilly's got a lot of catching up to do," Tara said.

"Brand," I said, looking up at him, "I need to speak with Tara for a minute."

"All right," he said before giving me a quick kiss. "Don't take long, please," he whispered in my ear.

I knew what he was thinking. I desperately wanted to be alone with him, too. But Tara needed to understand some things first.

I motioned for her to follow me into my bedroom.

"What's up, girl?" she said sitting on my bed.

I sat down beside her. "Listen, I know you're trying to protect me and I love you for it, but you're going to have to understand that I intend to spend a lot of my nights with Brand."

"But..."

I held up my hand to stop her from saying another word in protest.

"Listen, if for no other reason, I need him to protect me, at least until I can figure out how to phase on my own whenever I need to. He can get me out of harm's way a lot faster than I can myself right now. Plus, I had a lot of time to think about things while I was away. Life's too short, Tara. I'm going to squeeze as much time as I can out of my life, and I want to be with Brand for most of it. I hope you can understand that. And you don't have to worry about us doing anything physical other than kissing. I've already told him I don't want to make love until we're married, and I don't intend to get married until I'm out of school. And, sometimes, I might want to stay over at Brand's, like tonight. You're just going to have to trust me to do what's right."

"Well, I can't say I like it, but I can understand where you're coming from. I won't hound you too much about it anymore. You're a grown woman."

It seemed like people kept saying that to me. If I was so grown, why did they still feel the need to protect me like I was a child?

"Thanks," I said, hugging her.

I packed a small overnight bag and went back out into the living room. I said goodbye to my friends, and Brand and I got into his car and headed to his house.

"What are we going to do?" I asked.

"Well, my plan was to kiss you until you fell asleep."

"Sounds like an excellent plan to me."

Brand took one of my hands in his when we stopped at a stoplight on the highway and, before I knew it, we were in his driveway.

"I'm not sure I'll ever get used to traveling like that," I told him.

"It gets old after a while. You miss a lot of what's going on around you. Sometimes it's more fun to do it the slow way, but I'm too impatient and selfish when it comes to our alone time. I can't justify driving ten minutes when we could be doing this."

With his last word, he phased us to his bedroom, and helped me forget all my troubles, at least for one night.

CHAPTER 3

When I woke up the next morning, I found Brand sitting casually in a chair beside the bed, watching me.

"Why are you sitting way over there?" I asked. The last thing I remembered was falling asleep in his arms the night before.

"I thought it was more appropriate. Lying next to you all night could have caused a problem."

"What problem?"

Brand grinned like he wasn't sure how to explain what he was thinking. "It's hard enough to just kiss you without taking things further, Lilly. Trust me. Your chastity is much safer if I don't stay in bed with you all night every night."

"Oh." Now I understood and felt a slight thrill, knowing the effect I had on him.

Brand drove me back to my apartment so I could get ready for school. Tara didn't say anything or look at me funnily when we walked into the apartment together. Apparently, she'd accepted what I told her the previous night about wanting to spend as much time as I could with Brand far more easily than I'd thought she would. She'd always been my protector, and now she was willing to hand that job over to Brand, at least partly. I think she was secretly relieved I had him to watch over me. It was highly unlikely anything would happen to me while in his presence.

I wasn't looking forward to going to my classes. I was sure everyone would be looking at me strangely, thinking I was a scarlet woman for having spent a week with a man like Malcolm in Las Vegas. And, to be honest, if I were them, I would probably be thinking the same thing. I tried not to worry about what other people thought but, even though you want to pretend it doesn't matter what strangers think of you, there is always that small voice inside your head, yearning to be accepted by all. No matter how hard I tried, the butterflies in my stomach would not abate their fluttering.

Thankfully, my first class was with Brand. As long as I was with him, I could handle anything life put in my way, including a room full of curious stares and quiet gossiping.

When Dr. Floyd entered the room, I could see he was making an effort not to stare at me directly, but I did see him shake his head a bit as he handed out a set of papers to the class. When I looked at the papers, I realized it was a test. My heart began to pound inside my chest. Obviously, I hadn't studied or prepared to take the test at all. I did read the chapters he'd assigned, but I wasn't sure I could remember enough detail to answer the questions lain out before me in perfect type.

Everyone else around me was busily answering the questions, while I looked down at the test in front of me with a despondent heart. I felt a lot like you do when you dream you've shown up to class without any clothes on, except I had shown up without enough knowledge inside my head. Great, I really was going to be the bottom of the bell curve now. So much for Brand's grand idea that I was going to ace my first test in this class. I looked over at Brand and he nodded his head as if saying 'Come on, you can do it'. He began answering his own test questions with unimaginable speed.

I decided answering at least part of the questions I knew was better than not answering anything at all. I took a deep breath and read the first question.

And then it happened.

Just like the phasing I'd been able to do to get out of the prison Justin kept me in, I instantly knew the answer to the question like I had known it all my life. Without knowing why or how, I realized I knew all of the answers to every question.

It only took me half the class period to finish the test, and I knew I had done well on it. Almost at the same time, I noticed Brand look up from his work. We ended up turning our papers in together.

As we walked hand in hand out the door, Brand asked, "How did you do?"

"I think I aced it," I answered. "It was like the answers just came to me out of nowhere but, at the same time, it was like I had known the information forever. Does that make any sense?"

"Not really," he said, not being able to hide his worry over my new-found talent.

"It's not an angel trait?" I asked, having already assumed that was the reason and finding it troubling that my conclusion was false.

"No, not that I know of; we only know so much because we've lived so long. Having total recall about something you've never actually known is not something I've ever known anyone to be able to do."

"So, what can angels do besides phase?"

"Well, we're incredibly strong and agile."

"Hmm, I don't think I'm either one of those. I'm about as agile as a slug." I thought about fact for a minute. "Will said phasing was more of a mental ability than a physical one. Maybe my abilities are more mental than physical. Is that possible?"

"I think anything is possible with you, my love."

I smiled up at him and hugged his arm close. "That's the first time you've called me that."

He stopped me on the sidewalk and turned me so I was facing him. He looked deep into my eyes, as if making sure I fully heard his next words to me.

"You are my love," he said, bringing me in closer to his body and kissing me lightly on the lips, "and my life. It's hard for me to explain to you how dark my world was before we found each other. I need you so much, it scares me sometimes. I don't think I can tell you with words how much I love you, but I'll try my best to show you."

"You sure do make it hard on a girl," I said, ready to throw my books down and ravish him on the spot, not caring how such a scene might lower my already-tarnished reputation.

Brand's lips stretched into a roguish smile and his grey eyes lit up with joy.

"Well, I certainly hope I do," he said. "Otherwise, I would be concerned I was doing something wrong."

Brand walked me to my English Composition class. He couldn't go in with me, but he stayed outside the door. All I had to do was yell if something happened.

"I don't think they would try to snatch you in front of so many witnesses, especially since they wouldn't be able to slip in and out without you making a scene. It's an unspoken code among the other Watchers that exposing our existence is unforgivable," Brand tried to reassure me.

When I entered the classroom, I went to sit beside Tara at our usual desks.

Ever since the whole Michelle incident, Nora kept as far away from Tara and me as she could get. She now sat at the front of the classroom, close to Ms. Conner's desk. Being the best friend of a psychopath had a tremendously adverse effect on Nora's popularity. She pretty much kept to herself nowadays, from what I understood. I'd heard a few of my classmates say she was just trying to get through the semester here, and planned to transfer to a different college in January.

I pretty much got the same reception in my English class that I had in Biology. People stared at me and whispered quietly to each other, but didn't say much directly to Tara or me. Of course, it helped to have Tara sitting beside me like a guard dog, ready to rip into the first person who even thought about making a snide remark directly to me or stare for too long.

After class, Ms. Conner asked that I stay behind to give me an extra assignment to make up for the week I was out. Apparently, I had missed a pop quiz, so I had to take that in front of her, too. Luckily, I had finished reading *Taming of the Shrew* and passed the quiz without much trouble.

"Ms. Nightingale," Ms. Conner said hesitantly while handing me back my graded quiz. "I'm not sure what happened to you last week, but you don't seem like the type of girl who would just run off with a man to Las Vegas and not tell your friends or family. I know it's none of my business, but if you ever need to talk with someone, I'm here for you."

I wasn't sure what to say. Not even my mom had thought to disbelieve Malcolm's lie. Why did a veritable stranger understand me better than my own mother?

"Thank you, Ms. Conner. I appreciate that."

"I don't presume to know you but, from reading your journal, I think I have a fair idea of the type of person you are. I just wanted you to know how I felt."

I thanked her again and walked out of the room feeling a little better about the day.

Brand walked me to my chemistry class and afterward took me off campus for lunch so I wouldn't have to endure any more stares.

"Humans have a short memory," he told me as we drove back to campus for our Physics class. "They'll forget about everything in a few weeks."

"Well, to be honest, I thought I would be more upset about it than I am. It's actually just irritating. I don't see any reason for people I don't even know to treat me like some pariah of society, and they're so wishy-washy. After what happened with Michelle, I can't tell you how many people came up to me and told me how sorry they were that I had to go through what I did. Then, I spend one week in Las Vegas with a gorgeous guy, and I might as well wear a large, red 'A' on my chest."

"Do you think Malcolm is gorgeous?"

I looked at Brand and couldn't help but grin at the concerned look on his face.

"You have nothing to worry about, Brand. You're beyond gorgeous to me. But, yes, Malcolm is very nice to look at. I'm not going to lie to you and say he isn't."

"Well, as long as I'm better looking, it's ok I guess."

The vanity of men. Just when you think they're indestructible, you find a chink in their armor that you wouldn't have thought was there.

Physics went pretty well. Luckily, the week I was out, the night lab was cancelled due to the TA being sick. It was one of the few classes I wasn't behind in.

Brand walked me to Dr. Barry's office after class. "I have something planned for us to do Friday night."

"Oh?" I said excitedly. "Are we going to do my blood test then?"

"No, we have to wait on that. My friend said the earliest he could see us would be this Saturday. But we'll get it done. I promise."

I was disappointed. I wanted to know what my DNA might be able to tell us. It made me even more curious about my father. Who had he been? But, was that all that was different about me? From what Will had said, I should either be like Abby if my father had been a Watcher, or I shouldn't exist because angels like him, who only inhabited bodies, basically became sterile after the possession. So where did that leave me?

"Then what are we doing?" I asked, standing outside Dr. Barry's office.

"It's a surprise. And don't even bother trying to get any details from me, because my lips are sealed on the subject." He made the motion of locking his lips and throwing away the key.

I couldn't help but laugh at him, sneaking in one more kiss before going into work.

Dr. Barry ended up being very empathetic about me missing a week of work.

"After almost being killed by that lunatic, it's understandable you needed to get away for a while and blow off some steam," she said. "Just try to remember to tell someone next time. Although, I can see how you forgot. That sure was a handsome man you had escort you to Las Vegas."

When work was over, I was glad to go home.

Home. That word took on a completely different meaning for me now. It didn't exactly represent any particular place anymore. When I lived with my mother, Utha Mae's trailer was more a home to me than the place my possessions were actually kept. Now, home was wherever Brand was. He was my center, the very core of my happiness and future.

Will was at my apartment when we got there, waiting outside the door.

"I asked Will to come over and help you practice your phasing some more," Brand told me. "I need to go take care of some things for our date Friday night."

"Won't you give me just a little hint?" I begged, doing my best to obtain just a small bit of information from him.

"No, and don't ask anymore, my love." With a gentle kiss, he sent me on my way. "I shouldn't be more than a couple of hours."

"Hey," Will said when I walked up to him. "Any news on when Brand's friend can do those tests?"

I unlocked the door to the apartment, with Will following me inside. "Yes, we're supposed to go on Saturday."

"Cool. I'd like to go with you two when the results come in. I'm really curious about what they might tell us."

"Me and you both." I laid my books down on the kitchen table and opened the fridge to grab a couple of sodas for us.

"Oh, hey," I said, handing Will his soda and sitting down on the futon beside him. "I found another skill today."

I went on to explain how I had been able to answer the questions on my Biology test so easily.

"That's not something I've ever heard an angel being able to do. I always knew there was something weird about you, though," he said with a smile.

I popped him on the arm with my fist for his little joke at my expense.

Will tried to help me with my phasing, but I ended up sitting in the same spot, not being able to phase myself anywhere an hour later.

"I just don't understand why I can't do it whenever I want to," I said, frustrated by my inability to do what should just come naturally.

"Well, I'm sure you were more focused the first time, and you had a ton of adrenaline running through your system. It's just going to take more practice. It was hard for me, too, the first time I took someone's body over. It was like having to learn how to breathe again."

I heard a rattle of keys at the door and watched Tara step into the apartment. I jumped up in alarm as soon as I saw her.

Her hair looked like a pack of raccoons had fought on top of her head, and her shirt had been torn at the seams of both sleeves. There as a slight swelling across one of her cheekbones which indicated she'd been hit fairly hard, and a scratch along the side of her neck which stretched from her ear to her collarbone.

"What happened?" I asked, taking her books from her hands and setting them on the table.

"Got in a fight," she replied, slowly lowering herself onto the futon next to Will, as if it pained her to move so much.

"Who with?" Will asked.

"Some nosey-body girl outside the library."

"You weren't fighting about me, were you?" I asked, but already knew the answer to my question.

"She was mouthing off about stuff, and I just lost my cool."

"What was she saying?" I asked.

"You don't wanna know, girl. But she'll think twice about saying anything about you again, that much I can tell you."

"Tara, you need to just let it slide next time. I don't need you getting kicked out of school because of me. How do you think that would make me feel?"

"I know," Tara said, slightly chagrined. "I just have a hard time letting fools call you names in front of me. It just ain't right, Lilly Rayne."

I sat down beside Tara and hugged her close. I couldn't lecture her too much about trying to defend my honor. She had always been my protector. It would have been like asking the sun not to rise the next morning.

As a treat, I ordered out for Tara's favorite pizza, and invited Will to stay with us for supper. It felt so natural for the three of us to be together again. I missed the days when we would just hang out and talk about anything and everything. I hoped the new-found understanding between the three of us would last forever.

True to his word, as I could always depend on him to be, Brand came back to the apartment exactly two hours after he had left. He'd already made a trip back to his house to bathe, and had brought back some toiletries and extra clothes to spend the night at my apartment.

I saw Will raise an eyebrow at Brand's overnight bag, but he didn't say anything. He knew I needed someone close by who could phase me away from danger at a moment's notice.

As if knowing Tara would need a pick-me-up, Brand brought over the dirt he'd bought for her online from Georgia. She loved it, of course, and even got Will to try some of it. At least Will was on my side and agreed it was the worst thing he had ever put in his mouth.

When bedtime rolled around, Will left. Tara looked at Brand and me, with her arms crossed in front of her.

"I just want it made clear that I expect you to act like a gentleman with Lilly," she said, looking at Brand with her no-nonsense stance. "I understand why you gotta be close to her and all, but if I hear anything going on in her bedroom that shouldn't be, I'm coming in, is that understood?"

"The door will remain open. And after she falls asleep, I won't be staying in the bed with her," Brand promised. "I have no intentions of disrespecting Lilly, Tara. You know how much she means to me."

Tara dropped her arms to her sides. "I know. But you know I have to say what's on my mind, too."

Later in bed, Brand asked me, "Why is it so important to Tara for you to remain a virgin?"

"She lost her virginity our senior year of high school. The guy ended up being a real jerk about it, and she wants me to be the one who keeps to the purity pledge we took. I'm not sure why it's so important to her, exactly. I think it's just the fact that she had such a bad experience losing hers. It's made her put more importance on me keeping mine until I'm married."

"I'm glad you have someone like her in your life, but she needs to understand I wouldn't do anything you didn't want to do."

"I think she knows that," I said, tightening my hold around Brand as he lay next to me. I decided to change the subject. "So not even a hint about what we're doing Friday night? Can you at least tell me how to dress?"

"I'll arrange that. All I need you to do is be ready by seven that night. I'll ask Malcolm to come here and watch over you while you're getting ready."

"You trust him to do that?" I asked, surprised. "What about Will? I'm sure he'd be more than happy to come over."

"I'd rather Will didn't," Brand said cryptically.

"Why?"

"Having Will around would make the night feel odd for me, and I think it would be disrespectful to him in the long run."

Well, that certainly made me even more curious. What could he possibly have planned?

The next morning, I asked Brand to take me over to Malcolm's before my first class.

"Why?" he asked, not understanding my motives.

"He's my friend. I want to make sure he's all right. And I want to make sure he knows he can come see me when he needs to."

To be honest, I was worried Malcolm might fall off the wagon and kill someone because of the new rule Brand had made about seeing me. I knew I should be worried more about an innocent life being taken but, if I was honest with myself, I was more concerned about Malcolm's well-being. He had confessed to me that he didn't like the monster he had become. Killing people and drinking their blood was a weakness he detested about himself. I loved Malcolm as a friend, and didn't want to see him backslide into his old ways. I almost felt like I was his personal AA sponsor except, instead of alcohol, I was responsible for making sure he didn't indulge in his vampire cravings.

Brand phased us to Malcolm's house. When I knocked on the front door, a young man who looked closer to Brand's age than mine opened it. He was around six feet tall, with short-cropped white hair; hair exactly like Abby's. I could see a resemblance to Malcolm right away, but there was also a softness I had to presume came from his mother. I'd only seen Sebastian once before: the night Malcolm had come to Lakewood to kill me. At the time, Sebastian had been in his werewolf form. It was nice to see the human side of Malcolm's son before me.

"Lilly," Sebastian leaned down and gave me a quick peck on the cheek. "It's so good to see you again. My dad will be glad you came." Malcolm's son looked at Brand and just nodded. It wasn't a friendly nod; just one of acceptance that his presence was necessary.

"Where is he?" I asked.

"Here I am, dearest," Malcolm said, walking down the staircase from the second floor in a black T-shirt and faded jeans. It was the first time I'd seen Malcolm wearing a shirt that wasn't opened at the front to show off his well-defined chest.

"Brand," Malcolm acknowledged Brand much in the same way his son had, with a curt nod.

When Malcolm reached us, he picked me up and twirled me around like a father would a child, smiling his happiness.

"I've missed you the last couple of days," he admitted, holding me close before setting me down again on the floor.

I looked over at Brand, but didn't see the glower I had expected to on his face. It made me wonder what exactly had transpired between the two of them the other night.

"I just wanted to make sure you were all right," I told Malcolm, studying the color of his skin.

When we made our bargain that he could see me anytime he liked, as long as he didn't indulge in his craving for human blood, Malcolm told me his skin would become pinker if he ever consumed human blood, thus nullifying our agreement. It was a physical way for me to know he was keeping his end of our bargain. I noticed his skin looked as pale as ever, and let out a small sigh of relief.

"You shouldn't worry about me," he said, tenderly caressing my cheek with a crooked index finger. "I'm fine."

"Since we're here, Malcolm," Brand said, stepping up to my side, "I was wondering if you could watch over Lilly tomorrow evening at her apartment, say, from five to seven."

"Of course," Malcolm smiled down at me, obviously pleased he'd get to spend some time with me outside the presence of Brand.

"Would you mind if I talked with Malcolm alone for a few minutes?" I asked Brand.

"You don't have to ask my permission, Lilly." Brand looked uncomfortable with my request. I could see he felt awkward that I deemed it necessary to do such a thing. I simply didn't want to cause any more tension between the two of them.

I took Malcolm's hand and led him off to the study.

After closing the door to give us more privacy, I looked up at my friend and asked, "What happened when Brand came here the other night? He won't tell me much. I was afraid he might have ripped off an arm or a leg."

Malcolm chuckled while rubbing the side of his neck. "Not

quite. He just wanted to make sure I understood his feelings, and I got the message quite clearly."

"I'm so sorry. I didn't mean for him to find out about you seeing me that morning, but it just sort of ended up coming out."

"Don't worry so, dearest. If Brand hadn't come over here after learning about our little secret, I wouldn't have much respect for him. As it is, I'm surprised he controlled himself as well as he did. I can only imagine that it was the impact on your feelings that kept him from tearing me to shreds. He knew if he hurt me too badly it would upset you more than anything I did. He was only protecting your honor. I expected nothing less from him."

"What did he do to you exactly?"

"I'd rather not say, but he made his point."

"Well, I hope whatever happened won't affect our friendship. I care about you, Malcolm. You've become very important to me."

"Lilly," Malcolm moved his body closer to mine, taking my hands in his, and holding them close to his chest. "Are you sure Brand is the right one for you?"

I knew what Malcolm wanted. He wanted some small shred of hope that my concern over his well-being was really caused by some deep-seeded love I might harbor for him.

"He's the only one for me. I can't live without him. I can barely breathe when he isn't next to me."

"I see," Malcolm slowly stepped back, letting my hands go. "Well, if things ever change between the two of you, I hope you know I'll be here waiting."

"Things won't change," I told him, wanting him to understand the true connection Brand and I had. "You shouldn't wait for me, Malcolm."

"I can wait," he said. "It's not like I don't have the time."

When we left the study, I told Malcolm he should bring Sebastian to my apartment when he came over to be my bodyguard the next evening. Sebastian was delighted by my request. I got the feeling Malcolm was a bit more strict with his son than Brand was with Abby. The thought of Malcolm as an over-protective father made me smile.

CHAPTER 4

By Thursday, people at school seemed to stare at me less. I suppose Brand was right. In a few weeks, my classmates would forget about my scandal. I was sure they would move on to some other topic of interest and file me away in their minds as an afterthought. Dr. Barry was bugging me a bit though. She seemed extraordinarily interested in Malcolm. I didn't want to offend her, so I tried to answer what she asked as truthfully as I could about what he did for a living, where he lived, what he was like, and on and on. I got the distinct feeling she wanted to meet him and have me set it up, but she never actually came out and said it. I wasn't about to offer my services to her as a matchmaker. All I needed was to put a tempting treat in front of Malcolm to see him succumb to his bloodthirsty desires.

Dr. Barry would have been a good choice for Malcolm under any other circumstances. She was a pretty woman of around thirty-five, never married, no children, and rather brilliant. If Malcolm had been a regular person, I wouldn't have had any problem with setting the two of them up. But, Malcolm wasn't normal. Essentially, he was a vampire doing his best to abstain from his basic desire to drink human blood. I knew he tried to stay away from humans as much as he could so he wouldn't have to struggle as hard with the monster inside himself. I desperately wished Malcolm didn't have to live with such an affliction, but there simply wasn't anything I could do to help, except support him in his fight against himself.

Once Friday rolled around, I was a bucket of nerves. Brand still wouldn't give me a hint as to what we were going to be doing that night. By the time I got home from work at around five, Malcolm, Sebastian and Tara were already there waiting for me. Brand left me at the apartment, saying he would be back at seven, and that Abby would be dropping by to give me my dress sometime in between.

"Well, I'm glad this night has finally come," Malcolm grumbled as Tara brushed out my hair while I sat at the kitchen table. I had just spent a good twenty minutes taking a bath, washing my hair, and blowing it dry for her.

"What would make you say that?" I asked.

"Maybe we can get some peace and quiet at home now. All that banging and stuff was really getting on my nerves," Malcolm explained as he watched Tara brush my hair. "You should put it up for her. She never wears it up."

"I've never done that. You got any suggestions on how to do it?"

From the sarcastic way Tara asked her question, I don't think she was expecting what happened next.

Malcolm stood from his seat on the futon and handed the TV remote to his son. Even though Malcolm said most things on TV were drivel, he seemed to enjoy watching game shows for some reason. I assumed it must be the gambler inside him that found the shows interesting.

"I am an architect. Hair, steel, shouldn't make much of a difference. Give me a minute," he said, surveying the thick brown mass of hair on my head, like a general deciding on a strategic plan of attack.

"What makes you think you can style hair?" I asked him, completely amused by the prospect of Malcolm trying his hand at becoming a hair stylist.

He looked at me with one eyebrow raised. "I know how to do a lot of things, dearest. I would be more than willing to show you some that you might find interesting if you'd like," he said suggestively.

The next thing I heard was the whistle of a brush being slung in the air and a loud whack as it hit its projected target. Malcolm rubbed his injured forehead.

"That's for looking at Lilly naked," Tara told Malcolm, pointing a stern index finger at him. "I can't believe I almost forgot about that."

"What is it with people hitting me in the head over such an innocent little indiscretion?" Malcolm shook his head in dismay.

"Well, you deserve a lot more," Tara declared. "But we ain't got the time for it tonight. What are we gonna do about this hair?"

For the next forty minutes or so, Tara and Malcolm worked together on styling my hair into some sort of intricate up-do Malcolm had planned in his head. Tara seemed content to follow Malcolm's direction without complaint. I think she was impressed with his skill. She asked a lot of questions and seemed to enjoy working with my friend. Tara was never one to take instructions from people well. She was used to being the one who dished them out.

When they were finished, Malcolm stood in front of me and looked at his design with a critical eye.

"I think we did it," he said to Tara. "What do you think?"

Tara came to stand by him to look at me. "Yep, I'd say that's done. Now I just need to get some make-up on her."

About twenty minutes later, I was finally through being prodded and primped into perfection for my mystery date with Brand. I was basically just waiting for Abby to show up with my outfit for the night.

At about six-thirty, there was a soft knock at my door. When I answered it, I saw Brand's daughter standing on my doorstep, wearing a long blonde wig, a pink ruffled chiffon shirt, a pair of faded jeans and white leather ankle boots. Her eyes were bright blue tonight.

"Here you go, love," she said, handing me a clear bag with what looked like my black silk dress; the one I wore to the Black and White ball. "We had it dry cleaned for you. Your hair looks great, by the way!"

"Come on in, Abby. I have some people you should meet."

When Abby stepped into the room, I felt the air inside our little apartment take on a charged quality. After I shut the door behind her and turned around, I saw why.

Sebastian and Abby were staring at each other with an intensity I had never seen before. It was as if they were measuring each other up, while at the same time being totally absorbed by the other person's presence.

"Abby, this is Sebastian."

My voice seemed to break the spell they were both under. Sebastian stood and walked the short distance to Abby. She held her hand out for a shake but instead of merely shaking her hand he brushed his lips slowly across the top of it.

"Pleased to meet you," Sebastian said, never taking his eyes off Abby.

I think it was the first time I'd ever seen Abby speechless. She just stood there and stared at Sebastian.

"I'm Malcolm." Malcolm came to stand by his son, nudging him out of the way a bit. The maneuver made it appear that Malcolm was intentionally trying to break the connection between Abby and Sebastian.

"Oh, hey," Abby said, holding her hand out to Malcolm. "Dad's told me a lot about you."

"Hmm, I'm sure the negatives were completely over-exaggerated," Malcolm said.

"My dad doesn't over-exaggerate to me," Abby replied, a bit defensively.

Malcolm was about to retort with something I assumed would probably be completely inappropriate. Therefore, I stepped in before he had a chance to cause any more trouble.

"Thanks for bringing my dress," I told Abby. "I didn't even realize he had taken it."

"I gave it to him," Tara chimed in, continuing to pack away her hair-styling equipment into the clear plastic tub she kept it stored in. "He asked for it yesterday morning while you were still sleeping."

"So do you have any idea what he has planned for tonight?" I asked Abby.

"Can't say, love," she said with an impish smile on her face. "I promised not to."

"He made us all promise not to," Malcolm added irritably.

"All?" I asked looking at everyone in the room. Sebastian just smiled and Tara shrugged her shoulders.

"You'll know soon enough," Tara said. "But you better go put that dress on. He'll be here in a few minutes. You know that boy ain't never late."

Tara was definitely right about that. You could set the world clock to Brand's sense of punctuality.

I was almost dressed when I heard a knock on the front door.

"Anything happen?" were the first words out of Brand's mouth.

"No," Malcolm replied. "Everything's been normal so far."

I grabbed the shawl I had bought to go with my dress and draped it across my arm. The nights were starting to become chilly, and I wasn't sure how long we would be out.

When I walked into the front room, all eyes turned to me, but my eyes were drawn to Brand like starlings to the first rays of sunlight.

Brand was dressed in a black tuxedo with a white shirt and black bow tie. He looked a lot like he had at the Black and White ball, except this time he was smiling.

"You look beautiful," he said, walking up to me and giving me a quick kiss on the lips in front of our attentive audience.

"So do you," I replied, not being able to stop myself from running the palms of my hands down the lapels of his jacket. I could feel the rapid beating of his heart underneath my hands. It was pounding almost as fast as mine was.

He held his arm out to me. "Shall we?"

When we got into his car, he handed me a silky black blindfold.

"Would you mind putting this on?"

"Are we going somewhere secret?" I asked, putting the blind-fold over my eyes.

"No, but I don't want you to see my surprise until we're there."

I don't think we drove more than ten minutes before we came to a complete stop.

Brand asked me to stay put when he got out of the car. He opened the car door on my side and helped guide me out. I felt the sensation of grass underneath my two-inch heels, so I made sure to put most of my weight on the balls of my toes. About a minute later, the ground changed to a harder surface. The only thing I could hear was the clicking of my heels against the smooth, hard surface I was walking across.

"Ok, keep your eyes closed while I take the blindfold off," he instructed.

I couldn't help but smile. I could hear the excitement in his voice, but there was also a tinge of uncertainty, as if he was afraid I might not like what he had done.

Once he removed the blindfold, Brand whispered in my ear, "Ok, open your eyes."

When I opened my eyes, I thought we might have stepped into one of my dreams. We were standing in the middle of an exact replica of the Black and White ball, except everything had been set up in the middle of a forest clearing by the lake. At our feet were black and white tiles, identical to the ones that were used to assemble the dance floor at the ball. When I looked over my shoul-der, the same stage with a black backdrop and white floating musical notes and instruments was set up behind a band already in place.

"How did you do all of this?" I asked, amazed by all the work Brand did in such a short amount of time.

"You'd be surprised what you can accomplish with a lot of money and a little persuasion."

"But why would you go through all the trouble?"

Brand put his arms around my waist holding me close. The band started playing a song as if on cue, and we began to sway to the music.

"Because we never got to dance."

I almost started to cry. It was such a sentimental thing to do, and so indicative of the man I'd given my heart to.

"When I first saw you that night," Brand continued, "I couldn't breathe. I felt like my world was shattering all around me. All I wanted to do was take you in my arms and tell you how much I loved you. I almost went to you that night to beg for your forgiveness, but Will got to you first."

"When Will and I left and walked to the rose garden, I did see you on the terrace watching us, didn't I? That wasn't just in my imagination, was it?"

"I followed you," Brand confessed, almost as if he was ashamed of his behavior. "I still didn't trust Will, and I wanted to make sure you were safe. When I saw him lean in to kiss you, I thought my world was about to end. I wanted to *be* him so badly in that moment. Then, when you pushed him away and told him you couldn't go through with it, I felt a selfish sort of relief. I didn't want you to move on. I didn't want you to forget about me so quickly. My heart ached to be with you. There were moments when I couldn't understand how it kept beating through the pain."

The torment I saw in his eyes told me as much as his words did. He'd been as miserable as I had that night, and this re-creation was meant to wash away the last of our regrets. It was meant to symbolize a new beginning of treasured moments between the two of us.

"Thank you," I said, gazing up at the love of my life. "Thank you for giving us this."

"There isn't anything in this world I wouldn't give to you, Lilly. All you have to do is ask."

We danced for a couple of songs, just enjoying the way our bodies moved together in perfect unison, like we were made for each other.

When the third song began to play, Brand pulled away slightly and looked down at me. "I want to take you somewhere."

"Anywhere you want," I replied. And I meant it. I would follow Brand anywhere he ever wanted to go.

He took my hand and led me off the dance floor. I saw him look at the band and nod his head slightly. They seemed prepared for such a signal, and began packing up their equipment.

When we got back into Brand's car, he drove it off the grass back onto the highway, heading toward his home.

"Are we spending the rest of the night at your house?" I asked.

"No, we're just going to be dropping the car off," he answered. "We won't need it anymore tonight."

"Are we phasing somewhere else?"

"Yes, and please stop asking questions." He smiled at me, which made me unable to say another word. "Make sure to bring your shawl, though. It will probably be chilly where we're going."

We parked the car and got out. I placed my shawl around my shoulders as Brand came to my side and took hold of my hand. Before I knew it, we were standing in front of the largest Ferris Wheel I've ever seen. It was white, lit up with lights, and must have had over thirty large glass-enclosed oval pods attached to it with steel straps. There was a man standing in front of the wheel with his back to us, wearing a dark grey woolen newsboy cap and matching jacket.

"Hello, Jack," Brand said to the man.

Jack jumped a bit in surprise and turned to face us. He was an older man of about sixty and short of stature. Since I was 5'5", Jack could only have been an even five feet tall.

"Brandon, my boy! I should have known you would be right on time," Jack said, in a less-cultured British accent than Brand. He smiled at me with unabashed joy. "This must be the lovely Lilly you told me about. Jack Sneed," he said, holding out his hand to me.

I shook it. "Lilly Nightingale."

"She's as lovely as you described, my boy, just lovely."

"Are we ready?" Brand asked Jack.

"Go on in. I'll take care of everything else. It should be nice and warm in there. I turned the heat on for you."

Brand took my hand and escorted me into one of the glass pods of the Ferris Wheel.

"What is this?" I asked as he escorted me to the other side of the capsule.

"It's the London Eye."

"We're in England?"

"Yes, my love." He turned me so I could look out at the London skyline. He stood behind me with his chest at my back, and put his arms around me loosely.

I could barely feel us move as the wheel slowly turned and took us higher into the air. It soon became evident that the steel straps I had seen on the outside of the pod were used to keep the pod level while the wheel turned. From our vantage point, I could see the Thames River, Big Ben, the Houses of Parliament, and Buckingham Palace. It was a gorgeous view at night. The city was lit up with myriad lights, showcasing how lovely London really was.

"What time is it here?" I asked just as we were nearing the top of the wheel.

"Around two in the morning," Brand said, hugging me closer.

"Poor Jack! How did you talk him into doing this for us?"

Brand slowly turned me around to face him. He held both my hands in his and stared down at them for a few seconds before answering. He seemed shy to meet my eyes.

"Jack's been a friend of mine for a long time. I told him I needed his help to make this moment special for us, and he was more than willing to lend a hand."

Brand finally looked into my eyes, and I saw the uncertainty in his expression by the dim light of our glass bubble. There wasn't an actual light inside the pod, but the illumination of the wheel itself cast a soft glow around us.

Brand knelt in front of me on one knee. I thought my heart would stop beating from the implication of such a gesture.

"I know you want to wait until after you get out of school to get married, and I'm perfectly fine with that, Lilly. I've waited for centuries to find you. A few more years doesn't bother me. But I don't see any reason why I should wait to ask you to be my wife. Even if we don't actually say our vows for four more years, I want everyone to know how much we love each other. I don't want you to ever doubt that you are the center of my world and my life. Lilly, will you accept me, knowing all my faults, and grant me the honor of becoming my wife?"

I was speechless. How had my life led me to this moment?

Picture perfect was too clichéd to describe it, but no other words came to mind. How else do you describe the perfect setting, the perfect man, and the perfect question?

It was only the doubt in Brand's eyes at my continued silence that finally prodded me into giving him my answer.

"Yes."

Brand reached into an inner pocket of his tuxedo and slipped a ring onto my finger. I didn't even look at it before I made him stand up. I kissed him so hard I hoped he wouldn't have any more doubts about how much I loved and needed him.

When I finally let him go, I noticed we were back on the ground. Jack had his back to our pod, obviously trying to give us some privacy.

I looked up at Brand and smiled. "Did you really think I wouldn't say yes?"

"I hoped you would, but I wasn't sure how you would respond to me doing it so soon. I was a little worried you might think it was too early. We still have almost four years until we can make it official."

"It seems almost silly, doesn't it? Waiting so long," I said, wondering if I was making the right decision.

"No, it's not silly," Brand leaned down and kissed me softly. "I want to make your life as perfect as you've imagined it for yourself. If waiting until you have your degree is what you want, then that's what we'll do. I need you to feel good about yourself because, as long as you do, our life together will be that much richer. In a way, I'm actually being selfish by asking you now."

"Selfish?" I asked, confused. "What makes you say that?"

"I mostly wanted you to know how committed I am to you, but a small part of me wanted to let Will and Malcolm know how committed you are to me, too. I know that probably sounds completely childish, but I can't help it. I get a little jealous of your relationship with them."

I couldn't help but smile and shake my head at Brand. "It's not childish, but it does sound very human." He grinned at that. "They know how much I love you, and if making it official makes you feel more secure, I have no problem with that. I just wish you didn't feel jealous of them. They're my friends, nothing more. I've given myself to you, mind, body, heart, and soul, Brandon Cole. There's no reason for you to doubt my feelings for you."

"I don't doubt how you feel about me, Lilly. If I did, I wouldn't have had the courage to ask you to marry me. I just hope I'm worthy of you."

"Do you remember saying you thought we were meant for each other?"

"Yes."

"I think you're right. You need to stop doubting things and just accept them. Accept the happiness you've found with me, and stop questioning if you deserve it or not."

"I'll try," he said, but I could still see uncertainty in his eyes. I knew he had lived a long time, and I could only assume the guilt he felt from disobeying God and cursing Abby with her affliction was the reason it was hard for him to accept true happiness for himself. I hoped I could erase his pain in time and show him just how wonderful a person he was.

When we stepped out of the glass pod, Jack looked at us expectantly.

With an almost shy smile, Brand answered his friend's unasked question, "She said yes."

"Never doubted she would, my boy," Jack shook Brand's hand

in congratulations and raised himself on his tiptoes to give me a kiss on the cheek. "Now take her home before she catches a cold," he ordered, turning his back to us.

Brand phased us to a bedroom I had not been in before.

"Where are we now?" I asked.

"This is my house right outside of London. I thought we would stay here for the night, if that's all right with you."

"As long as we're together, I don't care where we are."

"I bought you some things to wear while we're here," he said, indicating a set of clothes laid out on the bed, with matching shoes sitting on the floor in front of them.

"Would you mind helping me get my hair down? I'm not sure what Tara did to it exactly. I just remember Malcolm instructing her to use a lot of bobby pins."

"Malcolm?" Brand asked, like he was sure he had heard me wrong.

"He thought my hair would look good up, so he came up with the design," I shrugged. "He's full of surprises."

"Hmm, yes, I guess he is."

Brand sat me down in a chair in front of a cherry-wood vanity table. It looked like the table had been prepared ahead of time, in anticipation of my visit. There were a silver-handled hairbrush, various perfumes, and a small make-up bag arranged on its surface. I watched him in the mirror as he carefully removed the pins from my hair, gently laying each section down onto my shoulders.

I still couldn't believe he asked me to marry him. Never in my wildest fantasies had I imagined feeling this all-consuming love for anyone. I became even more determined to make sure we got the chance to live a life filled with as much happiness as we could possibly have within my lifetime. I knew we still needed to find out what plans Lucifer had for me, and who was trying to stop him by killing me, but I needed this night, just one night where we didn't have to worry about things and could simply be together.

"Does Jack know what you are?" I asked, thinking back to how Brand's friend kept his back to us when Brand phased us to and from the London Eye.

"No, he doesn't know the complete truth. But he does know I'm different. He said he didn't need to know everything. Our friendship was enough for him."

"Do you have many human friends?"

"No."

I could see an unspoken sadness in his eyes and knew what he was thinking. Humans were fragile and died easily. I could well understand why he wouldn't want to grow attached too often. But tonight wasn't supposed to be about sadness or regrets.

After he removed all the pins, he picked up the hairbrush and began brushing my hair out for me. His touch was so delicate. I felt as though he was treating me like a porcelain doll, easily broken if not handled with care. After he was finished with my hair and put the brush back on the table, I stood from the chair and turned my back to him, lifting my hair over one shoulder.

"Would you mind unzipping it for me?"

I watched him in the mirror as he swallowed hard enough to make his Adam's apple move. He raised his hands to my shoulders in a tender caress, and slowly moved them inward over my bare shoulder blades to the zipper at the back of the dress. His eyes never left my back as he lowered the tab of the zipper. Once it was as low as it could go, he ran the palm of his hand down the newly-bared skin. His hand lingered at the small of my back as he looked into the mirror, meeting my gaze as I watched him.

There wasn't any mistaking what he wanted. I wanted it, too. Why shouldn't we? What could be more natural than two people who loved each other to share their bodies in the most intimate way possible?

As if knowing where my thoughts were going, Brand dropped his hand to his side and backed away.

"Why don't you go ahead and change?" he said in a hoarse voice. "I have supper prepared for us down in the kitchen."

He walked to a window on the other side of the room and turned his back to give me some privacy. He'd been doing the same thing since I escaped from Justin. There were times he actually left the room, but they were few. He was too scared to leave me alone, afraid I would be abducted again.

I quickly changed into the set of clothes on the bed and told him to turn around when I was putting the shoes on. It was then that I finally took notice of the ring on my finger.

I wasn't much for jewelry, but the ring Brand chose for me was breathtaking. It was either white gold or platinum, with a large square-cut diamond surrounded by smaller diamonds embedded in the setting, which extended halfway down the band. It sparkled brightly in the light of the room.

"Do you like it?" Brand asked, coming to sit beside me on the bed.

"It's gorgeous. Where did you get it?"

"I know a jeweler in France. He designed it especially for you. Does it feel comfortable on your finger?"

"It's fits perfectly. How did you know my size?"

"I took a measurement the other night while you slept."

"How long have you been planning this?"

"Since the moment you got back," he said with a guilty grin. "Come on. I have supper waiting in the oven downstairs."

On the way to the kitchen, Brand showed me some of his home. From what I could tell, it was large. We must have passed at least five bedrooms, and that was just on one side of the house on the second floor. It reminded me of an English manor you might see in a Merchant and Ivory film, full of grandeur and history, impeccably decorated in the Victorian style. As we descended the grand staircase, I felt like Scarlet O'Hara in *Gone with the Wind*.

The kitchen was very modern, and I could tell Brand spent a lot of time here from the easy way he moved around it. Besides the bedroom we had been in, it was the only room in the house, so far, which felt like home. It had dark cherry-wood cabinetry with brushed silver hardware, and black marble countertops with all the modern amenities, including stainless steel appliances. The center island was equipped with a built-in stove, sink, and bar. Brand pulled out a casserole dish from the double wall oven. Apparently, he'd found the time to come here in the two hours he was absent from me that day to make what looked like lasagna.

We ate at the small kitchen table, tucked away inside an attached circular room made of glass. From my seat, I could look out over a large green lawn with a winding river in the distance. Brand told me it was the Thames River, and that he'd bought the house just for the view. After we ate and cleaned up the kitchen, Brand took me to his study. The study was lined with bookshelves on all four walls and filled with leather- bound editions of all types of books. There was a brown leather couch and two matching wing-back chairs sitting in front of a fireplace, which had a black marble mantle.

In no time at all, Brand had a roaring fire going to drive away the chill in the room. When he came to sit beside me on the couch, I did what any newly-engaged female would do. I grabbed my man and pulled him down on top of me. I think what followed is called snogging, in England. Eventually, I fell asleep in his arms and didn't wake up until the next morning.

CHAPTER 5

Apparently, Brand had planned for everything I might need on our London excursion. When I woke up the next morning, he showed me a wardrobe full of clothes just for me, in his bedroom.

"I wasn't completely sure what you might want to wear, so I had Abby buy you a few things to keep here when we visit."

From the collection of clothes, I picked out a black and white abstract print shirt with a V-neck, flutter cap sleeves and banded empire waist with rushing at the sides, black slacks and black loafers to wear that day. Brand dressed simply in a light grey knit shirt with a darker grey trim along the V-neck and cuffs, dark blue jeans and black sneakers with grey stripes on the sides.

"Are we going to see your friend with the lab?" I asked him, sitting on the side of the bed, slipping on my shoes.

"Yes, he lives here in London. His house isn't very far away."

"Good. I hope he can find something. Otherwise, I'm not sure how we're going to figure out what's different about me."

Brand took me in his arms and kissed me. "We'll find the answers, Lilly. I know we will."

We went down to Brand's garage and got into his car. He told me it was a Weismann GT MF5. It was pearl-white with a black leather interior. It looked a bit like an old-fashioned road-ster with a modern twist. Almost everything inside was covered with premium black leather, except for the central panel where the gauges and radio were housed. Seeing expensive things like this car and Brand's house kept reminding me how different our worlds were from one another. Would I ever get used to it all?

As we drove out of the garage, I was finally able to see what Brand's home looked like from the outside. It was just as I had thought from the way things looked on the inside. It was a mansion built of dark red brick covered in English ivy. As we drove off the estate, I turned to Brand.

"What's your friend's name?"

"Allan Westwood."

"Does he live alone?"

"He has a daughter named Angela, who takes care of him. She and Abby are good friends. I think she might have helped Abby pick out the clothes for you."

"Is something wrong with him? Why does she need to take care of him?"

"Allan has a mental compulsive disorder. It makes it hard for him to go out in public. After you add in the fact that he has the same craving for human blood that all the Watchers like me do, you have your classic shut-in. It's one of the reasons we couldn't come here until today. Allan likes for everything to be in order, and he never starts a new project until he has every little detail worked out."

"He doesn't go anywhere?" I asked, never having heard of someone who didn't go out at all.

"He has to change residences every once in a while, so people don't get suspicious, of course, but Angela usually handles those details for him."

"Sounds like a lonely life for both of them."

"Angela has her friends. She's never acted like she minded taking care of Allan, at least not that I've seen."

The drive to Allan's took about twenty minutes through the lush green English countryside. I suddenly felt like a world traveler, having already traveled to Paris, Venice, Egypt, Hawaii, and now London. It still amazed me how much my world had broadened in just a few short weeks.

When we reached Allan's house, we were met by an imposing black iron security gate with two large Ws in the middle of each door. Brand rolled down his window to push the button on the intercom system.

"Yes," a very proper male British voice said through the speaker. "Can I help you?"

"Brandon Cole, here, to see Allan Westwood. I have an appointment."

"Come right in, Mister Cole. He's expecting you."

The gate swung open and we drove onto the property. Allan's house looked more like a medieval castle than a home. For someone with his phobias, I had to assume the formidable stone exterior made him feel more protected than just living in an ordinary home made of brick. Before we got out of the car, the front door opened and a young girl came bounding down the steps, which lead from the door to the gravel drive.

"Brand!"

The girl didn't look much older than sixteen, but I knew from what Brand and Abby had told me about the children of the Watchers that she was certainly much older. She flung herself into Brand's arms like a kid who was being visited by a favorite uncle.

Brand hugged her tenderly and turned her around to face me. "Angela, I want you to meet Lilly."

"Hiya," she said, holding out a slender hand to me in welcome. Angela was a pretty girl with naturally wavy, long white hair like Abby's.

I shook her hand. "It's nice to meet you, Angela."

Angela's light blue eyes took in the outfit I was wearing. "I'm glad to see the clothes Abby and I got you fit. You know how it is with clothing these days. You never know if anything's going to fit right until you try it on. Come on into the house. Dad's ready for you."

"Is he having a good day?" Brand asked, taking hold of my hand as we walked up the steps to the manor.

"As good as he gets," Angela shrugged. "I think he's looking forward to meeting Lilly, though. He's been intrigued ever since you told him about her, and you know how hard it is to get him excited about anything."

After we walked in, Angela shut the front door behind us and escorted us to a study to the left of the entrance. She went up to a wall of books beside an unlit fireplace, and tilted a series of them onto their bindings in what looked like a sequence. There was a rattling, which seemed to come from behind the shelves. Angela took a couple of steps back as the bookshelves swung open to reveal a metal door with an electronic key pad. After tapping in a numerical combination, the door slowly opened inward by itself. We walked into a small room with little white circular nozzles on the walls, floor, and ceiling.

"Decontamination chamber," Angela told me as the door to

the study closed behind us. "Don't be scared." She smiled reassuringly.

There was suddenly a draft of air hitting us from all sides, which only lasted for a few seconds. I had seen such things on movies and TV, but never thought I would actually ever be in one.

"Come on in," Angela said, opening the door on the far end of the chamber. "He's waiting for us."

When we walked across the threshold, it felt like I'd stepped inside a hospital. The antiseptic smell of bleach and other cleaners was almost overpowering. The floor was lined with white linoleum, and in the center of the room was a circular glass chamber where the man I assumed to be Allan was sitting on a silver stool in front of a white marble counter. The room contained a few pieces of equipment I didn't recognize, but assumed were used in Allan's genetic studies.

Allan was a handsome, slender man who looked no older than thirty-five, with neat short black hair and a clean-shaven face. He was of average build and height, dressed in a crisp white lab coat and shirt, black pants, shiny black dress shoes, and slim black tie.

Allan opened the door to the glass room and came out to greet us.

"Hello, Brand."

He may have been addressing Brand, but his eyes were locked on me. I could tell he felt the contentment my presence had on his kind by the welcoming smile he gave me. He held out his hand in greeting.

If Angela hadn't been standing across from me with a stunned look on her face as I shook her father's hand, I might not have known what a departure the handshake was from his usual routine.

"It's nice to meet you, Lilly, very nice indeed." Allen had a smooth, cultured English accent, which had a soft, almost innocent, quality to it.

"Thank you for helping me, Allen. I really hope you can answer some questions for us."

"Well, we'll see what we can do." He looked to Brand. "I assume you want the full work up?"

"If you can give us as much information as you can, it would be helpful. As I told you earlier, we don't have a full picture of Lilly's heritage since she never knew her father. I've met the mother and haven't detected anything out of the ordinary about her, but you may find something I can't sense."

"Please, come inside. I'll need to take some blood samples."

We all stepped inside the glass chamber. There was a central cabinet in the center of the room, where it looked like Allan did all his work. He walked over to the sink and took out a wrapped bar of soap from the glass cabinet which was suspended by wire cables over the counter space. He twisted the knob for cold water exactly twice and the knob for hot once. He opened a fresh bar of soap and threw the paper into a metal trashcan to his left. I watched as he rubbed the soap onto the palms of his hands exactly three times each before throwing the bar of soap into the trash. After rinsing his hands under the water at least ten times, he reached for a white towel to his right on the counter and dried his hands. He held the towel in his right hand as he turned off the water in the opposite order he had turned it on. He then threw the towel into the trashcan.

After putting on a fresh pair of green rubber gloves, he instructed me to sit in a metal chair that had an attached small glass table. He brought over a silver tray with two sterile syringes laying on its surface. It didn't take him long to draw the blood he needed for the tests. I was thankful for that. I hated being stuck with needles, mostly because the nurses and doctors who had taken my blood in the past always had a hard time finding a vein in my arm, and ended up making me feel like a pincushion by the end of the ordeal. Thankfully, Allan had no such problem and drew the blood in under a minute.

He put a cotton ball and piece of white tape on the puncture site.

"I should know something by tomorrow if you would like to come back. Same time?" The hopeful note in Allan's voice was hard to miss.

"We'll be here," Brand answered.

"Will said he would like to come with us," I said to Brand. "Would that be ok?"

"Is he the one you told me about?" Allan asked Brand in an aggressive tone I had not expected to hear.

"Yes."

"Then, no, he is not welcome in my home. I don't mean to sound rude, Lilly, but I would rather not have him around me or my daughter."

"No, that's fine," I said, slightly taken aback by Allan's vehement answer.

"We'll go so you can get to work," Brand said, taking my hand.

"See you tomorrow." Allan turned around and seemed to completely dismiss us from his mind as he set to work on my blood samples.

Angela escorted us back out to the front door.

"Hey, could you bring Abby with you when you come back?" Angela asked.

"Sure," Brand said, giving Angela a peck on her dimpled cheek. "I'm sure she'd love the visit."

"Ok, see you guys tomorrow then!"

When we got back into Brand's car and were driving away, I asked, "Why did he react like that when I asked if Will could come?"

"Most Watchers don't associate with Will's kind. We rarely associate with one another, much less his type."

"Why is that? Why don't you like each other?"

"Seeing them just reminds us of what we lost, so we don't seek out each other's company very often, usually only when we need help with something."

"Seems like a lonely existence. I would have thought you would want a friend who lived as long as you did."

"Not when it reminds you of why you were sent here in the first place. A lot of us still feel a lot of guilt over the decision we made."

"Yeah, that's what Malcolm basically said."

"He feels guilty?" Brand asked, surprised by my statement.

"Of course," I said, wishing Brand could see Malcolm the way I did. "He said he didn't like the monster he'd become through living here."

Brand seemed lost in thought after my statement. I turned my attention to the rolling hills of the green pastures we passed, lost in my own thoughts about the Pandora's Box we might have just opened by delving into my genetic background. What would Allan find out about me? Did I really want to know? If I were honest with myself, I was afraid he might find something I didn't want to know. What if it ended up being worse than anything I could imagine? What if there was something about me that would be repellant to Brand, causing him to fall out of love with me?

After a few minutes, I felt Brand take my hand and kiss the back of it with his warm lips, gently reminding me of his presence.

"What are you thinking about?" he asked softly.

"I'm scared." I admitted.

"Of what?"

"What if Allan finds out something I don't want to know?"

"He's only looking for the truth. There can't be anything wrong with that. And there's no denying that you are special, Lilly. Just look at how Allan accepted you. I don't think I've ever seen him shake anyone's hand before."

"What if he finds out something about me that you don't like?" I asked, finding it impossible to hide all of my worries now that I had started to voice them.

"Please stop worrying about the impossible," he gently chastised me. "There is nothing he could ever discover about you that would make me feel any less in love with you. *Nothing*."

His words helped ease the tension I was feeling. I knew Brand loved me. Why did I keep thinking he would change his mind? I suppose it was because true happiness was a hard thing for me to accept, even when it was staring me in the face and holding my hand. I needed to learn to accept the love Brand felt for me and not question whether it would last or not. The one thing my time in Justin's prison had taught me was that life was short. I needed to make the most of it while I still could.

Since it was lunchtime, Brand took me to a restaurant in Hyde Park called The Dell. We ate under the sun at a picnic table by the Serpentine River. It was such a beautiful day that there were loads of people in the park, trying to enjoy the last warmth of summer before fall rolled in and pushed the tranquil happiness of summertime to the side. After we ate, we took a stroll in the park and just talked.

I had never been very comfortable with guys before. Will was the only one I ever truly opened up to before Brand came into my life. It seemed odd to me that three of my four best friends were now men. I wasn't completely sure Malcolm was a best friend, but he was certainly a good one with the potential for best friend status. I just wished he would stop thinking of me romantically. I was flattered, of course, but I didn't think it was healthy for him. Perhaps after he learned Brand and I were engaged, he would understand that waiting for me to change my mind was a futile act.

When we got back to Brand's house, it was late in the afternoon, almost evening. We went up to his bedroom and retrieved my dress so I could take it back home. We then phased back to my apartment. Because of the time difference, I knew it was probably sometime around ten o'clock in the morning in Lakewood. I saw Simon's car parked beside my Mustang, and knew he must be visiting Tara. I decided to knock on the door before we barged in and possibly caught them making out on the futon.

Tara opened the door a few seconds after my knock.

"Hey y'all," she said, slightly out of breath, which made me glad I had decided to knock on the door first. I saw Simon tucking his shirt into his pants as he stood from the futon.

"Did you have a good time?" Tara asked, going to stand beside Simon, letting us inside the apartment.

"We had a great time," I answered, noticing the heightened hue of Tara's cheeks from being almost caught in a compromising position. "Did you?"

Choosing to ignore my question, Tara took Simon by the arm and escorted him to the door.

"Why don't you pick me up at five?" she told him.

"Could we make it six? I have a prior engagement."

"It's not another girl, is it?" Tara joked.

"Of course not," Simon said smoothly. "It's something for my mom."

"Ok, I'll be ready at six then. Don't make me wait for you, though."

"I won't," he kissed her on the cheek and left the apartment.

Tara leaned up against the door and sighed in contented bliss.

I really hoped things worked out with Simon. Tara seemed so happy with him in her life, and I desperately wanted her to be happy.

"So what are you and Simon doing tonight?" Brand asked.

The tone of his question instantly put me on alert that something was wrong. I could tell by the expression on his face that he was trying to hide what he was really thinking.

"We're just going out to dinner," Tara shrugged. "Nothing special."

Tara pushed herself away from the door and walked over to me. "So, where's the ring?"

"You knew?" I asked, completely astounded that Tara had known what Brand's intentions had been last night, and hadn't warned me or even hinted she knew about the proposal. I guess I was even more surprised that she didn't try to talk me out of accepting.

"Utha Mae told me a couple of days ago," Tara answered.

"How did she know?"

"What, you didn't tell her?" Tara asked Brand.

He grinned guiltily and simply shook his head.

"Lover boy over there asked her permission first."

"Was this the day after I got back?" I asked Brand. "Is that the secret you wanted to keep?"

"I wanted to have Utha Mae's blessing first. I felt it was important to have her approval before I asked you to marry me."

It all made sense now. That was why he wanted to stay behind when I went to talk to my mother, and it explained why they looked like they were sharing a secret when I got back. I could see Utha Mae and Brand keeping the secret, but I couldn't believe Tara had actually kept it, too.

I showed Tara the ring on my finger and her jaw almost dropped to the floor.

"Dang, girl, you better watch where you swing that thing. It could knock somebody out cold!"

I couldn't help but laugh a little. Tara was probably right, though.

"Ok, you two love birds behave while I'm gone. I need to go get some groceries. Shouldn't be gone too long, so don't get too comfortable," she said with a knowing grin.

"You're a big one to talk," I said. "It looked like you and Simon were getting awfully comfortable with each other before we arrived."

Tara waved her hand at me like it was nothing, but I saw the blush on her cheeks as she headed out the door.

"Lilly," Brand said after Tara left, "we have a problem."

This sent alarm bells ringing in my head. I knew I hadn't imagined his tone or misread his expression earlier. "What's wrong?"

"I think Simon is cheating on Tara."

"What would make you say that?"

"When she asked him if he was seeing another girl, he lied to her."

"Maybe he's just doing something for another girl who's a friend, and he doesn't want Tara to know." I knew I was grasping at straws, but I desperately wanted Brand to be wrong or to at least misunderstand his reading of Simon.

"I hope you're right, but I don't think so. I believe he's cheating on her."

I could tell Brand didn't like telling me this news because he knew I didn't want to hear it. If I didn't want to hear it, Tara surely didn't. Would she believe me if I told her the man she was falling in love with was a good-for-nothing cheat?

"We can't tell Tara what we suspect until we know for sure. She's so happy with him. I just can't make her unhappy without being absolutely positive."

"What do you suggest then?"

"Why don't we invite them to your house for supper? Maybe we can ask him some questions that'll tell us what's really going on."

"All right, but you should know that, if he *is* cheating on her, I won't let him stay inside my home."

"Oh, don't worry. If he's cheating on her, Tara will kick him out herself."

While we were waiting for Tara to get back, I took a shower and dressed simply in a pair of jeans and a white button-down shirt.

When Tara got home from the grocery store, we told her we wanted her and Simon to come to Brand's house for supper that evening. She thought it would be fun, and immediately phoned

Simon to tell him the change in their plans. Brand and I went back to his house to get things ready.

I was a bundle of nerves by the time Tara and Simon arrived at Brand's house that evening. Simon seemed impressed with Brand's home and couldn't seem to keep his eyes off my ring. I couldn't blame him for that. The way the light danced off the diamonds was a bit distracting, almost like a lighthouse mirror reflecting shafts of light in all directions.

Brand prepared roasted lamb, sautéed baby spinach leaves, couscous mixed with pine nuts and dried cranberries, and a dish of potatoes roasted in olive oil, garlic, and herbs. I was surprised by Brand's easygoing, almost-friendly banter with Simon throughout the meal. Tara knew I was nervous about something, though. I could never hide my feelings from her. She kept a wary eye on me and Brand during supper, listening intently to the conversation Brand was having with Simon. When the meal was over, Brand suggested to Simon that Tara might like a stroll by the lake while he and I prepared dessert.

Once they were gone, I asked Brand, "Well?"

"He lies easily," he answered, taking out a fruit trifle we had prepared earlier from the refrigerator.

"How are we going to know for sure that he's cheating on her?"

"I'm going to ask him."

"You're what?" I asked in disbelief.

"The easiest way for me to know for sure is to ask him a direct question, Lilly. There's really no other way to do it."

"Well, give me a minute with Tara first. I don't want her to be blindsided by this. She thinks he's a great guy. So did I, until you told me he was a liar."

"I'm sorry," Brand said, and I knew he was. "I can't help what I know. Sometimes it's not much of a blessing."

I sighed. "No, don't be sorry. It's better if she knows now before things get even more serious with him."

By the time Tara and Simon made it back in, Brand and I had dessert out in dishes on the table, waiting for their arrival. I pulled Tara aside and told her I wanted to show her something upstairs. I took her into Brand's bedroom and sat her down on the bed.

"What's wrong?" she immediately asked. "You've been walking on eggshells all night long."

I paced in front of her, not knowing exactly how to say what I needed to.

"Brand can tell when someone is lying to him," I finally said. "It's one of his powers as an angel."

"So?"

"He thinks Simon is cheating on you," I blurted out, seeing no other way to say what needed to be said.

"No, he's not."

The conviction with which Tara made this simple statement made me stop my pacing and look at her. I could see the doubt of Simon's fidelity on her face. She suspected what Brand thought might be true, yet her words completely contradicted it.

"Do you know that for a fact?" I asked.

Her silence only confirmed what her facial expression was telling me.

"He's going to ask Simon straight out if he's cheating on you. It's the surest way for him to know the truth. I just wanted you to know before he did it."

Without saying a word, Tara stood up and walked back down

to the dining room. Simon was eating his dessert when she walked up to him and said, "Are you seeing another girl?"

I thought Simon was going to choke on the food in his mouth. He took a drink from his water glass and cleared his throat.

"Why would you ask me something like that?" he asked.

"Just answer the question," Tara said, completely expressionless.

"No, honey, you know I don't want anyone else but you."

Tara looked at Brand. "Is he telling the truth?"

Brand hesitated for a moment and finally shook his head no, obviously regretting being the bearer of bad news. Simon looked scared all of a sudden. I watched Tara closely. I wasn't sure what her reaction would be.

I saw her eyes travel to the fireplace in the living room. Without saying a word, she stalked over to it and picked up the fire poker. I heard the scrape of Simon's chair as he hastily stood from it.

"Now, listen, Tara," he said, slowly making his way to the front door. "Who you gonna believe? Me or him?"

"Him," she said, walking toward Simon with a determination I've never seen in her.

Before I could stop her, she ran toward Simon and started hitting him across his back, yelling curses at him. Simon stumbled his way to the front door and ran for his car, once outside.

Tara stood on the front porch, brandishing the fire poker like a sword.

"You better run you good-for-nothing pile of dog crap! And don't ever let me see you again, or I'll make sure you regret ever meeting me!"

By the time I reached Tara, she was already crying. She leaned against me as I brought her back into the house and sat her down on one of the couches in the living room. Brand stood back from us, letting me comfort her as best I could. I knew he felt guilty for causing Tara so much pain. I would have to try to make sure she understood it was for the best. If their relationship had been allowed to progress much further, I knew it would have been that much harder for Tara to do what she just did.

As it was, I was glad I could be a comfort to her in her time of need. She'd held me so many times over the past couple of years after I lost Will, and then again when Brand broke up with me, mistakenly thinking I would be safer without him in my life. I was happy to just be there for her and hold her as the sting of Simon's betrayal sunk in. It was almost as if I could hear her heart break from losing someone she thought she could trust and build a relationship with. I knew in time she would find someone worthy of her love, and hoped it would be soon.

CHAPTER 6

It took about thirty minutes for Tara to stop crying. Brand busied himself in the kitchen to give us time alone. I'm not even sure what he was doing, to be honest. My complete focus was directed towards Tara. I told her she was better off knowing what kind of guy Simon really was before they got too serious.

She finally sat up and wiped the tears from her eyes.

"How come you ended up with Prince Charming and I got stuck with the toad?"

The rattling in the kitchen stopped. I glanced over at Brand and saw him smiling down at the glass plate in his hands, obviously pleased to be compared to Prince Charming, every girl's perfect standard for male courtship.

"Your Prince Charming is out there," I tried to reassure my best friend. "When the time is right for you to find him, he'll show up."

"I just don't understand how I could have been fooled like that," she said. "I'm usually better at telling if someone's just saying what I want to hear."

"I think you did know," I said truthfully. "You just didn't want to admit it to yourself because you wanted it to work out so badly. It's nothing to be ashamed of."

Brand came into the living room with a pile of cookies on the glass dish I had seen him holding earlier.

"Have one of these," he suggested to Tara. "I promise they'll make you feel better."

"What are they?" Tara asked, taking one of the dark chocolate cookies off the plate.

"They're chocolate, chocolate chip cookies with peanut butter and macadamia nuts."

Tara took a bite out of the one in her hand and immediately reached for another one. There were at least a dozen cookies on the plate Brand sat down in front of her on the coffee table, and I think she ate them all in half as many minutes. Brand brought her a glass of cold milk to help wash them all down.

"See?" Tara said, drinking the last of the milk. "Prince Charming knew exactly what I needed."

Brand took the now-empty plate and glass back into the kitchen with a satisfied smile on his face.

There was an unexpected knock on the door. Brand answered it and, without a word, motioned for our visitor to step inside.

"Hey," Will said to Brand, but quickly turned his attention to Tara and me when he saw us. "I just came by to see if you guys were able to go have those tests started today."

"Allan is performing them now," Brand answered, closing the door behind Will. "We're going back tomorrow to find out what he discovers."

"Mind if I tag along?" Will asked Brand.

"Not this time, Will," I answered, not wanting the news to come from Brand. I didn't want Will to think Brand was the one who didn't want him to join us. "Allan asked that we not bring you into his home."

Will seemed to accept this answer a lot better than I thought he would. I could only assume he had expected it.

"That's all right. Just let me know what he finds out when you can. What happened to you?" he asked Tara, seeing her puffy, watery eyes.

"She found out Simon was cheating on her," I answered, wanting to spare Tara from having to say the words aloud.

Will sat down beside Tara and put a comforting arm across her shoulders.

"You're better off without him then," he told her. "Don't waste your tears on a fool."

"I just need to stop thinking about it," Tara sighed.

It broke my heart to see her so dejected.

"Well, come on then." Will stood and pulled Tara to her feet. "I've got just the place to forget about stupid ex-boyfriends."

"Where are you taking me?" Tara asked, sounding excited and worried about Will's plans at the same time.

"Somewhere you've always wanted to go. Just keep a hold of my hand. See you guys later."

And they were gone.

"Where do you think he took her?" Brand asked, taking me into his arms and nibbling on my neck. How did he think I could answer coherently with him lighting every nerve in my body on fire?

"I have no idea," I said, wrapping my arms around his back, enjoying the sensations his touch always ignited in me. "But I hope they won't be back for a while."

"Mmm, me, too," Brand said, finding my lips with his.

Before I knew it, Brand had picked me up, laid me down on the couch, and gently lay down beside me, never breaking the contact of our lips. I felt his fingers run through my hair, holding my head as he gently plundered my mouth with his. One of his hands slowly made its way across my cheek and down my throat, to the buttons of my shirt. I felt him undo three of them and stop. His lips soon followed the same trail his hand just made, planting small warm, wet kisses across my chest.

I didn't want him to stop. I wanted him to keep going.

There was a loud knock on the front door. "Hello?"

We both let out a sigh of frustration at the sound of Malcolm's voice.

With a growl, Brand lifted his weight off me and practically stomped to the door. I couldn't help but giggle at him. He was like a bear that had been woken before the end of winter. He yanked the door open.

"What do you want, Malcolm?" Brand asked tersely.

"I did what you asked," Malcolm said, stepping across the threshold, ignoring Brand's openly-hostile glare. "You can't imagine what a pain it is to have to knock when I know you're both in here."

I quickly stood from the couch, and kept my back to Malcolm as I hastily re-buttoned my shirt. When I turned back around, Malcolm was taking in my disheveled appearance with a critical, unpleased look on his face.

"Did I interrupt something?" he asked innocently, knowing full well what we had been doing.

"What do you want, Malcolm?" Brand asked again, trying his best to contain his irritation with my friend.

I didn't think it was possible, but I loved Brand even more in that moment. I knew Malcolm got on his nerves, sometimes intentionally and sometimes unintentionally, but he suffered through it all for me. He knew how much I cared for Malcolm, and how much I wanted us all to get along. The effort he was making for me was never plainer.

"I just came by to tell you they removed everything from the clearing today. I thought you might want to know."

"It could have waited," Brand grumbled.

"Well, I'm not going to lie. I wanted to see Lilly, too," Malcolm said, leaving Brand's side and walking over to me. I guess I had a few stray hairs sticking out from my head, because Malcolm gently smoothed them down for me. His hand traveled down my left arm and took my hand. The smile on his face soon vanished as he felt what was on my ring finger. He looked down at it.

"What's this?" he asked confused.

"Brand asked me to marry him last night, and I said yes," I explained, hoping my news wouldn't hurt him too much.

"When are you supposed to be married?"

It was the first time I had ever seen Malcolm look worried.

"Not until I'm finished with school."

"Thank God," he said under his breath. I was sure Brand hadn't been able to hear it. He was still standing by the open door, eagerly awaiting his chance to throw Malcolm out of his home.

Malcolm let go of my hand, not wanting to look at the ring any longer. "Will said you were supposed to take Lilly to see your friend to do the genetic profile today. Who was it?"

"Allan Westwood," Brand answered.

"Allan?" Malcolm asked, surprised. "Does he still refuse to leave his house?"

"Yes."

"Did you at least take Lilly to the London Eye while you were there? I would hate to know that Allan's house was the only place she went to on her first visit to London."

"That's where I proposed." I could tell Brand felt a small bit of satisfaction telling Malcolm this, and it seemed to have the desired effect.

Malcolm kissed me on one cheek and walked back to the door. "Let me know what Allan finds out," Malcolm said to Brand. I heard Malcolm say something low to Brand, but it was too soft for me to make out what it was exactly. The only words I heard were 'four years'. The look of irritation on Brand's face quickly turned to the expression he used to hide his true feelings, completely unreadable.

"See you tomorrow, dearest," Malcolm turned to me and winked before walking out the front door.

Brand calmly closed the door and stood there for a moment, staring down at the doorknob still gripped in his hand.

"What did he say to you?" I asked, worried now by Brand's continued silence.

My question seemed to break his trance, and he finally looked at me.

"I'd rather not say, if that's ok with you. He's just jealous."

Brand came to me like a broken man and hugged me close. I wasn't sure what was wrong. I did the only thing I could think of to make him feel better.

"I love you," I said, hugging him as tightly as I could.

He pulled away from me just enough to look at my face, as if searching my eyes, almost expecting to see some doubt of my feelings for him there.

"I know," he whispered. "I love you, too."

"Then stop looking so sad." I cupped his face in both my hands, bringing his lips down to mine. It was the only prodding Brand needed in order to find his way back to where we left off before Malcolm's interruption.

We spent the rest of the night at Brand's house.

While I was taking my bath the next morning, I wondered where Will and Tara had phased to the night before. I could only assume Will had spent the night helping Tara forget about Simon. I was curious to know where he had taken her, though. When I stepped out of the shower and toweled off, the steam in the room was making it hard for me to see. I went to the small window by the vanity and opened it.

It was a beautiful late September day. The sun danced across the surface of the calm lake waters. The sweet sound of birds singing wafted through the window as a gentle breeze off the lake helped dissipate the steam in the room. It was an almost perfect morning. I quickly changed into the clothes I'd brought into the bathroom with me, and set about drying my hair with my towel.

The buzzing of a bee next to my ear first alerted me to its presence. As it flew past my face, I saw it was a yellow jacket. I swatted at it, trying to get it to go back out the window, but it nimbly avoided my hand. Before I knew it, the bee stung me on the side of my neck and promptly flew out the window. I looked in the mirror to see how bad the sting was. I could see the puffy red spot where it stung me, and watched in horror as it bulged into a large black polyp that soon disappeared as if it had been completely absorbed by my body. Once it was gone, you couldn't see any indication that I had been stung at all.

I felt the first effects almost immediately. My vision blurred and my head felt like it was about to explode off my shoulders.

The last thing I remembered was hitting my head against the tub as I fell unconscious.

Nothing made sense after that. I felt completely paralyzed. I couldn't hear, see, or feel anything around me. I had no concept of time. It felt like I was locked inside a dream with no way to wake up. I wanted to cry, but couldn't even find a way to do that.

After a long, long time, I finally saw Malcolm appear to me. He stood out like a beacon in the darkness of my mind. I wanted to run to him and ask him what was going on, but knew I didn't actually have a physical form to do such a thing with.

"Lilly?" he asked. "Are you here?"

I wanted to yell to him that I was here and to keep talking to me, but I couldn't.

"Listen, I'm not even sure this is working, but I had to try. We have you in the hospital. You're in a coma."

A coma?

"Dearest, try to tell me what happened. I pray you can see me now. I'm trying to share a dream with you. Honestly, I feel a bit stupid at the moment, but I had to try something. We can't figure out what's wrong with you. Brand found you lying on the floor of his bathroom a few days ago." The look of anguish on Malcolm's face told me that the situation was worse than I could have imagined. "The doctors here say you only have a few more days to live if they can't find out what's wrong. They've run tests but can't figure out what's causing the deterioration."

Deterioration? What was he talking about?

"Whatever is in your system is slowly shutting down all your organs. Brand and Will are out now, trying to find a way to cure you before it's too late."

I wanted to yell to Malcolm about the yellow jacket sting, but couldn't find my voice. There had to be a way to communicate with him and let him know what happened. But how?

"Dearest, please find a way to tell us what happened. I know you can do it. You have some of our abilities. Try to use the dream to show me what happened," he pleaded.

I could see that Malcolm was close to tears. It was then that I truly understood how dire my situation was. I tried to concentrate my thoughts and swim to the surface of my consciousness. But every time I thought I could feel a way to communicate with him, I fell even deeper into the darkness of my subconscious. Eventually, Malcolm faded from my mind, and I was left alone again.

I don't know how much time passed until I saw Brand appear. Unlike Malcolm, who simply appeared against a black backdrop, Brand recreated the moment he proposed to me on the London Eye. He stood alone in the glass bubble, so handsome in his tuxedo. Everything was perfect, except for the dead look in his eyes. I wanted to run to him and tell him everything would be all right.

"Lilly, come back to me," his forlorn voice broke my heart. I wanted to run into his arms and erase his pain. Why did I have to be the cause of so much heartache to my friends, my loved ones?

"You have to find a way to tell us what happened," he pleaded. "I can't lose you. I need you."

I wanted to tell Brand how much I loved him, in case it was the last time I ever saw him. Why couldn't I say something? I tried to think of some way to communicate. I decided to concentrate on the yellow jacket, the cause of the situation I found myself in now. If I couldn't speak in the dream, maybe I could project a picture of the reason I was in the state I was in. Maybe it would be enough for Brand to figure something out.

I saw Brand hang his head in complete hopelessness. My heart ached to be with him, to feel his body against mine one last time. I concentrated even harder on the image of the bee whose sting had propelled me into a coma. A buzzing noise filled my head. I saw Brand's head snap up at the sound. My image of an oversized yellow jacket hung in the air in front of him. I couldn't hold it for very long, but it seemed to be long enough for him to get the message.

"Hang on, Lilly. I love you," he said, filled with a new hope and sense of purpose.

He quickly vanished from my mind. The effort it had taken to project the image must have been great. I felt so tired and simply wanted to rest. I let the darkness drag me under to help me find some peace.

I wasn't sure what was happening to me. I'd been locked inside my dark prison for so long that it was a shock to my system when I finally did see light again. I slowly opened my eyes but quickly shut them again.

"Turn that dang light off," I heard Tara say. "It's bothering her eyes."

When I tried to open my eyes again, the first person I saw was Brand. He was looking at me expectantly, with tired grey eyes.

"Hey," I said, not being able to get much else out of my parched throat.

"Have her drink some more of this," I heard a strange male voice say. I looked to see who it was, and saw a tall black man in a dark blue suit and tie standing by Brand. He was handing him one of those nondescript beige plastic hospital cups with a straw in it.

"Drink this, my love," Brand said, placing the straw in my mouth. "It'll make you feel better."

The liquid inside the cup was sweet, almost like drinking sugar water. After I'd drained it of its contents, Brand handed the cup back to the stranger.

"What happened?" I asked, finally finding my voice.

"You were poisoned," Brand explained. "Malik was able to make the cure to save your life."

I turned my attention to the tall black man again. I could only assume he was Malik. He was a nice looking man, in an odd way. His hair was cropped short and his ears stuck out a bit far from his head, but it didn't detract from his handsome features too much. He had an open, friendly face that was only accentuated by his smile.

"I'm just glad Brand figured out what was happening before it was too late," Malik said with sincere humbleness.

"I don't understand," I said. "It was just a bee sting."

"It wasn't an ordinary bee," Brand replied. I saw his jaw muscles tighten, a sure sign he was trying very hard to keep his anger in check in front of me. "Don't worry about it right now. We're handling it."

"You need to get as much rest as you can," Malik advised me. "The effects of the poison will take at least a day to completely go away."

"How long was I in a coma?" I asked.

"Two weeks," Brand told me.

"Where are Will and Malcolm?"

"They're doing something for us. They'll be here when they can," Brand said in a controlled tone that told me he was deliberately hiding something from me.

"So what are we going tell the doctors?" Tara asked, looking at Malik for an answer. "They were pretty much telling us to make funeral arrangements just a few hours ago. How are we going explain a full recovery?"

Tara was always practical when it came to explaining the surreal world I found myself in to the real world around us.

"They'll just think it was a miracle," Malik told her. "As long as Lilly's healthy, they won't worry about it too much. They didn't understand what was wrong in the first place. Most likely, they'll just assume that whatever poison was running through her system made its way out."

"Well, I better go get Grandma and Lilly's mom," Tara said. "It was hard enough to convince them to leave her long enough for you to work your voodoo on her."

"I'll go with you," Malik quickly volunteered.

Tara seemed surprised by his offer but didn't tell him to stay behind. She turned to me and said, "We'll be back. Just be prepared for a lot of crying. You had us all worried, girl." Tara kissed me on the cheek and went to the door. I saw Malik open it for her and let her go out before him.

I looked at Brand and saw how much the past two weeks had drained him, not only emotionally but also physically. His face was paler than usual and his eyes were still haunted by the real possibility he had to face of losing me again.

"I'm sorry," I said.

"Why should you be sorry?" he asked, completely unprepared for my apology.

"All I seem to do is cause you and everyone else a lot of pain. Maybe you should have just let me go."

"Don't say that," he said with such vehemence it made me flinch. "I don't ever want to hear you say that again. Do you under-stand me?"

I couldn't say anything.

"You just don't understand," he said, running an agitated hand through his hair. "None of us would be the same without you in our lives. Don't ever say you'd rather be dead. If you had died, a piece of all of us would have died with you." He looked at me. I wanted to erase the pain I had placed on his face. "And it would have completely destroyed me, Lilly."

How could I have said such a selfish, thoughtless thing to him after everything he must have gone through the past few days? I immediately felt ashamed for my moment of self-pity.

"Forgive me," I said, putting my hand on his arm. "I wasn't thinking."

"I'll forgive you if you promise to never say something like that again."

"I promise."

Brand leaned down and gently kissed me on the lips. He touched his forehead to mine, and just sat there with his eyes closed, content just to be near me.

The door to my room opened, and I saw Utha Mae and my mom walk in. Brand left my bedside to allow them some time with me. I saw him walk over to Malik and say something. Malik nodded and left the room.

Tara had been right. Utha Mae and my mom ended up crying as soon as they saw that I was awake. Brand stayed in the background, keeping a watchful eye on me. A little while later, Malik came back into the room and said something to Brand. Brand nodded, but never took his eyes off me. Malik took a seat in the corner, obviously wanting to be out of the way of my family reunion.

I did, however, notice his eyes follow Tara wherever she went.

I wasn't sure how I felt about that. Yes, from what I knew, he had been the one who'd saved my life but, other than that, I didn't know anything else about him. After the fiasco that was Simon, I intended to make sure Malik's intentions were honorable, if indeed he had romantic designs toward my best friend.

A little while later, the team of doctors assigned to my case came into the room and hovered over me, pondering what had caused my miraculous recovery. Having no clue what had cured me, since they were never able to figure out why I was sick in the first place, they did what Malik said they would and agreed that whatever had been in my system was now out.

Utha Mae and my mom decided to leave about an hour later. Apparently, they had been staying with me in my hospital room a lot since my arrival, and both wanted to spend a night in their own beds for the first time in two weeks. I encouraged them to go home. Malik and Tara escorted Utha Mae down to her car. Before she left, my mom picked up my left hand, lightly touching the ring on my finger.

"When did this happen?" she asked.

"Not long before I got sick."

"When do you plan to get married?"

"After I'm out of school."

"I see," she put my hand back on the bed. "Well, you get some rest and call me if you need anything."

She turned from me, and I thought she was going to leave the room, but she walked over to Brand first.

"Take care of her," she told him and gave him a motherly hug.

After she left, Brand came and sat down beside me on my bed.

"She took that better than I thought she would," I said.

"Your mother loves you," Brand replied. "I know she hasn't

always shown you that in the past, in the best way possible, but you shouldn't doubt her love for you. I think she just wants to see you happy. Like we all do."

"What did Malik tell you earlier when he came back into the room?"

"He told me Malcolm and Will caught the person who poisoned you."

"Who was it?"

He paused as if he wasn't sure he wanted me to know, but he finally said, "Izzi."

"Izzi? Why would she want to kill me?"

How had I made Izzi mad enough to want me dead? I'd only met her maybe three times in my life.

"I'm not sure yet," Brand answered. "But I intend to find out." The menace in his voice worried me.

"And how exactly do you plan to do that?"

"Malik can force her to tell us the truth."

"How?"

"Do you remember me telling you that Izzi is a fairy?"

"Yes."

It was the night I went to Brand and declared my love to him. I'd asked him about his relationship with Izzi, and discovered it had all been a ruse to make me mad enough to forget about him.

"Malik is her leader. I guess you could say he's the king of the fairies. She's supposed to answer anything he asks her truthfully. But if she doesn't, I'll know."

"I don't understand. How did she poison me with a bee?"

"Fairies are shape-shifters. They're all born with the ability to shift into one particular animal. When you showed me the yellow jacket, I knew it had been Izzi who'd poisoned you."

"Is that like a skill of hers? The poison she put inside me?"

"No, she used a mixture of poisonous plants and coated her stinger with it. They're practically untraceable, since they can only be found deep inside the Amazon. Fairies know a lot about nature. They protect nature when they can and use it when it's advantageous to them. That's one reason they like to be naked whenever they can. It's a more natural state. After you showed me it was her, I went to Malik to ask for his help. When I told him what your symptoms were, he had me take him to the Amazon to find the antidote. However, involving Malik is going to change both of your lives I'm afraid."

"In a good or bad way?" I asked hesitantly.

Brand smiled. It was the first true smile I had seen on his face since I woke up.

"Depends on how you look at it, I suppose. When a fairy saves a human life, they become that human's godparent."

"So, what, Malik's like my fairy godfather now?"

"Basically, yes. He's going to be in your life a lot from this day forward. Fairies are very particular about how their charges are treated and looked after."

"How old is he?"

"Mid-twenties, I think. Why?"

"He's not like you then? He won't live forever?"

"No, fairies have life spans similar to humans now. There aren't any pureblooded fairies left in the world. Most fairies live to be a hundred or a little over that, but not much."

"Do they have powers?"

"Only the ability to shape-shift; their knowledge of plants and animals is passed down from generation to generation. They're skilled at making potions but not much else."

"Can I be there when you ask Izzi why she tried to kill me?"

"Why would you want to see her again?"

"I want to know why she did it, and I want her to tell me herself."

Brand was hesitant to honor my request but he finally said, "If that is what you want."

CHAPTER 7

The doctors reentered my room before Tara and Malik made it back from escorting Utha Mae to her car. They requested I stay in the hospital for a couple more days for further observation. I didn't want them to be any more suspicious than they already were about my recovery, so I agreed to stay and let them run their tests. Brand stayed close by my side while they talked with us. I began to wonder if he would ever feel comfortable leaving me alone again. It seemed like every time he did, something bad happened to me. Heck, I wasn't sure I wanted him to leave me alone either.

Tara and Malik came back to my room after the doctors left, and told me Utha Mae and my mom planned to visit again the next day to check on me.

"What day is it anyway?" I asked, having no concept of time anymore.

"It's Sunday," Tara answered.

"They're going to kick me out of school," I moaned, leaning my head back on my pillow, staring at the white tiled ceiling above my head. "And Dr. Barry is going to fire me."

"Girl, you worry too much," Tara sat down on the side of my bed. "I'll go get your assignments from your teachers tomorrow.

They know you were in the hospital. And don't worry about Dr. Barry." The confident smile on Tara's face had me intrigued.

"Why? Did something happen to her?"

"Oh, I had Malcolm go talk to her for you. From what he said, she'd pretty much do anything he asked her to. So, keeping your job isn't something you need to worry about."

Poor Dr. Barry. she had already been slightly infatuated with Malcolm even before meeting him. After being exposed to him, I was sure she thought herself head over heels in love with my friend now. I would need to make sure Malcolm didn't go see her again. It wasn't fair to use his power of attraction in such a selfish way.

"I need to head back to Washington to make some arrangements," Malik said to us. "But I'll be back as soon as I can." I couldn't help but notice his eyes were more on Tara than Brand and me when he said this.

"Would you mind taking me home? I'd like to get things taken care of quickly," Malik said to Brand.

"Of course," Brand reluctantly left my side and put his hand on Malik's shoulder. "I'll be right back," he said to me before they phased.

"So what's the story with Malik?" Tara asked. "He just sort of showed up and took over."

"He's my fairy godfather," I said, feeling a little silly saying it aloud. They were words I never could have imagined coming out of my mouth.

Tara's eyes widened. "You mean he's gay? Girl, that figures. Why do so many good-looking men end up liking other men?"

I couldn't help but giggle. "No, Malik's not gay, as far as I know. I mean he's literally my fairy godfather."

Tara looked completely confused, and I couldn't blame her. I wasn't all that confident I understood what it meant either.

"You mean like in Disney movies?" Tara questioned. "He's not going to be dancing around with a wand, singing Bibbity Bobbity Boo, is he?"

"No," I laughed. "At least, I hope that's not how it works."

Brand reappeared in the same spot he'd phased from, and seemed pleasantly surprised to return to see me laughing.

"What's so funny?" he asked, coming to reclaim his seat on the other side of my bed.

"I was just telling Tara that Malik is my fairy godfather."

"He's going to tell his firm that he's moving to Lakewood," Brand informed me.

"What type of work does he do?"

"He works for a private law firm. They handle environmental policies and things like that. He said it didn't really matter where his home was. He may have to make trips up to Washington D.C. every once in a while, but that would be about it. He mostly works from home anyway."

"So he's completely changing his life because of me?" I asked, wondering how many people I would end up affecting in some way. "When is he supposed to come back?" I asked.

"In a couple of days, when you're allowed to go home," Brand answered.

"When can we talk with Izzi? I want to know why she tried to kill me."

"We'll need to wait until you're out of here, since you want to be with us when we ask her."

Unexpectedly, Malcolm and Will walked through the door to

my room. Brand and Tara gave up their positions beside me so my two other fallen angel friends could give me hugs.

"Dearest," Malcolm said in an admonishing tone, "you really need to stop having these near-death experiences. I'm not sure I can handle them anymore."

Malcolm sat beside me, holding one of my hands.

"I'll see what I can do about that," I said, squeezing his hand, trying to reassure him that I was feeling better.

"Where is she?" Brand asked Will, who was standing on the other side of my bed. Will handed Brand what looked like a small metal box.

"She waited until the last possible second to change," Will said.

Brand put the box into one of his pants pockets.

It took me a minute to understand what they were talking about.

"Is Izzi in the box?" I asked.

"Yes," Brand answered, trying to keep his emotions in check, but I could see the anger simmering behind his grey eyes. "Fairies have to change into their animal form once a day for at least a few minutes, or they lose the ability to shape-shift. Malcolm and Will waited until Izzi had to change and then they trapped her."

"Why doesn't she just change back into her human form?" I asked. Surely, she could just bust out of her small prison that way.

"It's an iron box," Will told me, coming to stand on my left side once again. "It's like poison to fairies. She won't be able to change back until we let her out."

"Then why don't we just open it up now?" I asked. "I want to know why she did this to me."

"It was hard enough to catch her the first time, dearest," Malcolm said. "We'll have to do it at my house. The room I built for Sebastian to stay in at night has no openings for her to use as an escape. She can't simply change into the bee and run away from us there. It's where we've been holding her until she needed to shape-shift again."

"Shape-shift?" Tara asked. "What are y'all talking about?"

Brand explained to Tara about the shape-shifting ability of fairies.

"What's Malik turn into?" she asked.

"I think it's a black cat of some sort," Brand answered. "But you would have to ask him to confirm that. I don't know Malik all that well, to be honest. We've never spent much time together."

A nurse came into my room then to let us know that visiting hours were over. No one wanted to go, but the way the nurse stood at the door reminded me of a prison guard waiting for her charges to do what she said.

"I'll be back tomorrow," Malcolm whispered before kissing my hand and leaving the room under the watchful eyes of the nurse.

Will kissed me on the forehead. I noticed his eyes drop to the ring on my finger. When he looked back up at me, he lifted his eyebrows in a motion I had seen a lot during our childhood. I knew he would want to talk about the engagement ring when we had some time alone. I wasn't sure I really wanted to have that talk with him, though.

Tara told me she was going to go back home and start cleaning.

"You don't need to come home to a nasty apartment. I'll bring your school stuff to you tomorrow when I get out of my classes."

Finally, Brand and I were alone again, but I wasn't sure for how long. As soon as everyone was gone, I lifted my arm, holding out my hand to him in a silent plea to be held. It didn't take long before he was lying in bed beside me, holding me close. I guess I was more tired than I thought. Within a few short seconds, I was sound asleep.

I didn't wake up until the next morning. When I did, Will was sitting beside me in a chair, watching me.

"Hey," I said trying to sit up. "Where's Brand?"

Will stood and helped me. He grabbed an extra pillow from underneath the bed and placed it behind my back.

"He went to his house to change clothes. How are you feeling?" he asked, taking a seat beside me on the bed.

"I feel a lot better today. I guess I just needed some real sleep. Would you mind getting me some water, though? My throat feels scratchy."

Will poured some water from a pitcher beside my bed and handed me the cup. When I took the cup from him, I saw his eyes drop to the sparkling diamonds on my ring finger.

"Malcolm says you told Brand you didn't want to get married until after you were out of school."

"That's right," I took a sip of water from the cup, waiting for him to continue.

"Don't you think it's a little soon to be engaged to him?" The incredulity in Will's voice wasn't lost on me. "I mean, you've known him for like, what, a month?"

"I love him, Will. That's all I need to know."

"But," I could see the frustration on his face. There was a lot he wanted to say, but he didn't seem sure how to say it. "Ok, how do you know he loves you for who you are and not just because of the way you make him feel? I mean, does he really even know you? Does he know what you like and what you don't like? Does he know you cry at romantic movies and sappy

Hallmark commercials? Does he know you like to eat tomato sauce but not fresh tomatoes? Does he know chocolate fudge always makes you feel better when you're depressed? What if what he feels is just because you make him feel almost human? How do you know he's someone you want to spend the rest of your life with? I mean, have you even thought about that part? He'll never grow old, Lilly. Can you honestly say that won't bother you?"

Will's words had their desired effect. How did I know Brand loved me for who I was and not just for how I made him feel? The effect I had on all the Watchers couldn't be disputed. I knew they all felt a special contentment in my presence, that none of them had ever experienced before. Will was right about the fact that Brand really didn't know that much about me. Was his love for me just a byproduct of my peculiar nature? It was how I explained away Malcolm's feelings for me. I just assumed the effect I had on him was the cause of his infatuation. Could the same be said of Brand?

I hated the doubt Will had just planted. It made me question everything now.

"We have four years," I said, trying to sound reasonable. "It's plenty of time for us to get to know one another better, if I make it that long."

"Don't talk like that." Will's reaction resembled Brand's the previous day, when I thoughtlessly said it might have been better for everyone if I had just died. "We'll figure everything out. You'll live a long, full life, Lilly Rayne Nightingale. You have my word on that."

Brand phased into my room, dressed in a fresh blue polo shirt and jeans. He wasn't alone, though. Abby was with him, wearing her purple pigtailed wig, a white pin- tucked puff-sleeve shirt, black slacks, and lavender contact lenses.

"Hey, love," she said, walking up to me and kissing me on the cheek.

"Hey, Abby."

Will left soon after their arrival. I got the feeling he didn't like being around Abby. It was just as well. Our talk had put me in a pensive mood.

Abby and Brand had only been in my room for about thirty minutes when Brand got a call on his cell phone. From the look on his face, I could tell he was surprised by whoever it was on the other end of the line.

"Are you sure?" he asked the caller, as if he couldn't believe what he was hearing. "Ok, I'll be there in a few minutes."

"Who was it?" I asked after he ended the call.

"Allan," he replied in surprise, slipping his cell phone back into his pocket. "He wants to come here and tell us what he found out about you through the tests he ran."

"He what?" The complete astonishment on Abby's face was almost comical. "He actually wants to leave his bubble and come out into the real world?"

"I know. I can't believe it either," Brand replied, shaking his head in amazement.

"I almost forgot all about those tests," I said. It seemed like it had been longer than two weeks since my visit to Allan's house. "Why is he so anxious to tell me what he found?"

"He wouldn't say over the phone," Brand answered. "And now that you're awake, he doesn't want to wait to tell you what he discovered. I need to go get him."

"Why can't he just phase here himself?" I asked.

"Allan hasn't been many places," Brand answered. "We can only phase to locations we've physically been to before, unless we're following another angel's phase trail." He walked over to me and gave me a kiss to tide me over while he was gone.

"Oh, geez," Abby said, averting her eyes. "Do you really have to do that in front of me, Dad?"

"You'd better get used to it, daughter of mine." He smiled at her and gave me a wink. "I plan to do that a lot, whether you're around or not."

"Well, give a girl some warning next time, would ya? At least give me a chance to make myself scarce."

"I'll be right back," Brand said to me before he phased.

"I've never seen Dad smile so much before," Abby said to me after he was gone. "You make him happier than he's ever been."

It made me think about what Will had said. Why did he have to plant that seed of doubt in my head about Brand's true feelings for me? It was making everything seem tainted with uncertainty now.

It only took a minute for Brand to come back with Allan. Allan may have stepped out of his glass room for the first time in, I didn't know how long, but it didn't stop him from protecting himself as much as he could. He showed up wearing a black suit, black leather gloves, and a white mask over his nose and mouth, like the ones surgeons wear in operating rooms.

"Hello," he said, nodding his head to Abby and me in greeting.

"Hey, Allan." Abby didn't move from her spot on the bed. I think she was worried that any sudden movements might frighten Allan away.

"Brand said you have some news for us," I said to him, hoping to keep his mind on the mission at hand, and distract him from overanalyzing his new environment too much.

"Yes, I do," Allan replied.

I wasn't sure Allan was going to say anything else. He just stood there, staring at me.

"What did you find out, old friend?" Brand finally asked, trying to prod Allan into talking.

"Lilly shouldn't exist."

He said it so simply I almost missed its full meaning.

"What do you mean?" I asked.

"One of your paternal ancestors was an angel, but they were neither a Watcher nor a rebellion angel."

"Do you think you could expound some on what you're saying?" Brand asked, becoming visibly frustrated with his friend.

"Lilly's genetic code is similar to our own but large sections of it don't match at all, making it completely unique in sequence. However, it's not only your paternal genetic profile that is different. Your mitochondrial DNA sequence is unlike anything I have ever seen before as well."

"What does that mean?" I asked.

"Mitochondrial DNA is only maternally inherited. There has been a lot of research done by humans trying to find the 'Mitochondrial Eve', or the one common ancestor who is the mother of all humans. Because of that research, most every human can be classified into one of the known mitochondrial DNA groups, but I can't fit your results into any of them."

"Why do you think that is?" Brand asked.

"I'm not sure," Allan replied. I could hear an undertone of excitement in his voice. I think he was actually smiling underneath his mask. "I would really like a sample from Lilly's mother and grandmother, to verify that the mutation was inherited naturally from them and not through some byproduct of her angel DNA."

"We can probably get a sample from my mother, but I have no idea who my grandmother is, or where we can find her. I can try to get the information from Cora but that's going to be really iffy."

"Try to ask her again," Brand said. "If she doesn't tell you, I'll hire a private detective to find your grandparents for us."

My mother had always been adamant about not involving my grandparents in our lives. I was sure she wouldn't tell me where they were, even if I asked again. The possibility of meeting them was exciting, though. I'd always wanted to know who they were and why my mother turned her back on them so completely. But would they want to meet me? Would they want to have a relationship with a granddaughter they never wanted in the first place?

"Mom and Utha Mae are supposed to come by and see me today," I said. "I'll ask her then."

"Well," Allan looked around him with a critical eye, as if he imagined some microscopic organism landing on him at any moment, "that's really all the information I have for the time being. I brought you some buccal swab kits for the mother and grandmother," Allan handed Brand a clear plastic bag with what I assumed to be the swab kits. "Just take a sample from the inside of their cheeks. It should be enough to get the answers we need. I really need to be going now."

Allan looked at me and bowed slightly before phasing.

"I'm bloody surprised he lasted that long," Abby said after Allan's departure.

There was a light knock on my door.

"Hello," I heard Utha Mae call as she opened the door, warning us of her entry.

I saw my mother right behind her. Good, I could get things over with sooner than I thought. I was positive Cora wouldn't tell me where my grandparents were anyway. The sooner we knew that for sure, the faster we could get a private detective on the case.

"Good morning, child," Utha Mae came in with a few Tupperware bowls in her hands. "I hope you're hungry."

At the mention of food, I suddenly realized I was starving. I could only assume the needle stuck in my arm and the ever-present bags hanging at my side had been my only means of nutrition while I was in my coma. The idea of real food had my mouth involuntarily watering.

I introduced my mom and Utha Mae to Abby. I told them she was Brand's cousin, since the truth would be completely unbelievable, anyway, and quite a bit harder to explain. With my two new visitors, Abby made her goodbyes and asked Brand to walk her out to her car. I knew he would just be phasing her back home and didn't stress too much about his absence being long.

When I uncovered the bowls Utha Mae brought me, I sighed in total contentment. She had made me scrambled eggs with cheese, bacon, sausage, biscuits, and shrimp grits.

"I had to use the microwave they had here in the lounge to reheat it all," she told me. "Hopefully, it won't taste funny."

Well, it didn't taste funny at all. It tasted like a little bit of heaven swimming inside my mouth.

My mother surprised me by bringing in a stack of wedding magazines. I had never seen her so excited before. It was a completely different side to her. I suppose, since she never found a man of her own to marry, she was living out a fantasy through me. When Brand came back into the room, he smiled when he saw the way my mother was acting about our wedding. Even though I knew it wouldn't be taking place for quite some time, I simply couldn't bring myself to tell her she was planning way too far ahead. She was having so much fun talking about dresses and bridesmaid gowns that I didn't want to dampen her happy mood.

After I ate and listened to my mother talk about veils and how I should have my hair styled, I decided it was time to bring up the subject of my grandparents.

"Mom," I said, drawing her attention away from the magazine in her hands, "since I'm getting married and everything, I was wondering if you could tell me where I could find my grandparents. Maybe they would like to come."

"Even if they wanted to come, they'd never travel this far," my mom said, organizing the magazines scattered on my bed. "You know how I feel about them, Lilly. The subject is closed."

I decided not to push the matter, and let it drop.

"Oh, Ms. Nightingale," Brand said, picking up the clear plastic bag with the buccal kits in them. "Lilly needs to get a sample of your DNA for our biology class. We're doing a comparison of our DNA with a family member. Would you mind me taking it for her?"

"What do I need to do?" my mom asked hesitantly.

"Nothing but open your mouth. I just need to wipe the lining of one of your cheeks with a cotton swab."

Now why hadn't I thought to do that? I was sure my mom would be resistant to me asking her for a DNA sample, but Brand did it with such ease I couldn't help but be impressed.

It only took a few seconds, and Brand had what he needed. He made an excuse that he was taking the sample down to a cooler in his car, but I was sure he went directly to Allan's house as soon as he left the room.

At around lunchtime, my mom said she needed to get to work. She was still working at a dress shop in Dalton that a friend of hers owned. Since she had taken the previous two weeks off to be with me, she didn't want to impose on her friend's kindness anymore, and went in to work her regular hours. Utha Mae stayed with me for a little while longer, wanting to see Tara before she went back home.

"Brand, hon," Utha Mae said, rummaging through her purse and pulling out a crisp one dollar bill. "Would you mind going out to one of those vending machines and getting me a ginger ale?"

"No problem, Ms. Jenkins," Brand took her dollar and went out the door.

Once he was gone, Utha Mae turned to me. "Now, I want you to tell me the truth, baby. Do you love that man?"

Without hesitation, I said, "Yes."

"That's all I need to know then." She put her purse back on the chair beside my bed. "When he asked me for permission to marry you, I wasn't quite sure what you would want me to say. But the more I thought about it, the more I figured if you didn't want to marry him, you'd just tell him no. I kinda figured you would say yes, though." She smiled at me and came to see the ring on my finger. "I swear, child. You could knock somebody out cold with that ring."

I had to chuckle. "That's the exact same thing your grand-daughter said when she saw it."

When Brand came back into the room, Tara was with him. She had a book bag on her back that made her look like the Hunchback of Notre Dame. I groaned inwardly, knowing it would be filled with my homework assignments for school.

Tara showed me what I had to do for my classes before she

took Utha Mae down to the cafeteria to buy her some lunch. Brand helped me sort through my homework. While I was reading a chapter in my world civilization textbook, I couldn't help but think about my conversation with Will earlier. I think I read the same page five times without understanding a word of it.

Brand must have noticed my inability to concentrate, because he came to sit beside me and asked, "What's wrong?"

"It's nothing," I said, trying to brush off my doubts, but apparently they still lingered in my eyes.

"No, it's something; enough to worry you at least. Tell me what's wrong."

I let out a sigh, not knowing if I really wanted to tell Brand what I was thinking. But, if we were going to be married someday, I didn't need to start keeping secrets from him now.

"It's just something Will and I were talking about earlier."

"Which was?"

"He said our engagement seemed really fast, especially since you don't know me very well."

"I know you," Brand said confidently. "I may not know the things he does, but I know a lot about you."

"Like what?"

"I know you are thoughtful, kind-hearted, and loyal. I know when you give someone your friendship that it's forever. And I know the most important thing I need to know - you love me."

"But there's so much about me that you don't know."

"Everything else will come in time. I plan to spend every day of your life with you. I'm bound to learn a few things."

"He said something else which bothers me even more than you not knowing the little things about me."

"And what was that?"

I could tell Brand was suspicious, but I'd already opened up the subject. I couldn't back out now.

"He said your feelings for me may just be a side effect of the way I make all the Watchers feel. That maybe you're mistaking the contentment you feel around me for being in love."

"Do you honestly think that's true?"

The expression of hurt on Brand's face made me wish I didn't have doubts about his love for me. But I refused to lie to him.

"I don't know. It's not so much that I doubt you love me, but you can't deny the effect I have on Malcolm, too."

"You can't possibly compare my feelings with that buffoon's." Brand sounded so offended I wasn't sure I wanted this conversation to continue. "He's completely infatuated with you. It's not the same thing as love."

"But you said yourself you've never been around anyone like me before. How can you be so sure that what you feel for me is real?"

Brand cupped the side of my face with one of his hands. The look in his eyes told me how much what I said hurt him, but I think he understood how my doubts were hurting me, too.

"You do have an effect on me. I freely admit that. But my love for you goes so far beyond just feeling content. I don't know how to tell you how much I love you to make you truly understand. Even if you didn't have the ability to curb the hunger for blood I've felt since I was exiled here, I would still love you. I would still want to marry you. The connection we have with one another goes beyond any physical pleasure. Don't let Will's jealousy taint the love you have for me. You have to know how much he wants you for himself. He's still in love with you, Lilly. I don't know if he said these things to provide a way to change your feelings for me, or if he said them to hurt me because I'm taking you even further away from him. But, please, don't doubt my love for you. I can't stand to think you consider my love so feeble."

I felt ashamed. How could I have admitted to him that I doubted his feelings were real?

"I'm sorry," I said, pulling him to me, hugging him tight. "I'm so sorry. Forget what I just said."

Brand pulled away from me and looked into my eyes. "No, I can't. I won't. If I have to spend every day for the rest of your life proving how much I love you, I will."

"I know you love me." I could tell he knew I was telling him the truth. "It's probably just the fact that you're so perfect. I can't understand why you would want to be with someone like me, except for this power I have that makes you feel almost human."

Brand just shook his head at me, like I still didn't understand the true depth of his feelings for me.

"One day you'll know that isn't why I love you. For now, all I can do is tell you and show you how much you mean to me."

He held me close. We stayed like that, silently willing the other person to physically feel the love we had for the other, until Tara came back into the room.

CHAPTER 8

I spent the rest of the afternoon catching up on my schoolwork. Brand ended up helping me understand more than just reading the pages in my text books did. Since he had lived through the things my world civilization class discussed, he was able to give me a first-hand account of the events I needed to know about. And his knowledge of math and science helped me understand a few concepts that had been eluding me all semester. Catching up on my schoolwork didn't take nearly as long as I had feared at first.

Malcolm came to visit me near suppertime, and brought in some contraband food for us to eat from a local restaurant. He also happened to bring his chess set.

We told him about the results of Allan's genetic work-up on me. He seemed as excited about the intriguing data as Allan had been.

"I was hoping I could talk you into a game," he said to me while Tara and Brand were cleaning up after our meal.

"That sounds like a good idea," Brand said. "I need to go help Malik move his things into his new apartment."

"Which apartments is he moving into?" I asked.

"Lakewood Gardens," Brand said. "He's anxious to get settled as soon as he can."

"Mind if I come with you to help?" Tara asked.

"I'm sure he wouldn't mind that," Brand replied, trying to hide his smile. He came over to me, and gave me a kiss that literally took my breath away.

I heard Malcolm clear his throat loudly. Brand pulled away with a satisfied grin on his face. "I'll be back as soon as we're through. Don't tire her out," he said to Malcolm. "I plan to continue that kiss when I get back."

Malcolm lifted a dubious eyebrow at Brand. "I'll try not to think about that while we enjoy some private time together. You know I don't get Lilly to myself very often these days."

"Just keep her safe," Brand almost ordered, going to stand beside Tara.

"Ready?" he asked, laying a hand on her shoulder.

"Yep."

When they left, Malcolm set up the chessboard on the wheeled bed table I usually ate my meals on.

"Malcolm," I eyed my friend hesitantly, not sure I should open up this can of worms but needing to know the answer, "how would you describe your feelings for me?"

Malcolm stopped what he was doing and looked at me quizzically. "What exactly do you mean, dearest?"

"Would you say you feel like you're in love with me?"

"Why are you asking me this? Are you having doubts about marrying Brand?" he asked hopefully.

"No," I quickly said, not wanting to give him the impression that my feelings for Brand were wavering, "something Will said to me this morning keeps bugging me."

"And what would that be?"

"He said Brand's feelings for me are just because of the way I make him feel when he's around me. So, I wanted to know what your true feelings were for me. Would you say you *think* you're in love with me?"

Malcolm was thoughtful for a moment and crossed his arms over his semi-bared chest as he considered my question.

"I wouldn't take the things Will says to heart if I were you, dearest. His kind is so used to twisting the truth to get what they want. I doubt even he realizes he's doing it. I admit that the way you make me feel content with myself is extremely addictive. I've made no secret about that. But it's not the reason I care for you."

"Why do you care for me so much?"

"Well, we have a lot of fun together, don't we, at least when your over-protective fiancé isn't around? I can be myself around you, which is something I haven't been able to do in quite some time. You're my friend. I don't have many of those."

"But would you say you're in love with me?" I pressed. I needed to know.

"Are you asking me because you have those feeling for me, or because you're just trying to judge how true Brand's feelings are for you?"

"I love you as a friend," I replied, not wanting to give him the wrong impression.

"Well, that's something I suppose," Malcolm murmured, somewhat disappointed. "If those feelings ever change into something deeper, I'll answer your question." He continued to set up the chessboard. "Until then, dearest, I'd rather keep my feelings to myself. You'll either have to believe Brand or not. There isn't much I can do to prove that he loves you. He has to do that himself."

S.J. WEST

I was slightly frustrated with Malcolm's obtuse answer. Why was it so hard to just tell me how he felt? He either felt like he was in love with me or not. However, I didn't want to push the issue. He wasn't the only one who had few friends. I enjoyed his company, too.

About an hour and a half later, Brand, Tara, and Malik appeared in my room.

"Hey," I said to the trio. "Get everything moved?"

"Just need to move my car," Malik answered, eyeing Malcolm with open distrust. "Everything all right here?" he asked, keeping his eyes on Malcolm as he began to pack up the chess game.

"You don't have to worry about me, Malik," Malcolm said, unable to hide his irritation. "I'm a reformed vampire, or hasn't that been explained to you?"

"No, I've been told about you," Malik answered, sounding like he didn't quite believe what he had heard. "It doesn't mean I trust you around Lilly. I don't know you that well yet."

"And then there were three," Malcolm mumbled, continuing to pack up the game, but handling the pieces more roughly than before.

"Malcolm is a good friend of mine," I told Malik. "He'd never do anything to harm me."

"If you say so," Malik replied, keeping his eyes on Malcolm, not trying to conceal his disapproval of the friend I had chosen.

"I think I'll be going, dearest," Malcolm said, giving me a quick kiss on the lips.

My eyes fell on Brand as Malcolm stood upright and tucked his chess game under an arm. Brand was displeased with Malcolm's show of affection, but kept his emotions reigned in.

"What time are we going to interrogate Izzi?" Malcolm asked.

"As soon as Lilly is discharged," Brand answered, keeping his voice level. "I'll call you tomorrow when we have a more definite time."

"Then I'll see you all tomorrow." Malcolm said before phasing.

"Listen," I said to Malik, "I know you're supposed to be my fairy godfather, or whatever, but you need to understand how important Malcolm is to me. He's my friend. If you're going to be a part of my life now, you need to understand that. He gets enough grief from Brand and Will. He doesn't need to be getting it from you, too, especially since I know him a hell of a lot better than I know you. He's earned my friendship and loyalty. You haven't."

"I'm sorry if I upset you, Lilly," Malik said, seeing how irritated I was at his treatment of my friend. "It's just my nature to be suspicious of anyone my charge comes into contact with. Malcolm's a vampire. I'm sorry, but that puts him at the top of my list of suspicious characters."

"I don't like him that much either," Brand admitted. "But Lilly's right. He is her friend, whether I like it or not. He wouldn't hurt her, or I wouldn't leave her alone with him. If I can trust him, you can trust him."

"I'll give him the benefit of the doubt, for now. He would be the first Watcher I've ever heard of who's successfully stopped drinking human blood after he's tasted it. It'll take a while for me to fully believe he isn't a danger to anyone."

I noticed Malik glance Tara's way as he said his last sentence.

"We just came to drop Tara off," Brand said to me. "I'll help Malik move his car and come right back. It shouldn't take but a few minutes."

"I'll be fine," I reassured him.

Once Malik and Brand were gone, Tara came and sat on the side of my bed.

"Ok, spill, girl."

"What are you talking about?" I asked.

"What was going on when I came in here this afternoon? It looked like you and Brand were making up from a fight or something."

"I guess we were, sort of."

"What happened?"

I explained Will's theory of why Brand fell in love with me so fast to Tara, and my subsequent talk with Brand about the subject. I also mentioned my talk with Malcolm.

"Well, I'm glad you didn't try to keep it from Brand," she said. "But Will's gonna get an earful the next time I see him. I swear that boy just doesn't know when to give up. You know I love him like a brother, but I agree with Malcolm. I think the demon part of him just wins out sometimes. Brand loves you, girl. I don't know why you feel like you're not good enough for him, or whatever. Just be happy that he does."

I didn't want to linger on the subject anymore. So, I decided to change it.

"Hey, you never told me where Will took you the other night after that business with Simon."

"He took me to Disneyland. You know how I've always wanted to go to Disney World, but it was just too late to go to Florida. So he took me to the one over in California, since it was still open."

"That was nice of him."

It reminded me of how thoughtful Will could be. Was he just acting out his jealousy, by casting doubt on Brand's feelings for me like everyone seemed to think, or was he acting like the best friend I once knew so well? What Will had said was plausible. Brand and Malcolm might not even realize that their feelings were being clouded by my power over them. We still didn't know everything about me. Could there be something else about me that would cause Watchers to fall in love with me? Even Justin had said he wanted to keep me for himself when I was his prisoner. And Robert, well, I didn't want to think about that episode in my life, but even he had been affected by me enough to almost go against Justin. Maybe Will wasn't that far off the mark. How could I know for sure?

When Brand made it back to my room, Tara gathered up her belongings and said she would be back the next day to help me check out of the hospital.

After she was gone, I silently watched Brand as he packed up my schoolbooks and the few personal belongings I had. I think he wanted to make my departure from my sterile prison as fast as possible the next day.

Did Brand really love me?

It was a question that kept running through my mind, even though I didn't want it to. And I felt like a traitor to his love for doubting it. I knew he thought he loved me, but was it real? I hadn't doubted it until Will brought up the possibility that his feelings for me were just a byproduct of what I was. Did it matter if that were the case, though? Wasn't love usually caused by feeling comfortable in someone else's presence? So comfortable that you could relax and simply be yourself? Perhaps I shouldn't worry about why Brand loved me and just accept the fact that he did.

"Could you stop that for a minute?" I said to him.

He dropped the book in his hand and came to me. "Is something wrong?"

"No, I just wanted you closer."

With a pleased smile, he crawled into the small bed, wrapping his arms around me.

"I'm really tired of being here," I sighed, tightening my hold around him and sinking deeper into his warm embrace. "I want to be home."

"It's only one more night," he said soothingly, rubbing his hand up and down my back.

"But your bed is so much more comfortable than this one."

His hand stopped moving against my back. He drew away from me slightly to look into my eyes. "Is my house home for you?"

"Yeah, I guess it is," I said, surprised by the fact that I did indeed think of Brand's house as my home. Honestly, wherever Brand was seemed like home to me, but his house was where we spent the most intimate of our time together. "Is that all right?"

"It's more than all right, Lilly." He hugged me even tighter. Before I knew it, we were laying in Brand's bed. The room was dark, but that didn't bother me.

"Thank you," I sighed, relaxing completely for the first time since I had woken up from my coma. I fell asleep in his arms, but our night together didn't end there. Brand shared a dream with me that followed through with his earlier promise about continuing a certain kiss.

When I awoke the next morning, I was back in my hospital bed. Brand was still holding me.

"Good morning," I said, smiling up at him.

"How did you sleep?" he asked, with a roguish grin on his face.

"Well, besides feeling like I need a cold shower this morning, very well."

"Cold shower, huh?" He kissed my lips gently and started to trail a series of warm kisses down my neck. "I have a better idea, if you're interested."

My pulse raced. I was glad they didn't have me hooked up to a heart monitor anymore. I was sure it would cause an alarm to go off at the nurses' station. I felt like I might hyperventilate under the assault his lips were making across my throat.

I heard the distinct sound of a man clearing his throat come from somewhere inside my room.

Why did it seem like we were always being interrupted? It was almost as if we had a big neon sign going off over our heads every time we tried to have an intimate moment together, alerting whoever was paying attention that we were getting too close.

Brand sat up and looked behind him. When I looked around Brand, I saw Allan standing in the exact spot he'd stood the last time he visited.

"Sorry," he said in an honestly contrite voice. He was wearing his lab coat this time, with a pair of green rubber gloves, and the same white facemask he'd used on his previous visit over his mouth. "I suppose I should have called first. Please accept my sincerest apologies for interrupting."

Brand stood from my bed, discreetly adjusting his clothing. "No, Allan, it's good of you to come. Do you have the results for us?"

"Yes, I thought you would want to know what I found out right away."

"What did you discover?" Brand asked.

"Her mother has the same mitochondrial DNA sequence as Lilly, but she doesn't have any of the angelic DNA sequences which give Lilly her powers. It has to be assumed that Lilly inherited those from her father. I would still like to get a sample of the grandmother's DNA, if at all possible," Allan requested, "just to confirm my findings."

"We need to find your grandparents," Brand said to me. "It's the only way we'll be able to figure out where your mother's family originated."

"How long will you be in this location, if I might ask?"

"We're leaving this morning, I hope," Brand answered. "But you are welcome to come to my home anytime you want. Just call me and I'll take you there so you know where it is."

"Very thoughtful of you," Allan looked at me. I think he was smiling beneath the mask. "Glad to see you made a full recovery, Lilly. Please don't hesitate to call on me if I can be of further assistance to you in the future."

"Thank you, Allan."

"Well, I'll let you two get back to what you were doing."

After Allan left, I couldn't help but laugh a little.

"Well, you heard the man," I said to Brand, trying to look as alluring as I could in a hospital gown. "We should get back to what we were doing."

Just as Brand was about to crawl back into bed with me, a nurse came into the room and completely spoiled the mood. A little while later, Malcolm, Tara, Will and Malik came in, dooming my chances of another romantic interlude with Brand before I left the hospital. It was just as well. I would rather be in our own bed to continue further explorations anyway.

It didn't take very long to check out of the hospital. Some of my doctors came by to wish me well before I left, but if you'd asked me any of their names, I couldn't tell you one. All I wanted to do was get out.

As soon as we got into Brand's car, he phased us to Malcolm's house. Malik traveled with Malcolm and Tara with Will, in their respective vehicles. We were all pretty anxious to find out what information Izzi could tell us.

"Stay close to Malcolm and Will," Brand told me. "I need to go get Izzi."

"Where did you put her?"

"Somewhere safe back home. I won't be long," he gave me a kiss and disappeared.

We all walked into Malcolm's house together. When we were about to head down to his basement, I saw Brand walk through the front door with the small iron box in his hands. Once we were in the basement, I saw where Malcolm's son spent most of his nights. It was a 20'x20' room. Malcolm hadn't exaggerated one bit. The room was completely devoid of windows or any other openings, except for the door. When we stepped across the threshold, I noticed the walls must have been made of at least ten- inch of steel.

After we were all inside the room and the door was secured, Brand opened the box and dumped its contents onto the floor, laying the box down beside the bee in front of us. We were all in a semi-circle around the yellow jacket, which lay motionless on the steel floor before us.

"Is she dead?" I asked, not seeing any movement from the bee.

"No," Malik answered. "She just needs some time to recover from being in the iron box for so long."

I'm not sure how long we stood there, but it couldn't have been more than five minutes. Finally, I saw the transparent wings begin to flutter. Then suddenly, the creature was in the air, buzzing from wall to wall, desperately trying to find a way to escape.

"It's no use, Izzi," Malik told her. "It would be better for you to just change shape and answer our questions. Otherwise, this might go a lot less smoothly for you."

After a couple more minutes, I guess Izzi realized there was no escaping her fate. She changed back into the form I was more used to. She stood tall and proud in front of us, wearing absolutely nothing.

"What are you going to do to me?" Izzi asked Malik, lifting her chin a little in defiance.

"You know the punishment for attempting to murder someone," Malik replied. I could tell his words frightened her, but she refused to let it show for more than a second. "However, if you answer our questions, I will consider sending you into private exile instead. Otherwise, I'll send you to the others, and I think you know what they'll do to you."

"What do you want to know?" Izzi kept her eyes locked on Malik, as if the rest of us weren't even in the room.

"I think I'll let Lilly ask you herself."

Izzi finally let her gaze fall on me. Her eyes raked me up and down, with complete and total undisguised hatred.

"Why did you try to kill me?" I asked.

"I was bribed," she answered with a shrug, as if my death meant nothing in the grand scheme of things.

"By whom?" I asked. "And why did they want me dead?"

"How should I know why he wanted you out of the way? It's not like I really cared about the reason."

I heard a growl come from beside me and saw Brand grip Malcolm's arm, restraining him from taking another step toward Izzi.

"Wait," Brand said, though I could tell by his expression that he had to exert a lot of control on his own emotional response to Izzi's words.

"Then who was it? And what did you have to gain by my death?" I asked.

Izzi looked at Malik. "If I tell you the answers, do you promise not to send me to them?"

"You have my word," Malik said. "If you tell us the truth," he amended.

"It was Faust. He's the one who wanted me to kill Lilly. He said if I did, he'd arrange for Malik's death so I could become the leader of the fairies. Since you don't have an heir yet, I would be next in line."

Malik looked to Brand. "It sounds true. Is it?"

Brand nodded his head once. "But she's holding something back. There was more to the bargain."

"What was the rest of the deal?" Malik demanded.

Izzi looked at Brand. "He said he could make you fall in love with me; though that was just a perk, not my main reason for helping him."

"He doesn't have that type of power," Brand told her. "You should know that."

Izzi shrugged her shoulders. "I figured as much. But I didn't think it would hurt to try. If you can fall in love with such an ordinary human, I thought he could at least steer you in my direction and make you finally notice me for once. I mean, seriously, Brand, you could do so much better."

Before I knew it, Brand was holding Izzi up by the neck, against a wall. She was desperately trying to pry his fingers away from her throat, unable to even gasp for breath.

"It's only because of Lilly you're even still alive," he hissed at her. "Don't ever disrespect her in front of me again. As it is, I'm having a hard time restraining myself from just snapping you in two for trying to take her away from me."

I wasn't sure what to do. I'd never seen Brand so upset before. The fierceness of his anger actually shocked me. It was a side of him I had never had to deal with.

As quickly as he'd snatched her up, he let her go and returned to my side. I could hear his ragged breathing as he attempted to get his raw emotions under control. I put a hand on his arm and felt him relax slightly under my touch.

"Where is Faust now?" Malik asked Izzi as she struggled to take a few breaths. I was sure Brand had been close to breaking her neck. I could only imagine how sore her throat felt. I could see the red outline of Brand's handprint around her neck.

"I don't know," she rasped. "He contacted me, not the other way around."

"And you have no idea why he wanted you to murder Lilly for him?"

"No."

Izzi leaned against the wall, trying to breathe normally even though it sounded more like wheezing.

"She's telling the truth," Brand said in a disgusted voice. I wasn't sure if he was repulsed by Izzi or himself. I assumed it was probably a little of both.

"Very well," Malik said. "Transform, Izzi, and get back into the box."

"You're not going to put me with the others, are you?" she asked in a hoarse voice, but I could still hear her fear.

"No, I'll do what I said. You have my word."

Without protest or another word to anyone, Izzi transformed

back into the yellow jacket and flew back into the iron box sitting on the floor.

Malik closed the lid and held it securely in his hand.

"Is the plane ready?" he asked Brand.

"Yes, it's waiting for you at the airport. Just give the coordinates to the pilot when you get there."

"I'll take you to the airport," Will offered.

"I'll be back as soon as I can," Malik said to us before Will phased them both out of the room.

I turned to Brand, concerned about him. He tried to smile at me to show he was all right, but I could see the anger he was attempting to contain.

"Take me home," I said to him, though it sounded more like an order than a request.

He took my hand, and we were standing in his living room before I knew it.

"Come here." I pulled him to me, hoping to erase the rage our conversation with Izzi had awakened in him.

"I'm sorry you had to see me like that," he whispered.

"Don't apologize," I told him. I pulled away from him and looked into his eyes. He was trying so hard to control the anger he felt, but his eyes could never lie to me. "It was a natural reaction. If the tables had been turned, I probably wouldn't have had the strength to control myself the way you did."

Brand closed his eyes and hung his head. "I've never felt that close to killing someone before," he confessed. "If you hadn't been there, I'm not sure what would have happened."

"You wouldn't have done it," I told him. "That's not you."

"But it could have been, Lilly," he said, opening his eyes, looking to me for understanding. "She almost killed you."

"But she didn't," I tried to reassure him. "I'm right here, with you."

I'm not sure if it was the reminder of my mortality or just a need to erase the anger he felt but, when Brand kissed me, I felt his desperation. I matched it with my own. I could still hear Izzi's words about me being an 'ordinary human' and how Brand could 'do so much better'. Her words mirrored the thoughts I'd been having lately. But I didn't want to think about that. I wanted to enjoy the feeling of being completely adored by the man kissing me, even if I *was* just ordinary, and didn't really deserve to have him love me so completely.

Before I knew it, we were lying in bed. I felt Brand reach under my shirt, brushing his warms hands against the bare skin of my back. His lips left mine. I heard him whisper, "I love you" in my ear before he kissed his way down my neck to the little bit of chest revealed by my V-neck T-shirt. He pushed the bottom of my shirt up to reveal my stomach, and continued his assault there, exciting every nerve in my body.

"Brand," I whispered, "I don't want to wait."

He looked up at me, and I could see the hunger he had in his eyes for me, but there was something else there I couldn't quite identify.

He pulled my shirt back down and stood up from the bed.

"What's wrong?" I asked, not understanding why he was leaving.

"Nothing's wrong," he said, standing a couple of feet away, looking at me like he was afraid to come any closer.

"Oh," I said, assuming I had completely misread his desire for me. "If you don't want to..." I couldn't continue what I was going to say. It was just too embarrassing. I tried to look away, but I felt

Brand's hand under my chin as he sat down beside me on the bed, forcing me to look at him.

"How can you even think that?" he asked, dropping his hand from my chin. "I think I've made it pretty clear how much I want you."

"But why did you stop?"

"You're going to think I'm being completely paranoid." He ran an agitated hand through is hair, like he wasn't sure how to say what was on his mind. "But, it's important to me that we do everything right. I don't want to give Him any excuses to not bless our marriage."

"Who? God?"

Brand nodded. "I truly think He brought us together, and I want to do everything right this time. Can you understand that?"

Actually, I could. I'd always imagined my wedding night to be this one perfect moment in time with the man I finally gave my heart to. I knew, without a shadow of a doubt, that Brand would do his best to make it even more beautiful for me than I could have ever dreamt it to be. To know he was willing to put aside his own desires in order to provide us with the best chance of a happy life together made my doubts about his true feelings for me lessen.

"Well, I guess I'll just have to plan on a lot of cold showers over the next few years," I tried to joke, feeling a need to lighten the mood.

"Or we could try to not take things as far," Brand suggested, but I could tell he was as resistant to that idea as I was.

"I think I'd rather just take cold showers," I told him, pulling him back down on the bed so we could continue where we left off.

CHAPTER 9

When I went to take a shower, Brand went downstairs to start preparing lunch. Fearing for my safety, he kept phasing into the bathroom asking, "Lilly, are you all right?"

I would simply reply, "I'm fine", from behind the shower curtain. I think I did that at least ten times before I'd enough of it and stepped out of my shower early. I toweled off quickly and put some clothes on before he had another chance to pop in on me and check on my welfare. I understood his worry, and wished there was some way I could at least remove that burden from him. There was really only one way to do that... learn to phase by myself.

If I could do that one simple thing, Brand wouldn't feel like he had to be with me every minute of the day to keep me out of harm's way. Not that I minded his company; I loved it, but doing little things like taking a shower alone without having to worry about someone seeing me in a compromising position would be comforting.

By the time I made it downstairs, Brand was setting the table for lunch. He'd made poached salmon with apple-tomato chutney. I discreetly scraped the tomatoes off, hoping he wouldn't notice.

"You don't like tomatoes?" he asked.

"No, I don't," I confessed, "which is really weird, because I like tomato sauce, like in spaghetti sauce or sauce on a pizza. I'm sorry I can't eat this. It looks really pretty, like something most people would love."

"Don't feel like you owe me an apology, Lilly. The more I learn about what you like and don't like, the better. I want to know everything there is to know about you."

I couldn't help but smile at his heartfelt statement.

"So, tell me," I said, continuing to eat the salmon, "who is Faust and why would he want to kill me?"

"Faust is a jinn."

"What's that?"

"You've heard of genies right?"

"Like the one in the Aladdin story?"

"Yes, that's basically a jinn. God made them after He made angels but before He made humans. When Lucifer rebelled, they joined his side and were banished down here with the rest of them. They all adopted a particular human form, but they can also travel undetected as shadows. Sometimes they like to scare humans, so they let them see their shadow forms. Humans who have seen the jinn call them shadow people."

"Do they really grant wishes?"

"In a way," Brand sat back in his seat, idly flaking off pieces of his salmon with his fork. "They're able to grant two wishes to whomever they trick into making them."

"Why would they have to trick someone? I would think most people would jump at the chance to wish for whatever they wanted."

"A jinn's services aren't free. Most people lose more than they gain in the end."

"Why only two wishes?"

"People usually use the first wish on something small, like wishing for a car or something physical that proves the jinn can do what he says. After they're fooled into thinking they can get whatever they want for nothing, they wish for something bigger, like wealth or fame, and then the jinn has them trapped."

"What do you mean?"

"In order to keep what they've wished for, they have to provide the jinn with a comfortable life. If the jinn ever leaves them, they lose everything, even more than what they lost in order to make their wishes come true."

"Why doesn't the jinn just wish for things for himself?"

"It doesn't work that way. They can't grant their own wishes, only the wishes of others."

"So do they really live in oil lamps?"

"Not exactly." Brand smiled at me, as if he found my naïveté endearing. "Their spirits are bound to certain objects. It's different for each jinn. Faust's is bound to a double-sided coin. It's how he fools people into becoming his patron. He strikes up a conversation with someone, and tricks them into playing a game with the coin. Once the person touches it, they're locked into a game they'll never win."

"So what do the people lose to get what they wish for?"

"Family and friends; everyone who ever truly cared for or loved them. They lose their old lives completely to gain the new life they wished for."

"Is that why they only get two wishes? So they can't use a third one to un-wish what they asked for?"

"That's how it usually works. Some people use the first wish more wisely and can use the second one to undo what their first wish did, but most people don't."

"Why would this Faust want to kill me?"

"I'm not sure," Brand leaned his elbows on the table, pushing his plate away, completely uninterested in his lunch now. "But it might explain who's been responsible for the accidents Will's been saving you from."

"What do you mean?"

"Someone could have been using a jinn's power to kill you. It makes sense. All of the accidents were planned ahead of time, and a jinn would have had the power to put all of the accidents you've escaped from into motion. They're able to see into the future a small bit in order to make things that need to happen occur at specific points in time. They can set the events into motion, but since Will knew when to pull you out of harm's way, you were never where you were supposed to be to have them affect you."

"So how do we find this Faust?"

"I'm not sure yet. But we'll find a way," he reassured me. "We also need to find your grandparents. I know a private investigator in New York. I'll call him today and get him on the case. Hopefully, it won't take him long to locate them."

"I never thought I'd ever get the chance to meet my mother's parents," I admitted, pushing my own plate of half-eaten salmon away, having lost my appetite. "My mom was always so insistent about not having them in our lives. I'd just given up hope of ever knowing who they were."

"You do want to meet them, don't you?"

"Yes," I said hesitantly. "I'm just not sure if they want to meet me."

"I'm sure once they see you in person and all grown up, they'll love you."

"We'll see, I guess." I didn't realize until that moment how important it was for me to have my grandparents want to meet me as much as I had always wanted to meet them. The possibility of their rejection wasn't something I had considered until now.

Brand stood from his chair and took my hand, urging me to stand. It seemed like he always knew when I needed to be hugged.

"I'll be with you when we meet them," he said, kissing my forehead. "Don't look so worried, my love."

I looked up into his warm grey eyes, reminding me of his total and complete love for me, and quickly forgot about my trepidations. I brought his lips down to mine, wanting to lose myself in him.

"Good grief, is that all the two of you do?"

I broke off the kiss at the sound of Malcolm's agitated voice. He, Will, and Tara were standing only a couple of feet away from us.

I saw Tara prod Malcolm's side with her elbow. "Quit picking on them. That's what people do when they're in love. Stop acting like a jealous fool."

"I thought I asked you to knock first," Brand said, putting a possessive arm across my shoulders.

"I forgot," Malcolm shrugged, completely unapologetic about his unannounced appearance inside Brand's home. "Besides, it wasn't just me coming to visit."

"I told him to bring me over," Tara said. "He was trying to explain about angel DNA and completely lost me. I was hoping you could dumb it down for me some so I could understand."

This was the first opportunity we had to tell Tara and Will

about Allan's findings. It was also the first time we had a chance to tell Malcolm about Allan testing my mother. Brand and I sat them all down and explained what we knew. We told them about hiring an investigator to search for my grandparents, to see if they could shed some light on my mother's family origins.

"Wow," Tara said when we were finished. "After all these years, you're gonna finally meet them? What's your mom say about that?"

"I haven't told her," I admitted. "I'm not sure I will until after I meet them and see what kind of people they are. I'm sure she's had her reasons for not contacting them after all this time. After I meet them, I might not want to see them again either. If that's the case, I don't see any reason to tell her."

"Ok, so who wants to explain to me what that business between Malik and Izzi was all about?" Tara asked. "Who was she so scared of going to?"

I was glad Tara asked about Izzi. I didn't feel comfortable asking, since I was the reason she was being punished.

"Fairies have their own laws," Brand explained. "If one of them breaks a law, they have to go before their leader, in this case Malik, and he decides their punishment. There is one particular uncharted island in the Pacific Ocean where all fairies who have committed unforgivable crimes are sent. Izzi probably wouldn't have survived very well or very long there. So Malik took her to another island, where she could live the rest of her life out by herself."

"She'll die there?" I asked. I don't know why, but I felt guilt over Izzi's lonely fate. Intellectually, I knew it was a just sentence for trying to kill me, but emotionally I couldn't help but feel sorry for her having to live out the rest of her days alone, on some forgotten island.

Brand squeezed my hand, knowing me well enough to realize how upset I would be by learning this new information.

"It's only what she deserves. She's lucky he gave her the chance to go there. If she hadn't provided us with the information we needed, she would have been sent to the others, and I can assure you that would have been a fate much worse."

"Well, I think I need to go check on my son," Malcolm announced, standing from his seat at the table. "Oh," he said, turning his attention to Brand, "before I forget. Have you had a talk with your daughter yet?"

"Why would I need to have a talk with her?" Brand asked, clueless as to what Malcolm was talking about.

"Because of all the time she and Sebastian have been spending with one another," Malcolm's eyes narrowed. "Haven't you been paying attention?"

"I've been a little busy," Brand said defensively. "How long has this been going on?"

"Since your trip to London. I've told Sebastian how I feel about it, but he won't listen to me. Maybe if you can talk Abby into not seeing him anymore, his feelings for her will cool off."

"I'll have a talk with her."

"Good. The sooner we get this handled, the better. I'll be back tomorrow to check on Lilly."

"I'll be at school most of the day tomorrow," I told him.

"Are you sure?" Brand asked me.

I loved his concern for my wellbeing, but school was important to me. The sooner I graduated, the sooner we could be married. I was even considering summer school now to make things go a little quicker, and I never thought I'd have a good enough reason to willing give up my free summers.

"Yes, I feel like going," I told him, even though one more day of rest did sound very tempting. But I knew if I gave in to one more day it could turn into two more days or even three. The sooner I got back into a normal schedule, the better.

"Hey, you mind taking me back to my apartment?" Tara asked Malcolm, standing from her chair.

"No problem."

Malcolm put his hand on her shoulder. He winked at me before he phased her back home.

Will sat at the table, completely silent. He'd been quiet through most of our discussion.

"Would you mind if I talked with Lilly alone?" he asked Brand.

"I'm not the one you should be asking," Brand answered, looking to me. I could tell he was worried about something, but he didn't say anything else. I got the distinct impression he really didn't want me talking to Will, but was unwilling to say anything that would stop me from doing it.

"I'll be right back," I said to Brand, kissing him to help banish whatever it was he was worrying about. I stood from my seat. "Let's go talk outside, Will."

Will followed me out the French doors that led to the back patio. We walked down to the lakeshore in mutual silence. When we got close to the water's edge, I stopped and turned to face him.

"What's bothering you?" I asked him.

"Lilly," he said, coming to stand a little too close to me, making the conversation take on an intimate tone I wasn't comfortable with, "have you thought about what I said to you in the hospital?"

"Thanks to you, that's all I've thought about," I said irritably.

"Then you know it's true."

"No," I said, taking two involuntary steps back from Will. "I don't know if it's true or just your way to cast doubt on Brand's love for me."

"You know I love you for who you are," he said. "At least with me you wouldn't have to worry about becoming pregnant and dying because of it. Hell, I don't even want you to have sex with him. How do you know you won't end up pregnant, even if you are on birth control? It's not one hundred percent, you know. There's always a chance it could fail, and you could end up being killed by one of those things growing inside you. How far have you two gone, anyway? You always seem so close."

I could feel my temper flare. "That's none of your business, Will Allen. And you need to get the ideas you have about you and me out of your head! I thought you understood. I'm not in love with you anymore."

"But..."

"No buts!" I couldn't stop myself from yelling at him. He was making me crazy and confused with all his ideas. "If you can't accept the fact that I love Brand, then we can't be friends anymore, Will. I can't keep having this conversation with you. I love Brand. I don't know how to make it any plainer."

Will stepped closer to me, putting his hands on my shoulders. I could tell by the look in his eyes that he wasn't willing to give up so easily.

"I know you think you love him, and maybe you really do. But, you loved me at one time, too. Just think about what I said, Lilly. That's all I'm asking."

"I need you to leave," I said, shaking his hands off my shoulders.

He stepped back from me. "Just think about it," he implored before he phased.

When I went back inside, Brand was leaning back against the dining table, waiting for me. His arms were crossed over his chest, and he had a brooding expression on his beautiful, pale face.

"Mind me asking what he wanted to talk to you about?" he asked in a voice so low I had to strain to hear him.

I could tell he wanted to know about the conversation I'd just had with Will but, at the same time, he wasn't sure he wanted to hear it. Apparently, his curiosity won out.

I closed the French doors behind me and leaned back against them, shaking my head in disbelief.

"He's still trying to convince me his love for me is more real than yours."

"I see," Brand sighed heavily. "Will does have one advantage over me. He could grow old with you. I can't do that. You would have a more natural life with him than with me. I wouldn't blame you if you wanted to take his offer."

"You always try to think about what would make me happy, but what you don't realize is you're all I need for that to be true."

"I feel like I'm cheating you out of a real life," Brand confessed. "Most people get to plan to have a family and live a relatively normal existence with one another. I can't give you either, only myself."

"You're all I want," I told him.

"But will you be able to say that in twenty years? Or even ten? People's feelings change, Lilly. I've seen it happen time and time again. What if you end up resenting me because of what I am?"

"You know how you told me I shouldn't doubt your love for me?" I asked him. "Well, I'm asking you to not doubt the love I feel for you either. You make me complete, Brand. I don't know how else to say it. When we're together, I feel like there's nothing we can't do. And who's to say we can't have children one day?" My words had the desired effect on him. "Remember, I'm part angel. Who knows what would happen if I actually did become pregnant? Maybe your curse doesn't include me."

"I can't take that chance," he said, firm in his resolve. "I refuse to even think about doing anything that would cause me to lose you like that."

I didn't want to push the subject. I knew how adamant he was about me not becoming pregnant, and losing my life like Abby's mother did. But, for me, the option of a child with Brand was still not out of the realm of possibility. I'm not sure why it hadn't occurred to me before now. I was part angel. It was possible Brand and I could conceive a child not burdened with the curse Abby had to live with.

We stood there quietly, looking at one another.

"Promise me you won't ask me to take that kind of risk with your life, Lilly, please."

I didn't want to make a promise I might not be able to keep. I simply pulled him to me and hugged him tight.

"Don't ever think I would leave you," I told him instead. "I could never be happier with someone else. I wish you and everyone else could understand that."

Brand's arms tightened around me, silently assuring me that he would never willingly let me go.

Brand called the private investigator in New York after our talk. It was a short conversation, since we didn't know anything about my mother's parents. All we had to go on was the little information I knew about my mother. I knew her birth date and her full name, but that was it. It occurred to me that I really didn't know my mother at all. I didn't know where she had grown up, who her friends were when she was younger, nothing that would help us in our search for my grandparents. The woman I knew as my mother was a stranger to me.

"That's odd," Brand said, closing his cell phone at the end of his conversation with the private investigator. "Larry did a quick search on your mother while we were on the phone. He said it was as if she didn't exist until a little bit before you were born. He'll have to dig a little deeper than what he could do over the phone to find out what's going on."

"What do you think that means?"

"I don't know, but Larry is good at what he does. He'll find out what we need to know."

I sat back on the couch with a disappointed sigh. I had hoped this part of our quest for the truth would be relatively easy. Brand came and sat down beside me.

"How long does he think it will take?"

"He wasn't sure, but I offered him a sizable bonus to do it as fast as he can."

Having done all he could about finding my grandparents, I could tell Brand's thoughts were shifting to something else by the change of the expression on his face.

"What are you worried about?" I asked.

"Abby."

I had meant to ask Brand about Malcolm's reaction to a budding romance between their children.

"What's wrong with her and Sebastian liking each other?"

"It could get complicated."

"Mind elaborating on that some?"

"Our children are a lot like regular wolves. They mate for life once they find someone and decide to commit to them."

"Is that such a bad thing? Since they live so long, I would think you would want her to find someone she could be happy with."

"She's tried it once before," Brand's mood quickly darkened. "I thought it would be good for her, but in the end it hurt her more than it helped."

"What happened?"

"His name was Nathaniel. He was the son of a Watcher named Remington. Remington and I became friends after Abby and Nathaniel committed to one another. Remington eventually decided abstaining from drinking human blood was just denying who he really was. He came to believe it was a futile act of contrition. I don't think he ever truly believed we could be forgiven. After he killed his first victim, he became someone I didn't recognize anymore. He was like a madman afterwards. It seemed like he always had blood on his hands."

"What did Nathaniel think about his father becoming a murderer?"

"Nathaniel was a good boy, but the bond we have with our children is very strong. Eventually, Remington wanted his son to join him on his hunts, but Nathaniel didn't want to. He wanted to stay with Abby. It wasn't hard for Remington to make Nathaniel into the same kind of monster he was."

"What did he do?"

"Since Abby and Nathaniel were mated, they slept in the same cell at night. Remington released them one night after they

BLESSED

had transformed, and made sure they had a victim nearby to tempt them into a hunt."

"Abby didn't..."

"No. I was able to stop her before she tasted human blood, but I was too late to save Nathaniel."

"So is that the person you were talking about when you first moved here? You said Abby had just broken up with someone she was trying to forget."

"Do you remember everything I tell you?" Brand smiled wistfully at me.

"I try to."

"Yes, that was the person I was referring to."

"If you're concerned about Sebastian doing the same thing, you don't have anything to worry about. I know how much it means to Malcolm that his son doesn't end up like him. If Malcolm loves anyone in this world, he loves his son."

"I just worry about Abby," Brand admitted. "I know how much pain she went through trying to forget Nathaniel. I don't want to see her go through that again."

"Wouldn't you want her to find happiness, though? You can't protect her from everything, even though you want to. Sometimes you have to let the people you love make their own decisions. Besides, Abby seems very independent. Even if you did forbid her from seeing Sebastian, do you think she would obey you?"

"No," Brand sighed in resignation. "She would do what she wanted to anyway."

"Then maybe you should just have a talk with her and tell her your concerns for her safety and happiness. I think she would respond to that a lot better."

"You're probably right." Brand looked at me with an almost

149

confused expression. "How did you know I was going to forbid her from seeing Sebastian?"

I shrugged. "It seemed like something you would try, even though you know in your heart it would be the wrong thing to do."

"Sometimes I think you know me better than I do myself."

"Maybe I'm coming into my wifely intuition early," I teased, absently twirling the hair at the nape of Brand's neck, wondering what it would feel like to call him my husband. "What else is bothering you about Abby and Sebastian?"

"If they do decide to be together, I'll be stuck with Malcolm for a very long time," Brand grumbled. "I was hoping that, after we figured out what Lucifer wants with you, he would be out of our lives."

"You should give him a chance," I said in defense of my friend. "Even after we solve everything, I would still want him in my life. Can you understand that?"

"If he wasn't trying to take you away from me every chance he got, I might be able to find a way to get along with him," Brand said in his own defense. "But, as things are, I can't completely trust him, Lilly."

It reminded me of Brand's reaction to whatever Malcolm had said to him the night before Izzi attacked me. "Tell me what he said to you the other night."

"Do you really want to know?"

"Yes."

Brand took a deep breath like he was steeling himself against repeating Malcolm's words to me. "He said that he still had four years to change your mind and that he had to believe you have some doubts about marrying me if you're willing to wait that long."

"You know that isn't true, don't you?" I couldn't believe

Malcolm had said such things to Brand. I was definitely going to have a talk with him the first chance I got.

Brand was silent.

"Look at me," I said to him, forcing him to look into my eyes. "I would marry you right now if that would prove to you and everyone else once and for all that you are all I want. I'm really thinking about just dragging you down to the justice of the peace this minute and putting an end to this foolishness today!"

Brand smiled. "No, we don't have to change your plans just because of Malcolm and Will. But thank you for offering." He drew me into his arms. "It means a lot to me. More than you can know."

"Well I would, you know," I said, snuggling against him. "I would marry you today if that would make you happy."

He tightened his arms around me. "No, I can wait."

After a few minutes, Brand asked, "Would you mind coming with me to talk with Abby? I might need your support to keep me focused."

I stood up from the couch and reached out for his hand. "No time like the present. Let's go talk to her."

Brand's talk with Abby went smoothly. She seemed to have been expecting it, and was pleasantly surprised when Brand told her he just wanted her to be happy and careful before choosing Sebastian as a mate.

"I don't suppose I could talk you into speaking with Malcolm on our behalf," Abby said to me after her discussion with Brand. "If you can bring my father around, maybe you could get Malcolm off of Sebastian's case."

"I could try, Abby," I said. "But Malcolm is extremely overprotective of Sebastian. I'm not sure anything I say will make him feel comfortable with the situation."

"Could you just try, *please?*" she pleaded. I almost felt like Abby's mother then. She was acting like a love-struck teenager begging her mom for help with her boyfriend's parent.

"I'll do what I can," I told Abby, not knowing how I would talk Malcolm into letting Sebastian court Brand's daughter.

CHAPTER 10

After our talk with Abby, I had Brand take me back to my apartment. I felt a little guilty for leaving Tara alone so much, especially so soon after her break-up with Simon. Brand understood my need to be with Tara and simply sat in the background while she and I did girly things, like paint each other's fingernails and toenails while she caught me up on campus gossip.

Brand sat on the futon, scribbling in a notebook he had brought with him.

"What are you doing?" I asked, hobbling over to him with the toe spacers still on my feet, coming to sit beside him.

"Working on something," he said, closing the book before I had a chance to take a peek at what he was writing.

"Is it a secret?" I asked, intrigued by his behavior.

"Sort of," he said with a shy grin. "I'm still working on that poem for you."

I remembered inadvertently reading the first two lines of the poem that day in Biology class, before we'd even gone on our first official date. I'd almost forgotten about it.

"How's it coming?" My curiosity was piqued now at the reminder.

"Slow," Brand admitted, dragging the word out to emphasize just how slow it was going. "In all of the hobbies I've had over the years, writing poetry has never been one of them. I think I know why now," he chuckled, scratching his head.

"So when do you think it will be ready for me to read?"

"Maybe by the time we get married." He grinned uncertainly. I couldn't stop myself from kissing him. He just looked too cute.

"Malcolm's right," I heard Tara say from her seat at the table, blowing on her nails to help them dry faster. "That's all y'all do."

I pulled away from Brand and stuck my tongue out at her.

"When you fall in love, I'll remember you said that," I told her.

"Pfft, that'll be a while off. I don't need a man in my life right now. They're nothing but trouble."

There was a loud knock at the door. Brand got up to answer it.

"Might have known you would be here," I heard Malcolm say. "May I come in?"

Brand stood away from the doorway to allow Malcolm entry into the apartment.

Malcolm walked in dressed in a long black leather coat, black jeans, and a blood- red button-down shirt.

"I had an idea," Malcolm announced. "I think I might know of a way to find Faust."

"How?" I asked, unable to conceal my excitement.

"You remember Horace, don't you?" Malcolm asked Brand.

"Is he still looking for his ring?"

"Yes. He runs a pawnshop in New York now. He might be able to tell us where Faust is hiding out."

"It's worth a try, I guess," Brand said, obviously thinking it was a long shot.

"I think you and I both know he won't tell *you* anything,"

Malcolm replied. "I thought I might take Lilly to see what we could learn from him."

"Lilly doesn't need to be with you when you speak to him," Brand said, instantly suspicious of Malcolm's true motives for requesting my company.

"Well, before I decide if I'm going anywhere, who is Horace?" I asked.

"He's a jinn," Malcolm replied. "But he lost the ring his powers are attached to. Without it, he can't start a new contract with someone."

"What happened to the ring?"

"His last patron took it so Horace couldn't trick anyone else into making wishes. I think he might have thrown it into the ocean or down a volcano. Poor Horace has been searching for it ever since."

"I would like to go," I told Brand. If this jinn could help me find Faust, I wanted to meet him for myself.

"What makes you think he'll talk to you?" Brand asked Malcolm.

"There's no guarantee he will," Malcolm admitted with a shrug of his shoulders. "But he'd be more willing to talk to me than you. Plus," Malcolm pulled out a small blue velvet bag from his coat pocket and jingled it. "I have a collection of antique rings to bribe him with. Who knows, one of them might be Horace's. Do you have a better idea on how to find Faust?"

I could see Brand was reluctant to admit he didn't. Finally, he said, "No."

"Good," Malcolm looked down at the toe spacers still on my feet. "You might want to take those off before we go, dearest," he suggested. "People in New York are progressive, but those things might draw the wrong type of attention."

I just rolled my eyes at Malcolm and went to my room to change my clothes for our trip to New York. Malcolm was about to follow me, but Brand put a restraining hand on his arm.

"That's my job," he reminded my friend. "Not yours."

Before we left for New York, Brand kissed me lightly on the lips.

"Take care of her," he said, looking into my eyes but obviously speaking to Malcolm.

"You don't have to worry about that." Malcolm grabbed my hand and phased us before I had a chance to say goodbye.

In an instant, we were standing on the corner of a busy street in front of a store. I looked up over the door and saw the storefront sign: 'Horace's Pawn and Trade, Rings of All Kind Welcomed'.

It didn't look like we were in the most fashionable part of town. The street and buildings around us looked old and unkempt. I saw a few women who looked like streetwalkers only a few yards away from us, smoking cigarettes. They eyed Malcolm like he was a rare piece of chocolate they wanted to devour whole.

Malcolm tugged on my hand, which was still firmly clasped in his. "Come, dearest. Let's see what Horace might be able to tell us."

As we walked into the dilapidated building, a bell attached to the front door rang, announcing our arrival into the shop. I had never been in a pawnshop before, but I thought this one seemed extremely untidy. There were various items ranging from stereo systems to cowboy boots piled onto shelves, without seeming to have any discernable order to their placement. A glass-enclosed counter, containing various pieces of jewelry, ran from the front door to the middle of the shop.

I heard a door open somewhere near the back of the shop and saw a man hurriedly shuffle his way to the other side of the glass counter we stood in front of. He was only a little bit taller than me, slightly overweight with balding light brown hair, a mustache and goatee that seemed to be the home of more than a few bread- crumbs, and thick, black- framed glasses. He was dressed shabbily in a grey and blue-checkered shirt that had a fresh mustard stain down the front, a thin blue zippered jacket, and matching pants.

"How can I help you today?" he asked, coming to stand across from us behind the counter before he even looked up. He talked in a hurried, irritated tone, as though we were disturbing him from doing something more important.

"Hello, Horace," Malcolm said, leaning his hip against the glass counter.

When Horace's eyes finally met Malcolm's, I saw him wince.

"What brings you here, Malcolm?" Horace said, tapping his fingers against the counter nervously.

"I thought you might be able to help me and my friend out. Lilly, I'd like to introduce you to Horace."

Like I would anyone I was meeting for the first time, I extended a hand out to the jinn. He looked at my hand, and quickly glanced at Malcolm before deciding to follow through with what was meant to be a polite handshake. He shook my hand so fast I wasn't completely sure it had actually happened.

"What do you want?" Horace asked. "I'm kind of busy, you know."

Malcolm lifted a dubious eyebrow in Horace's direction and slowly surveyed his establishment.

"So I see," he said. "We were wondering if you could tell us where Faust is hiding out these days."

"F-f-faust?" Horace stammered in a whisper. He acted like just saying the name would bring the building down around our heads. "What do you need with him?"

"He's been trying to kill this beautiful young woman next to me. I want to ask him why."

"I don't know where he is," Horace said quickly. "You need to leave."

Even I could tell Horace was lying. He did know where Faust was. He was just too scared to tell us.

"Not even for a bag full of antique rings?" Malcolm said, bringing out the bag from his coat and tossing it onto the counter in front of Horace.

Before Horace could snatch up the bag, Malcolm grabbed his hand.

"Where is Faust?" Malcolm demanded. "If you just tell us that, I'll let you have the rings. I'm sure even if one of them isn't yours, you can sell them for a tidy profit."

Horace snatched his hand out of Malcolm's, eyeing the bag with an obsessive lust I had never seen on anyone's face before.

"You go to the movies much?" Horace asked.

"Why?" Malcolm asked.

"If you do, you've probably heard of an actor named Lloyd Cushing. If you find him, you'll find Faust."

"That's his new patron, I assume?"

"Yes."

Malcolm pushed the bag closer to Horace. "Thank you, Horace. Now, was that so difficult?"

Horace snatched the bag of rings to his chest. "Is that all you want?"

"Yes. We'll be going. Good luck in your search."

Malcolm took my hand again and, before I knew it, we were standing outside the Statue of Liberty, on the platform beneath the flame of her torch.

I couldn't help but shiver from the cold wind coming off the water, making the early evening air even colder.

"Oh, I'm sorry," Malcolm said, opening his long leather coat and bringing me in close to his body to keep me warm. "I forgot to tell you to bring a coat. I wanted to show you the view from here while we were in New York."

The only view I was seeing at the moment were the pecs of Malcolm's muscular chest. I looked up at my friend and saw him smiling down at me. The tenderness in his expression as he gazed at me instantly made me feel uneasy.

"I think I'd rather just go home," I said through the chatter of my teeth.

"Nonsense," he said, holding me tighter in an effort to provide me with what warmth he could. In actuality, it just made me have to turn my face to the side and lay my cheek against his bare skin.

"I can't bring you to New York and not try to show you some of the city. It just wouldn't be right, dearest."

"Could we at least go somewhere a little bit warmer?" I asked, unable to keep myself from wrapping my arms around Malcolm's waist to absorb more heat from his body.

After what was probably only a minute but seemed like forever, I heard him mumble, "If you wish."

The air around us quickly warmed up, and Malcolm reluctantly let me go.

We were standing in front of a *maître d'* podium.

"Oh, I'm sorry. I didn't see the two of you standing there. Welcome to the Russian Tea Room," the lady behind the podium said to us. "A cozy booth for two, perhaps?"

"Yes, thank you," Malcolm said, extending his arm for me to take.

We followed the woman up to the second floor into a room with mirrors on all four walls. There was a 15-foot revolving glass aquarium at the front end of the room and a spectacular gold tree with Venetian glass eggs hanging from its limbs at the other end. The woman sat us down at a booth made for only two people and handed us each menus.

"I think we'll start out with the Imperial black caviar, if you don't mind," Malcolm said smoothly, "and a couple glasses of white wine."

"Just water for me," I told the woman. "I'm not twenty-one yet," I reminded Malcolm.

"Ahh, I forget that," he said. "Fine, wine for me and water for the lady."

"Yes, sir."

After the woman walked away, I reached for my phone. I was glad I had thought to bring it along.

"Who are you calling?" Malcolm asked, eyeing me over the top of his menu, even though I could tell he knew perfectly well who I would be calling.

"I want to let Brand know where we are," I answered, finding his number on my contact list. "He'll worry if he doesn't hear from me."

I told Brand that Malcolm asked me out to dinner while we

were in New York. I could tell he wasn't pleased, by the restrained tone of his voice, but his words told me to have a good time.

I had, of course, heard of the Russian Tea Room before, but my limited experience was confined to what I had seen on TV and movies. I tried my best to find one entree on the menu and ended up thinking they all sounded equally good. I finally settled on the chicken tabaka. Malcolm had the aged New York strip steak.

While we ate our caviar, waiting for our meals to be served, I felt it was a good time to have a little discussion with Malcolm.

"Brand told me what you said to him the other night about me having doubts about marrying him," I said.

Malcolm didn't seem too surprised and just shrugged.

"I stand by what I told him," he replied.

"Do you like hurting him like that?" I asked, not wanting to believe Malcolm could purposely be so heartless.

"I'm just being honest with him. Why else would you willingly wait so long to marry him?"

"I want to finish school first, Malcolm. Why is that so hard to understand?"

"It sounds like an excuse, if you ask me."

"If you knew my mother, you would understand."

"What does your mother have to do with it?" I could tell Malcolm hadn't expected this turn in the conversation.

"I don't want to end up like her," I admitted. It was the first time I'd said it to anyone out loud. "I don't want to be an uneducated woman whose only purpose in life is a man or men in my mother's case. I don't want marriage to be the only thing of real substance about me. I don't want it to define who I am. I need to prove to myself that I'm more than that and can take care of myself before I can commit my life to someone else. Does that make sense to you? Can you understand that?"

"I suppose," Malcolm conceded. "But it doesn't change the fact that I still have four years to try to change your mind." He wiggled his eyebrows at me in a suggestive manner, and I couldn't help but shake my head at him and grin. He was hopelessly incorrigible.

"I love Brand," I said to him. "You're never going to change that."

"You should have the cheesecake for dessert," was all Malcolm said in reply, obviously trying to change the subject.

Seeing that I wasn't making much of a dent in his resolve to change my mind about marrying Brand, I decided to try attacking another front.

"Brand talked with Abby today," I told him.

"Did he have any luck changing her mind about Sebastian? I know I haven't been able to get my pig-headed son to listen to reason."

"He basically told her to do what would make her happy."

"He did what?" Malcolm almost yelled.

Everyone in the room looked at us, but quickly returned to their meals out of common decency.

"You need to do the same thing for Sebastian," I told him. "He's your son. Don't you want to see him happy?"

"Well, of course I do," Malcolm mumbled, sitting back in his chair and throwing his napkin on the table in disgust. "But how do I know being with that girl is the right thing for him? He's been perfectly happy with the way things have been so far in his life."

"Everyone needs someone to love," I told him. "If Sebastian

and Abby think they are in love, let them have their chance. Wouldn't you do everything you could for the person you loved?"

Malcolm sighed, letting my words sink in.

"Yes. I would do anything for her." He glanced up at me.

"Then let Sebastian decide if Abby is the one for him for himself. If you don't, you might cause a rift in your relationship with your son that can't be mended, and I don't think you want that to happen."

"No," Malcolm pinched the bridge of his nose with his index finger and thumb as if our conversation were giving him a headache. "I couldn't stand losing him like that."

"Then you need to let go," I said. "Let him know you trust him to be the man you raised and make his own decisions. Don't try to be his lord and master. He's a grown man. He has the right to make his own decisions, even if you don't agree with them."

"And Brand's ok with what it all means? He does realize we'll be in each other's lives for the rest of our children's lives, doesn't he?"

"He's fully aware of that," I said. "No, he's not extremely happy about that part of the arrangement, but he wants Abby to be happy. He's willing to make the sacrifice."

"Well, I just want to go on record and say that I don't like it. But, I know you're right. I shouldn't try to hold Sebastian back. He's been alone for a long time. He's too good a person not to share his life with someone else besides me."

I put my hand over the one Malcolm had resting on the table. "I'm proud of you."

He picked my hand up with his free one and kissed it gently. "You seem to keep changing me, dearest."

"For the better, I hope."

"Only time will tell."

I made sure to bring home a whole cheesecake for Tara and Brand from the restaurant. Tara was all over it, but Brand simply said he didn't like plain cheesecake. I suspected he just didn't want anything Malcolm had paid for.

Malcolm told them both what we had learned from Horace.

"I'll go to California tomorrow," Malcolm said. "It shouldn't be hard to find this actor. Wherever he is, Faust won't be too far behind."

"Let us know what you find out," Brand requested.

Malcolm didn't stay long. I got the feeling he wanted to think about what he would say to Sebastian the next day, after he changed back into his human form. I was glad to see he was taking my advice.

After Tara went to bed, I sat Brand down on the futon.

"Ok, I'm tired of not being able to phase myself. I want you to help me."

"I'm not sure I can tell you what you need to know," Brand confessed. "That was the main reason I was letting Will handle it. He has to relearn it each time he enters a new body. I've done it for so long, I don't even think about it anymore. I just do it."

"There has to be something you can do to help," I said, desperately needing the independence being able to phase on my own would give me.

"Well, I *was* thinking about trying something," he admitted, with an uncertain look on his face.

"What?" I asked, instantly grabbing onto the small window of hope he had opened.

"When you phased, you were upset. Maybe if we could stimulate you in some way that makes you want to phase somewhere else, it would work."

"Like what?"

"Well, obviously I can't frighten you," Brand said, standing up and pacing in front of me, trying to think of a way to trigger an emotional response from me.

"What else is there?" I asked, standing too.

Brand had his back to me when I stood, but quickly spun around and pinned me to the wall beside the front door. He kissed me in a way that was unlike any other he'd ever shared with me. It was as if he shed the quiet reserve he usually had to be gentle and loving and let me see the primeval side of him. It was a kiss filled with all his physical passion for me, telling me with his lips and tongue how much he desired me. All I could think about was how much I loved him and wanted him, too.

For some reason, my mind traveled back to the night of the Black and White ball. I remembered wanting to share my first kiss with Brand in the rose garden in front of the Commons that night. It would have been a perfect place to share the type of kiss we were having right now, completely raw and true to our passion for each other.

I felt Brand's hands fall to my back as if supporting me while our kiss continued, and didn't realize why until his lips reluctantly left my mouth.

When I looked around us, we were standing in the middle of the rose garden in front of the Commons building. Now that fall was almost upon us, the flowers had shed most of their petals, and the bushes were preparing themselves for a long winter nap.

"Did I phase us here?" I asked, trying to catch my breath and let my passion for the man in front of me calm.

"Yes," Brand answered, sounding slightly out of breath also. "What were you thinking about?"

"The night of the Black and White ball. I had planned to kiss you at the end, but you had broken up with me by then. In my mind, I pictured us doing it here in this spot that night."

Brand brought his head back down to mine and tenderly kissed my lips.

"Can you picture where we'll make love for the first time?" he whispered against my mouth, his breath sending shivers of delight all over my body. I felt his hands go up the back of my shirt and stroke the bare skin, causing me to moan and lose the ability to breathe.

An image of Brand's bed quickly came to mind, and I knew there was nowhere else I wanted to be. We were soon standing beside it, falling onto the mattress, with no plans to phase anywhere else for the rest of the night.

CHAPTER 11

I phased back to the apartment early the next morning to get ready
for school. When I told Tara I could now phase myself, I think she
was more excited than I was.

"Do you think we could go to Disney World?"

"I haven't been there either. I can only phase to places I've
been. Or at least that's what I've been told."

"Oh, what about Paris then? I heard Oprah talk about these
croissants she had there once."

"That I can do, but right now I need to go to school."

Tara always tickled me with the way she thought about things
sometimes. When I told her I could phase, it was like she was a kid
given carte blanche to the world.

Brand met me at school. I told him I wanted to drive my car
some. It had been so long since I had real freedom that I was
feeling a little high with my new-found independence. He was
waiting for me outside on the steps of our Biology class.

"I'm not sure I like being away from you so much," he said,
taking my books as I sat down beside him.

"And here I thought you might be getting tired of me," I
teased.

"Never," he murmured, taking my hand in his.

My first day back to school went pretty well. I didn't have any unexpected tests. They were all planned for the following week, so I had plenty of time to study. Dr. Barry was still over the moon from meeting Malcolm in person, and kept asking if he might come by to pay me a visit while I was working. I told her I thought he was probably too busy to do something like that, hoping to cool her infatuation some. Other than that, my day was fairly ordinary, something which hadn't happened in a long time.

At least everything was normal until I got back to my apartment. Malcolm and Will were standing outside the door to my place, waiting for us when Brand and I parked our cars.

"Did you find him?" Brand asked as soon as he got out of his car, immediately knowing what their presence meant.

"Yeah," Malcolm said. "I thought we should all go together, just in case there's trouble. You never can tell when you're dealing with a jinn, especially one as powerful as Faust."

"What's that supposed to mean?" I asked. "Is he dangerous?"

"He could be," Will replied. It was the first time I had seen him since our last discussion. I wasn't feeling extremely comfortable around him, knowing the way he viewed our relationship. "It's just safer if we all go together."

"We won't be long." Brand kissed me and went to stand beside Malcolm.

"What?" I asked. Did he seriously think I was just going to stay behind? "I'm coming with you."

"That's probably not the wisest thing, dearest," Malcolm said, trying to cajole me into staying behind. "He *has* been trying to kill you, after all."

"I can phase myself out of danger if I have to," I defended.

"Brand helped me figure out what I was doing wrong last night. Listen," I said, unable to keep the frustration out of my voice, "I'm the one whose life is in danger. Don't you think I've earned the right to meet the person who's been trying to kill me?"

Brand held his hand out to me. Without another word of protest, Malcolm phased us all to Faust's location.

We stood beside a large pool, behind a mansion of glass and stone. There was a man lying on a modernized version of an outdoor chaise longue with a tall sunbrella at the head of the chair, shielding him from the full effects of the sun directly overhead. He wore only a pair of white swim trunks. His light brown hair was streaked with patches of blonde and slicked back against his head. He looked like he was enjoying a pleasant afternoon siesta with his eyes closed against the sun, unaware of our presence.

If he hadn't been the person trying to kill me the past few years, I might have thought him handsome. He had a debonair quality to him, even in his relaxed pose. I could easily see him being an actor himself, possibly playing James Bond or a romantic lead in an epic. He was definitely not someone I could see in a romantic comedy. He was far too serious-looking for such light-hearted fair.

"Hello, Faust," Malcolm greeted. Both Brand and Malcolm made sure to stand between Faust and me. They left me a small space in between them in order to watch the jinn.

Faust opened his eyes and looked at the four of us. When he saw me, a knowing smile spread his lips.

"Well, gentlemen," he said, raising himself up on his elbows as if he was talking to a trio of old friends. "Or should I say fellow Fallen? Well, except for you, of course, dear Lilly. My, my, you're even lovelier than the pictures I've seen of you." He looked back at the three fallen angels in front of him. "I suspect you've come to ask me some questions. I had a feeling Izzi would botch things up and lead you back to me."

"Who's been using you to make attempts on Lilly's life?" Brand demanded.

Faust sat up and reached for a white terrycloth bathrobe lying across a steel chair beside him.

"I really wish you hadn't found me," Faust said as he stood, putting the robe on, clearly deciding to ignore Brand's question. "I finally found someone who could provide me with the lifestyle I deserve. You don't realize how hard that is to do."

"That's not our concern," Will said. "Are you the one who's been telling Lucifer what I needed to know to protect Lilly all these years?"

"Do I really need to justify that with an answer?" Faust asked. With our continued silence, he said, "Very well. Yes, of course it's been me."

"Why?" I asked.

Faust looked at me and half grinned. "Well, that's the question of the century, isn't it, dear one?"

"Maybe you should answer the question," Malcolm said gruffly, narrowing his eyes on Faust.

Faust pulled out a lighter and a pack of cigarettes from a pocket in his robe. After lighting one and taking a couple of puffs, he just shook his head. "If Lucifer wanted you to know, he would tell you. As it is, I promised him I wouldn't say. But," he said pointing a finger at me, "I *can* say he'll need you for something very soon."

"How soon?" I asked, unable to hide the trepidation I felt by his statement.

Faust looked up to the sky as if he were looking at a mental calendar. "Oh, I would say you have a little over two months."

"What does that mean?" Brand asked, not trying to hide his worry. "What does he plan to do with her?"

Faust shrugged his shoulders, taking another drag on his cigarette. "Can't tell you, I'm afraid. You see, I want him to succeed in what he's planning."

"Then why have you been trying to kill me?" I asked. He wasn't making any sense.

"It's been a delicate balance, you see. Working for one person while trying to help another, very hard to do. I'm surprised he's had this much patience with me. It's why I used Izzi this last time."

"What do you mean?" Will asked.

Faust flicked his finished cigarette into to the pool and immediately lit another one. "He was getting impatient, since Justin failed to take care of things for him, and he thought my little orchestrated accidents were a waste of time now, since Lilly kept side- stepping them somehow. I didn't want him to think I was botching my own work on purpose. So, I decided to show him I was really trying, and convinced Izzi to kill Lilly for me. I didn't know it would take you people so long to figure things out on your own. Your incompetence almost caused quite a hitch in Lucifer's plans. He wasn't very pleased with me after that little episode, as you well know, Will."

"Yeah, I know," Will agreed.

I pushed Brand and Malcolm out of my way and walked up to Faust.

"Please," I begged, "tell me who's been using you to try to kill me."

Faust took a long drag on his cigarette, watching me closely.

Slowly, he let the smoke dribble out of his mouth from his lungs. "I wish I could, dear one, but I can't."

"Why not?" I asked, unable to conceal my frustration. Here was someone who could finally tell us everything we needed to know, and he wasn't telling us anything.

"If I gave you that answer, your friends would know too much," Faust looked at the three fallen angels behind me. "Keep her safe," he advised them. "Time is running out, and he's become too impatient to wait on me any longer. He's finding other means to get rid of Lilly before time runs out." Faust looked down at me with pity. "I'm sorry. Your fate was decided a long time ago. There isn't anything anyone can do for you. You'll either die or be used by Lucifer. I don't see any other direction for your life."

Before I could ask another question, Faust disappeared, leaving behind his robe, swim trunks, and unfinished cigarette in an empty pile at my feet.

"Damn it," I heard Malcolm grumble, watching something I couldn't see go by us. I saw his eyes follow whatever it was as it quickly disappeared into the house.

"What happened?" I asked.

"He switched forms," Brand said, running for the sliding glass doors leading into the house. "But he has to get his coin before he can leave."

We all ran as fast as we could into the house. We ended up finding Lloyd Cushing sitting on a stool by himself at a built-in bar in his living room, with his head hanging low between his shoulders. I had seen a couple of his movies in the past few years. He made a lot of comedies, and people seemed to enjoy them a lot. Their humor always seemed a bit too juvenile and crude for my taste though.

"Where is Faust?" Will demanded. "Where's the coin?"

"They're both gone, dude," Lloyd said. When he turned around to face us, I could see that he was crying. "It's finally over. It's over."

"You know you'll lose everything now," Will said to him.

"I know, dude, but you just can't believe how much I just don't care."

Lloyd stood up and walked out the front door of his house, with us watching. He left the door open as if he didn't care who might walk in off the street and take his possessions. He was a man who wanted nothing but to leave his old life behind, only taking the clothes on his back to start a new one.

"Great," Will threw his hands up into the air, looking completely disgusted. "We lost our best lead on figuring out what the hell's going on. Now what are we going to do?"

"We stick to our plan and find Lilly's grandparents," Brand said, with a calm I wish I felt. "It's the only other lead we have right now. Faust isn't going to resurface again until everything has played itself out."

"Which means I only have a little over two months," I said, more to myself than to anyone else.

"We're going to find out what's going on well before then," Brand promised.

I felt like I had just been given a death sentence. I knew my time was short because of what Justin had said to me while I was imprisoned with him, but I guess I didn't realize just how little time I actually had left. To have it put into terms of months seemed almost surreal to me, like I was watching things from outside my own body. How do you come to terms with the reality of knowing you might only have a few more weeks to live?

When we phased back to my apartment, none of us was in a very good mood. After telling Tara what we had learned, her giddiness about my phasing abilities was cast aside.

"Two months?" she asked us. "What's that mean? I mean, Lucifer wants Lilly alive, right? So he's not gonna kill her if he goes through with whatever he's got up his sleeve. Is he?"

"That's the problem," Will said. "We don't know what he has planned exactly."

"Why can't you find out?" Tara asked Will, but it sounded more like an accusation, like maybe Will was holding out on us.

"I've tried, Tara," Will replied, obviously agitated. "I love Lilly. Don't you think I've tried everything I can to find out what he wants her for?"

"Well, try harder!" Tara shot back. "Hell, you're a demon. Don't you have some kinda demon magic or something to make him tell you?"

"He's an archangel, Tara. He's a lot more powerful than I am. I can't *make* him do anything. Why do you think I've followed his orders all these years?"

"What do you mean?" I asked. "What would he do to you if you didn't do what he told you to?"

"Destroy me," Will replied. "He can destroy my spirit, like I never existed."

"He can do that?" It was the first time I had actually thought about why it was that Will followed Lucifer's orders so obediently. It never occurred to me he could kill Will.

"I'm not sure he'll be contacting me anymore anyway," Will said. "He only came to me when he knew Lilly's life was in danger. Now that Faust is out of the picture, I doubt I see him again until he needs her for whatever it is he has planned."

"Well, you're not gonna give her to him, are you?"

"Not willingly, Tara, but I doubt it will be something any of us can prevent."

"We still need to figure out who's trying to kill Lilly," Brand said, trying to redirect the conversation. "If we can at least stop whoever it is, that'll be half the war won. We'll have to deal with Lucifer when the time comes, but until then we need to focus on things we can control."

"Have you spoken to your private investigator friend today?" Malcolm asked Brand.

"No. He said he'd call as soon as he had something to report. If I haven't heard anything by tomorrow, I'll contact him and see what's taking so long."

I stopped listening to everyone else talk and became lost in my own thoughts.

Did I really only have a little over two months to live? I couldn't see any other explanation for the way Faust had told me about my fate. He acted and sounded like someone who was handing down a death sentence.

I didn't want to die. I didn't want to have my life end just when it was beginning. It never occurred to me I would have so little time left. I suppose all of the narrow escapes I'd had over the years should have clued me in to the fact that I might have a shorter lifespan than a normal person, but when you're eighteen, death seems so far away. Even though I *could* have died in any number of accidents during the past few years, planned or not, I never really thought I could.

I had already cheated death so many times. I suppose I felt a false sense of invincibility. The closest I had come to actually dying was when I was with Justin, and even then, I found a way to escape a certain death sentence. It was that experience which showed me how short life can be. The information Faust just gave us made me realize my life could be shorter than I ever thought possible.

"Are you all right?"

I looked at Brand sitting beside me and shook my head slowly. I wasn't going to sit there and lie to him. I was most definitely not all right.

Brand stood and took my hand, making me stand beside him.

"If you will all excuse us, Lilly and I need to talk privately."

It wasn't really a request, and Brand didn't feel any need to wait for them to give us their permission to leave. He phased us to the lakeshore at the back of his house. The sun was just setting in the background. Any other day, I would have thought it romantic, but today I couldn't shake the doomed feeling I had that it might be the last sunset I ever saw.

"Lilly," Brand put his hand underneath my chin, making me look into his eyes. I could tell he was worried, but I also knew he understood what I was going through and wanted to help me in some way. He didn't want me to give up.

"Don't lose hope," he begged. "You have to believe we'll find a way to have the life we want together."

"The more we learn, the harder it is for me to keep hoping everything will work out," I admitted, not intending to hold anything back from him, not now. Not when I might not have a lot of time left to share all of me with him. "You heard him. Whether or not whoever is trying to kill me succeeds doesn't really matter. Whatever Lucifer has planned for me isn't going to be any better."

"Neither of them is going to win." The fierce determination on Brand's face made me want to hope.

"How can you be so sure?" I whispered.

"Because I stand by what I've always told you. I refuse to believe we met by chance. We were meant to find one another, and I was meant to help you. There's no other explanation for me. I have to have faith that together we can make things right, but I need you to trust me and believe in us and what we have together. If you don't trust in us, we might fail."

"I trust you," I said.

"Are you willing to prove that?"

"Do you really need me to prove it to you?"

"No, but I think you need to prove it to yourself," he said gently. "To erase your doubts. I get the feeling you're still not completely sure you believe what I just said, even though you want to."

"How am I supposed to prove it?"

Brand held my hand tighter and pulled me after him toward his boat moored to the dock a few yards away.

"What are we doing?" I asked, not completely understanding what his intentions were.

"It might be easier if you didn't think about it too much," he said. "Just trust me."

Brand settled me in the seat beside the wheel of his sailboat before untying the rope that held it secured to the platform. He jumped into the boat and started the engines. Before I knew it, we were heading toward the middle of the lake. I tried to steady my nerves by keeping my eyes and attention focused on my hands in my lap.

What was he thinking? He knew I hated the water. Ever since almost drowning in the lake back home when I was eight, I had avoided any activity that would put me too close to deep water.

Lake Serenity wasn't a large lake, probably only a mile long and half again as wide, but it was big enough to make the muscles of my stomach knot into a tense ball and make me feel like I couldn't breathe.

I think we were in the middle of the lake, its deepest point, by the time Brand shut off the engines. He knelt down in front of me.

"Are you ok?" He asked.

I nodded my head but didn't look at him. I just kept focusing on my hands in my lap. As long as I did that, I could handle being suspended on top of something that could kill me and almost did ten years ago.

"Take my hand," he said, holding out his left hand, palm-up.

"Why?" I asked, not seeing the point. I didn't see the point to any of this. Why was he inflicting this torture on me?

"Trust me, Lilly. I won't let anything happen to you."

He held his hand steady, waiting for me to take it. It took me a good minute to even look at him. He was watching me as if he wasn't sure what I was going to do, but hoping I would put my faith and trust in him.

Was this supposed to be my way of proving I trusted him? Well, we were on a boat. It wasn't like I was in the water exactly. The force it would take to capsize us would have to be more like winds you would face on the open sea. There probably wasn't any real danger on such a small lake, just my fear. I took a deep breath and put my hand in his. When I stood, I didn't feel the boat shift. That had to be a good sign that it was big enough to move around on without worrying about falling overboard, right?

"Come with me," he said, waiting for me to take a step closer to him.

I took a small shuffling step forward, unable to make my feet move too far from each other. We slowly made our way to the side of the boat.

"Do you trust me?" he asked, staring down at me.

"Yes," I replied. "Why do you keep asking me that?"

Brand let go of my hand. I immediately grabbed the steel rail on the side to steady myself. The wind picked up, making the boat move slightly, but not enough to make me lose my balance. I watched Brand as he quickly shed his shoes, shirt, and pants. He stood in front of me, in just his underwear. In any other situation, the sight of him almost naked would have riveted my attention but, as it was, all I could think about was keeping my balance and not falling overboard.

"Trying to distract me?" I tried to joke.

"No," he grinned. "You need to prove to yourself that you really do trust me. That you believe in us."

He dove into the water, bobbing up to the surface a few feet away.

"Jump, Lilly, and I'll catch you. Trust me."

"Have you lost your mind?" I yelled at him, trying to control my growing hysterics. "Isn't it enough I came out here with you?"

I hadn't stepped foot in water higher than my knees in ten years, and now he wanted me to jump in water that was probably a mile deep? There wasn't any other explanation. Brand had most definitely lost his mind.

"I can't," I murmured, not sure if he could hear me. I could feel my body start to tremble at the thought of flinging myself overboard. Just imagining the pressure of the water against my chest, pushing out the last bit of air from my lungs, made me spasm involuntarily. Even if my mind wanted to, I didn't think my body would let me put myself in such mortal danger.

The sun was almost completely set now. Darkness was quickly falling. In a few more minutes, I probably wouldn't be able to see Brand bobbing in the water in front of me.

"Jump, Lilly," he implored.

Why was he doing this to me? Why did this have to be his test of my trust? He picked the one thing I feared as much as I did the mystery I found myself involved in. I guess that was the point. If I didn't trust him to keep me from drowning, something he could definitely control, how could I trust him to save me from something he couldn't control at all?

I closed my eyes, unable to look at him watching me anymore. I couldn't stand to see his face filled with so much uncertainty and longing for me to put all of my faith in him...in us. There was only one thing I knew without a shadow of a doubt. Brand loved me and I loved him. Did I really believe what he said about us being brought together for a purpose? Did I dare to hope he was right, and put my trust in his belief that everything would turn out in our favor?

I'm not sure how long I stood there with my eyes closed trying to decide what it was I believed. When I opened them again, all I could see of Brand was a dark shadow in the water still watching me. I couldn't make out his face anymore, but I didn't have to see it to know what his expression would be. He would be losing hope that I did, indeed, trust him. It was that more than anything else that made up my mind for me.

I slowly let go of the rail, relinquishing my hold on the known, and trusting my fate to the one person in the world who held my heart completely. I took off my shoes, not wanting their added weight making what I was about to do any more difficult or cumbersome. It would be my luck to trip on a shoelace, hit my head on something, and sink like a rock.

I looked to the outline of Brand still treading water in the near darkness.

"I trust you," I whispered, unable to make myself speak much louder. I closed my eyes, unwilling to watch what I was about to do. I put one foot over the side of the boat, letting gravity pull me the rest of the way forward. I felt a slight breeze lift my hair off my shoulders in my moment of freefall. My body tensed involuntarily, preparing to feel the water envelop me, but that moment never came.

I felt Brand's arms around me almost as soon as my feet left the safety of the boat's deck.

"I've got you," he whispered, holding me tight against his cold, wet chest.

I wrapped my arms around him and started to cry. In that moment, I knew that, as long as we had each other, we could accomplish anything we set our minds to. Brand had been right. Until the moment I put my fate into his hands, I hadn't completely believed in us. I hadn't completely trusted in our ability to conqueror the obstacles that lay in our way. It was a freeing moment and one that ignited a determination inside me that I had never felt before. We would figure out what was happening and find a way to live out the rest of my life with one another. There was no other option for me now.

I stopped crying and looked up at Brand. I couldn't see his face clearly, but I could feel how hopeful he was.

"Can we go home now?" I asked. "I still don't like the water."

I heard him chuckle and, before I knew it, he phased us, boat and all, back home.

CHAPTER 12

Not long after we got back home and settled in for the night, Brand got a call from Malik.

"Lilly..." Brand called to me with the phone still to his ear.

I was sitting at the kitchen table, working on a jigsaw puzzle Brand had stored in a closet full of them. He said he picked them up along his travels but never seemed to find the time to sit down and do any of them.

"Malik wants to know if we would like to come to his apartment tomorrow night for supper."

"Sure, that would be nice."

"What time do you want us there?" I heard Brand ask.

Once the arrangements were made, Brand joined me at the table and started helping me with the puzzle.

"Malik said we could invite Tara over if we thought she would like to come, too."

"Yeah..." I said, not really knowing if that was such a good idea.

"What's wrong? You think she doesn't like him?" Brand asked, taking my reserved response as a negative.

"I'm more worried about Malik liking Tara too much. It's just not the right time for her to get tangled up with someone else. She's still trying to get over what Simon did to her. According to you, Malik will be in my life for a long time, and Tara will always be a part of my life. I would hate for him to try to start something with her now. Odds are it wouldn't work out."

"Why not?"

"Tara's emotions are just too raw. She might end up using Malik as someone to get over Simon. I'd rather see him wait a little while before he tries to start a relationship with her."

"Well, why don't we invite her anyway? You never know; Malik may just want a friend."

I raised a quizzical eyebrow in Brand's direction. "Fairy godfather or not, he's still a man. How many men just want to be friends with a woman they find attractive?"

Brand grinned. "You're right. He probably does want more than just friendship, but why don't we let Tara make that decision for herself? She's not exactly timid. If she doesn't want him to make any moves on her, she'll let him know in her own special way, I'm sure."

I didn't see Tara again until the next morning, when I returned home to get ready for school. When I asked her if she wanted to go to Malik's with us, she told me she already had a date planned for that evening.

"You do?" I asked. This was the first I had heard of someone new.

"Yeah, he's in the same class Simon and I have. I guess he figured out we weren't dating anymore after I threw my book at Simon when the fool tried talk to me. Leroy picked my book up and asked me out right there on the spot."

"What do you know about him?" I was surprised Tara wasn't

eagerly giving me the 411 on this Leroy character, and she didn't seem very enthusiastic about going out with him.

Tara shrugged. "He seems ok."

I didn't push the issue. Maybe this was what Tara needed; a distraction to get over Simon quickly. At least, that was what I hoped.

When Brand and I went to Malik's apartment that evening, I kept having this strange feeling that someone was watching me. Nevertheless, every time I looked behind me, there wasn't anyone there. Brand noticed my nervous behavior, so I had to tell him what was putting me on edge. After that, he kept a more watchful eye on our surroundings.

Malik's apartment complex was much swankier than the one Tara and I could afford to live in. The complex was divided up into ten two-story buildings, with only two apartments to each building. When Brand pushed the doorbell, Malik opened the door within in few seconds, wearing a white apron that said 'Kiss the Cook' in black script on the front.

"Welcome to Casa Malik," he said, sweeping a hand, inviting us to enter his home. "Tara couldn't make it?" he asked, closing the door behind us.

"No, she already had a date planned for tonight," I told him, watching his reaction.

"Oh," he said, clearly disappointed but quickly recovering. "Well, I hope you guys came hungry. I think I made enough food to feed the whole complex."

Malik's statement wasn't an exaggeration. It felt like we were sitting down to a Thanksgiving dinner. I was sure Tara would be disappointed she didn't come with us. Malik had made a feast of food she would have enjoyed, including beef tongue with caramelized onions, her favorite dish.

"So," I said, while eating some of the best chicken and dumplings I'd ever tasted. They rivaled Utha Mae's and that was a compliment in itself. "Brand didn't really tell me the reason saving my life makes you feel obligated to watch over me."

"I think it's just something programmed into our DNA," Malik said with a slight shrug of his shoulders as he cut up a piece of ham. "It's just the way we are. My mom saved this woman's life once while we were on vacation, and we ended up moving from California to Washington, D.C. We found a house right next door to Netty. They're still best friends to this day. I asked my mom why she felt like she needed to be so close to Netty, and she said it was similar to the way she felt about me, like she always wanted to be close by to keep me out of harm's way. Now I understand what she meant. It's not like it's something I can control. I just feel this overwhelming need to be close to you and protect you as much as I can. I think the more time we spend together the more you'll feel our connection, too."

"You do know what's going on with me, right?" I asked, hoping Malik understood the danger he might be putting himself into by getting involved in my life.

"Brand told me about it before I helped save you," Malik said. "So don't worry about me. I'm a big boy. I can take care of myself just fine."

It was one less thing I had to worry about at least.

After supper, I felt like doing something fun. It had been a while since I did something that was silly and more appropriate to my age. It didn't take me long before I had the boys talked into checking out the new miniature golf course that opened in town just that summer. Tara and I had planned to check it out when we first moved to Lakewood, but considering everything that happened since we moved, we just never found the time.

Malik drove us in his silver Lexus RX hybrid. On the way, he suggested to Brand and me that we might want to think about switching to hybrid vehicles because of how much better it was for the environment in the long run. I didn't mention my Mustang was over forty years old and probably one of the worst offenders of exhaust emissions in the world.

Since it was Friday night, the miniature golf place was packed with families and students. We ended up having to wait about fifteen minutes before we were allowed onto the course. Initially, I felt bad for dragging the boys out with me. Miniature golf isn't really a manly sport, after all. However, after we started playing, my guilt quickly faded. You would have thought we were playing in a PGA championship game the way Brand and Malik transitioned into competition mode as soon as we stepped onto the Astroturf. The golf course was called Fantasy Land. It featured creatures ranging from dragons to gnomes. At the end of the course, on the eighteenth hole, was a large castle similar in design to Cinderella's castle at Disney World.

With my coordination, I wasn't planning to win or even come close to winning. I just wanted to have fun and forget about our problems for a night. I tried not to laugh at how seriously Brand and Malik were taking the game, but when Malik got on all fours to line up his shot on the tenth hole into the gaping jaws of a fierce looking red dragon, I lost it. I giggled so hard I started to cry.

"Hey, Lilly!"

I looked a couple of holes ahead of us and saw Tara for the first time. My laughter must have traveled far enough for her to hear.

She waved at me, and I waved back. I assumed the boy standing next to her was her date, Leroy. He definitely wasn't what I expected.

Leroy looked like the type of person I hoped Tara would never go out with again. Although Simon turned out to be a total jerk, even though he dressed appropriately and showed a maturity I thought was real, I had hoped Tara's taste in men was changing for the better.

Unfortunately, Leroy looked like one of those people who would be stuck in teenager mode for the rest of his life. He was wearing clothes which were at least three sizes too large for his frame, a baseball cap that sat backwards on his head, and at least five different-sized gold chains around his neck. I think the style is called hip-hop, but since I wasn't that hip on the latest styles, I couldn't be sure. One of the necklaces had a large gold 'L' dangling from it, hitting Leroy in the stomach every time he moved. Another word, which started with an 'L', immediately came to my mind at the sight of him. I was definitely going to have a talk with Tara when she got home.

What made me worry even more than Leroy's sense of style was the fact that he brought along one of his friends, who looked just like him. I didn't like the fact that Tara was out numbered two to one.

"That's her boyfriend?" Malik asked incredulously, apparently having thoughts which paralleled my own.

"Not her boyfriend, per se. It's their first date and hopefully their last, if I have anything to say about it," I grumbled, wanting to go grab Tara and stand her safely by my side.

"She could do better," Malik said matter-of-factly, trying to take his eyes off Tara and Leroy as they progressed to their next hole.

For the next few holes, neither Malik nor I could stop looking after Tara. He completely forgot about his competition with Brand, and ended up missing more holes than he made. The more I watched Leroy and his friend leer at Tara behind her back as she played, the more I wanted to just go over and smack them upside their heads.

On our sixteenth hole, Tara was lining up to shoot her ball over the bridge through the castle doors, and Malik was preparing to shoot his into the king's crown when we both saw Leroy make a completely inappropriate sexual gesture in Tara's direction with his hips, causing his friend to laugh heartily.

I was sure what happened next would be hotly debated in the years to come. Was it an accident or did Malik intentionally ricochet his ball off the king's crown causing it to hit a tower of the castle, which propelled it into Leroy's forehead hard enough for us to hear a distinct 'crack'?

"Sorry," Malik called to them, sounding sincere, waving an apologetic hand in the air. "My hand slipped."

Leroy picked up Malik's ball and threw it back at him as hard as he could. Malik ducked, but the ball ended up hitting a small girl of about ten behind us on the leg.

"Is she ok?" Malik asked the mother of the girl.

"She'll be fine," the mother replied, rubbing the spot on her daughter's calf, trying to alleviate the sting of the ball. It would probably leave a bruise, but nothing more.

Malik quickly jumped over the two hip-high brick walls between him and Leroy.

"Listen, man, I said I was sorry. You could have hurt someone with that little stunt of yours."

"Oh yeah? Come on, punk," Leroy said, putting on a show of bravery, bouncing around like he was Rocky Balboa, with his hands fisted. "Let's go."

"Are you serious?" Malik said, trying to hold in his laughter at Leroy's preposterous stance. Seeing that Leroy was indeed serious, Malik's demeanor hardened. "Listen, there's no way you would win a fight with me. It would be in your best interest to stop acting like a fool."

Leroy swung one of his fists at Malik. Malik caught it in mid-air and held it. He used it to twist Leroy's arm around his back and hold him in what I could only assume was a painful position.

"That's enough," Malik scolded him. "Now both you and your friend can leave on your own two feet, or you can be wheeled out of here on stretchers after I get through with you. Take your pick."

Malik pushed Leroy away from him, into his gawking friend's arms.

"Whatever, man," Leroy said, puffing out his chest, trying to act like leaving was his idea and not the better of the two options Malik just gave him. "Come on, let's go," he said to Tara.

"Have you lost your mind?" she said to him, walking over to stand by Malik. "I'll have my friends take me home. I've had about enough of you acting the town idiot for one night."

"Whatever," Leroy said, giving Malik a disgusted look before he turned to leave. Leroy attempted to walk away, looking cool, with some sort of shuffling gate. Unfortunately, it just made him look physically challenged.

With our fun game of golf completely forgotten, Brand and I skipped the remaining holes and walked over to Tara and Malik.

"Sorry if I ruined your date," I heard Malik say to Tara.

"I wasn't having fun with them anyway," Tara replied. "They were acting like they were thirteen years old."

"Ok, I'm making an official rule," I told Tara. "The next guy you go out with has to be approved by me."

"Are you serious?" Tara asked, completely caught off guard by my announcement.

"Yes, I'm completely serious. Maybe if I give them the interrogation you gave Brand before we went out, we can weed out losers like that."

Tara rolled her eyes at me. "Girl, you're crazy."

"No, just trying to prevent any more Leroys and Simons."

"Who's Simon?" Malik asked.

"That's a long story," I said. "Let's head back to your apartment for that dessert you promised first. Tara can tell you about him if she wants."

Tara sat up front with Malik while Brand and I found a cozy spot together in the backseat of Malik's Lexus.

"So who's Simon?" I heard Malik ask Tara as we pulled out onto the highway.

After that, I completely lost track of their conversation. Brand had one arm around my shoulders, hugging me close to him, and his other hand on my thigh, slowly rubbing a warm path back and forth between my hip and knee.

He leaned down and whispered in my ear, "I love you," while tugging lightly on my earlobe with his teeth and lips.

I turned to face him. Even in the dim light spilling into the car from the streetlights on the highway, I could see Brand's thoughts were running along the same lines as my own. I restrained myself from just falling against him and making out with him in the back of Malik's car, like any other girl my age would with her fiancé. I forced myself to tune back into the conversation Tara and Malik were having, to get my mind off just phasing Brand and me back to his house so we could be alone.

I heard Tara tell Malik about her relationship with Simon and why it ended.

"Lilly might be right," Malik said. "Maybe another set of eyes on the next man you date would be better for you."

"Maybe," Tara shrugged.

"She won't have a choice," I called out from the backseat, desperately trying to ignore the warmth of Brand's hand as it continued along its path against my leg.

"You don't have to worry about me going out with anybody for a while," Tara told me over her shoulder. "I'm swearing off men. All they do is get me crazy."

"Well, since you'll have some free time," Malik said. "Could I talk you into showing me around the area tomorrow? I haven't been much farther than my front door."

"Sure," Tara said nonchalantly. "I can do that."

I was pretty sure Malik had just hidden a date behind something that sounded innocuous, but it didn't feel appropriate to point that fact out to Tara right in front of him.

When we got to Malik's apartment, Brand's small play at seduction on the ride back had me ready to take him home and ravish him until the sun came up the next morning or I passed out from exhaustion, whichever came first. But, I tried to place Tara's needs in the forefront of my mind to keep me sober from the intoxication I was feeling from Brand's attention.

Malik had made an apple cobbler for dessert and served it a la mode. He dug out a deck of cards and invited us to play a game of gin rummy. It wasn't something I wanted to do, but couldn't think of a polite way to say 'No, thanks. I'd rather go home and make out with my fiancé, if you don't mind.'

So, we played gin rummy. At least Tara was having a good time. She won most of the hands. After the fifth hand, I excused myself and went to use Malik's bathroom. When I walked out, I felt someone grab one of my wrists. Before I knew it, Brand had me pinned up against the wall of the hallway, kissing me just as he did when he helped me learn how to focus my attention and energy to phase on my own.

When he finally let me breathe, he looked around us.

"Hmm," he sounded disappointed. "I was hoping you might instinctually phase us back home." He began to nibble on the tender flesh at the base of my neck, making it almost impossible for me to think, much less speak.

"We can't just leave Tara," I whispered, trying my hardest to keep myself from phasing.

"Couldn't you say you have a headache or something," he suggested, "so we can leave?"

"I'm not going to lie." I put my hands on either side of his head and pulled his lips to mine, kissing him so he wouldn't have any doubts that I desperately wanted to be alone with him, too. "I'll just ask if she wants to leave."

Brand and I eventually untangled ourselves from one another and walked back out to where Malik and Tara were still playing cards. When I asked Tara if she was ready to leave, she just waved me off.

"Y'all go on. Malik said he'd drive me home."

"Are you sure?" I asked, not feeling comfortable leaving her with a veritable stranger.

"I'll see her home safely," Malik promised. "You have my word as your godfather."

"Besides," Tara looked up at Brand and me with a knowing smile. "Y'all looked like you could use some alone time from what I just saw in the hallway a minute ago." To which she started making kissing noises, causing both Brand and me to blush profusely at being caught in the act.

"Well," Brand said, trying not to look too embarrassed, but looking completely flustered. "On that note, I think we'll be saying goodnight."

As Brand and I left Malik's apartment hand in hand, I got the same eerie feeling I had earlier in the evening. Someone was definitely watching me. Brand opened the passenger door of his Porsche for me. Just as I was about to get in, I felt the hairs on the back of my neck stand up. I quickly looked behind me, and saw a man standing in front of the line of trees at the back of the apartment complex. It was dark, but I could see who it was by the light cast from the apartments around us. It was Robert.

"What's wrong?" Brand asked, following my gaze to the now-empty tree line.

Had Robert actually been there or had I just imagined him? Since seeing Robert again wasn't something I would want to imagine, I had to assume he had actually been there.

I looked up and down the tree line, searching for him. I felt a hand land on my shoulder and jumped.

"Lilly," Brand said, worried by my reaction to his touch. "What's wrong?"

"Take me home," I said, unable to keep the fear out of my voice.

Before I knew it, we were standing in Brand's driveway. He

closed the door of his car and phased us to his living room. I sat down on the couch facing the fireplace and tried to control my trembling.

Brand put his arms around me, doing what he could to bring me comfort, but all I could see in my head was Robert laying on top of me, trying to force himself on me in that dank little prison cell Justin kept me in.

I quickly stood up, leaving Brand's arms empty. He looked up at me in confusion.

"I'm sorry," I said. "Please, don't touch me right now. I don't want to associate anything about you with him."

"Who, Lilly?" Brand asked, desperately wanting to understand what was wrong with me.

How could I tell him? I hadn't mentioned it to anyone, not even Tara. I had hoped to just forget about it and pretend it had never happened, but I couldn't. It was too fresh in my memory to become one of the forgotten scenes in my past. Seeing Robert again brought my fear back to the surface, even though I had buried it as far as I could in my subconscious. How could I tell Brand what had almost happened with Robert?

I suppose one reason I hadn't told him before now was because I felt ashamed, like I should have been able to fight harder to keep him from almost raping me. I knew that was foolish. I knew I had done all I could at the time to keep it from happening, but that didn't stop me from wondering if maybe there had been something else I could have done to stop it. Why hadn't that experience triggered my phasing capability? I was lucky Justin came back in time to pull Robert off me.

"Please, Lilly," I could hear the fear and worry in Brand's voice. "Tell me what's wrong."

I slowly sat back down beside Brand. I could tell he wanted to put his arms around me, but was stopping himself from doing something so natural. It was time he knew. I couldn't lie to him and I didn't want to.

"When Justin had me," I began, "there was another Watcher who was helping him."

"What was his name?"

"Robert."

I saw Brand's hands tighten into fists involuntarily. "Did he do anything to you?"

The deadly tone in his voice forced me to look at him. He already knew something had happened, or I wouldn't be acting so strangely. There wasn't any going back now.

"Justin had Robert bring me my food while I was there. He was concerned Malcolm might not trust him when he said he didn't know where I was, and try to follow him when he phased. Right before I was supposed to meet the person who wanted Justin to kill me, Robert came to the room and tried to..." I couldn't say it. The words simply wouldn't come out of my mouth.

"You don't have to say anything else," Brand told me. "I can imagine what he tried to do. It wouldn't be the first time. Lilly. Did he..."

I looked at Brand and saw the pain on his face from just thinking about what he wanted to ask.

"No," I said, answering his unasked question. "Justin came back in time and stopped him."

Brand let out a sigh of relief, but his hands remained fisted. I could tell he wanted to hit something and hug me all at the same time.

"Why didn't you tell me this before now?" he asked.

I shook my head, unable to stop the tears from falling. "I felt ashamed. I didn't want you to know."

"Lilly," the love and understanding as he said my name made me start to cry even harder. I felt his arms go around me. I put my arms around him as tight as I could, sobbing into his chest, telling him I was sorry.

"You have nothing to be sorry about," he whispered. "I just wish you had told me sooner so I could help you work through it. You don't need to hide things from me."

"I wasn't just hiding it from you," I cried. "I've been trying to hide it from myself too. I didn't want to think about it."

I'm not sure how long we sat there. Brand held me until I couldn't cry anymore. It felt good to finally share my ordeal concerning Robert with him. I hadn't meant to keep it a secret. I just didn't want to dwell on something that would cause me pain when I had someone like Brand, who only wanted to bring happiness into my life.

When I finally pulled away from Brand to sit up and wipe the tears from my face, I looked at him and winced inwardly. He looked like he wanted to kill someone. I assumed that someone was Robert.

"You're not going to do anything, are you?" I asked. I couldn't imagine what Brand would do to Robert if he ever saw him. His reaction to the news that Malcolm saw me stepping out of the shower was nothing compared to the look on his face now.

"You don't need to worry about that," he said in an ominous tone. "Just know that I love you and I will protect you. Did you see Robert tonight? Was he at Malik's?"

I nodded my head. "He was standing by the trees when we were leaving, watching us."

Brand pulled out his cell phone and called someone.

"Get over here," he ordered. "We need to talk."

Almost instantly, there was a knock at the door.

"Come in," Brand called.

Malcolm strolled in, wearing only a pair of red silk pajama pants.

"I really don't appreciate being summoned," Malcolm said as he stepped into the house. His anger quickly dissipated as soon as he saw my tear-stained face.

"What happened?" He rushed over to me and took me in his arms. "Are you all right, dearest?"

"Yes, I'm fine," I said, pulling away from Malcolm's embrace as gently as I could without hurting his feelings.

"No, she isn't fine," Brand said, telling Malcolm what I had just revealed to him, and that Robert was apparently stalking me.

If there was one thing Brand and Malcolm had in common, it was their protectiveness over me. Malcolm's mood became as dark as Brand's after learning what Robert had tried to do while I was being held captive. I almost pitied Robert if the two of them ever found out where he was.

"Can you find him?" Brand asked.

"I haven't seen him for quite some time; not since Justin disappeared."

"Disappeared?" I asked. This was the first I had heard this news.

"I tried to find him after you returned and told us what happened," Malcolm replied. "But no one has seen him. Since he can't be found, the others chose Robert to take his place as leader of the Watchers, at least my side of Watchers."

"How hard would it be to get to him?" Brand asked.

"We'll have to find him first. I'll ask around and see what I can find out."

"When you locate Robert, let me know."

"I just want to forget about him," I said, desperately hoping we could just leave the past behind us.

"I'm afraid that won't be an option," Brand told me. "Even if I were to let what he did slide, which I won't, he seems to have taken Justin's place, and we have to assume whoever it is trying to kill you has Robert working for him now. You heard what Faust said. The person behind everything is trying to find alternative ways to kill you. We have to assume Robert is waiting for his chance."

"And you can't possibly think we would just let him go unpunished for what he did to you, dearest. It's not in our nature."

I sat back on the couch with a heavy sigh. "I just want this all to be over." One way or the other, I thought, but didn't dare say to the two beside me.

Malcolm told us he would contact us if and when he found Robert's location. After he left, Brand led me upstairs. We lay on his bed together, cradled in each other's arms without saying a word for the rest of the night. I fell asleep at some point, wondering what Robert had planned for me.

CHAPTER 13

When I woke up early the next morning, I could feel Brand lying behind me, holding me tight. Apparently, neither of us moved during the night. He must have realized I was awake because his arms loosened their hold. I turned around to face him. The look of sadness on his face instantly woke me up.

"What's wrong?" I asked, raising my hand to smooth out the wrinkles of worry from his forehead.

"I should have been there to protect you," he whispered.

"There wasn't anything you could have done," I said. "And he didn't get what he wanted. You can't protect me from everything, Brand. It's impossible to keep someone from being harmed at all. Besides, I can take care of myself now. They won't be able to just keep me locked up like that anymore."

"It doesn't help the guilt I feel," he admitted.

"Do you really want to help me?" I said, running my hand down the front of his shirt. "Then help me erase what he did, from my mind."

Instead of the passion we'd felt for one another the previous night, Brand kissed me with a tenderness that shattered my world in a totally different way. The lightness of his touch and the gentle way he ran his hand against my skin was completely opposite of the rough, savage way Robert had treated me. Brand treasured me, while Robert had simply wanted to use me for his own selfish needs. Brand could never be that heartless or selfish when he made love to me.

Making love with Brand was becoming harder and harder not to do. We pushed the boundaries as far as we could without becoming overtly sexual, but the thought of enduring another four years of just heavy petting wasn't exactly pleasant. What if I didn't have four years? What if I really only had two months? These were questions I had to seriously consider. I knew Brand thought we would find a way to stop what was happening to me, but I had always been a realist. I had to consider the very real possibility that things wouldn't work out the way we wanted.

My experience with Robert was a prime example. It was a situation that neither Brand nor I could have foreseen happening. What if Robert had succeeded that night and taken my virginity in such a brutish way? I would have regretted it for the rest of my life, no matter how short that life might actually be. What was the point of waiting to marry Brand if I only had two months left, and never got to live out at least part of the beautiful dream Brand had for our wedding day and night?

Later that morning, I phased back to my apartment to shower and change clothes. Brand said he wanted to make an in-person visit to our private investigator to see what he had been able to find out so far. When he tried to call Larry the previous day, his secretary said she hadn't seen him, but left a message for Larry to call Brand the first opportunity he got. Since he never got a phone call back, Brand wanted to check on Larry himself. I told him I wanted to go along and made him promise not to leave until I got back.

Tara was sitting at the kitchen table, thumbing through a local newspaper when I got back home. She smiled at me broadly as I took a seat beside her.

"Well, did y'all get all that kissing out of your system last night?"

"Not exactly," I said. "Listen, I need to tell you something."

I didn't see any reason to keep the secret of Robert from Tara any longer. She would find out eventually, and I wanted her to hear the story from me.

"Lilly Rayne Nightingale, I could strangle you for keeping this from me. Girl," she stood from her seat and came over to give me a hug, "you should have told me."

"I know. I'm sorry. I shouldn't have tried to forget about it, I guess. I should have told all of you, since it seems like Robert has taken Justin's place now."

"Well," Tara said, pulling away from me. "You have three angels and a fairy on your side. Plus me, for whatever I'm worth."

"You're worth everything to me," I told her, squeezing her hand. "But I really don't want to talk about it anymore. I've thought about it enough. Tell me how the rest of your night with Malik went."

"Oh, it went fine. We played a couple of hands of gin rummy after y'all left and then we watched a movie. I was actually looking through the paper to see what movies are playing. I thought he might like to go to the new theater they just built. I heard it has stadium seating."

"So, you like him?" I asked, hoping she would get the subtle hint in my question.

"He seems nice, but don't get any romantic notions in your

head about us, Lilly Rayne. We're just friends. I don't want anything else right now."

I decided to leave it at that. Tara needed someone to pal around with, since I spent so much time with Brand. Malik seemed like a nice guy, and I couldn't see any reason why she shouldn't have him as a friend, even though I was pretty sure he would eventually want more than just friendship from her. Hopefully, by that time, Tara would have completely forgotten about Simon, and be emotionally ready for a real relationship. But it wouldn't hurt to make it plain to Malik how I expected him to treat Tara. I decided to make a quick trip to his apartment before I went back to Brand.

After I showered and got ready, I told Tara where Brand and I were going that day.

"New York?" she asked. "Man, you gotta take me there someday."

"I will. I promise."

I phased to Malik's front door and pushed the doorbell. He quickly answered, wearing a nice polo shirt, jeans, and sneakers, appropriate clothing for a casual day out with a friend.

"Hey, Lilly, I wasn't expecting to see you today." He smiled and seemed genuinely happy to see me. "Come on in."

I walked into Malik's apartment. "Listen, I don't have long. I just wanted to come over and set a couple of things straight with you."

Malik crossed his arms in front of him with a serious look on his face. "Ok, what is it you feel like you need to tell me?"

I took a deep breath. "If I'm wrong, let me know, but I get the feeling that your intentions toward Tara are leaning toward the romantic side more than just the friendship side."

Malik grinned. "I'll never lie to you, Lilly. I was hoping to ask Tara out on a real date at some point."

"Well, what do you call spending the day with her?"

Malik shrugged. "I thought it might be nice for her to get out and have a fun day, after what she went through last night. I don't plan to do anything but make sure she has a nice time."

"So you're not going to try anything, right?"

"Oh, I think I know what you're getting at." He smiled and shook his head, "No, I won't try to make a pass at her. In fact," it was almost as if I could see a light bulb come on over his head, "I'll make you a promise. I promise to keep my relationship with Tara on a friendship level unless she decides she wants it to progress further. How's that? Will that keep you from worrying?"

"That works for me."

Since I knew Tara wouldn't be interested in a new relationship for a while, Malik's promise seemed like the perfect solution to keep him from pushing her into a dating situation she wasn't ready for yet. Besides, if they became friends and then decided to change it to a romance, it would be better for the both of them. It always seemed like people who were friends and in love had the most lasting relationships.

Before I left, I told Malik what Brand and I were going to be doing that day. He asked that I keep him informed on what we found out.

By the time I made it back to Brand, he was sitting at the table, working on our puzzle.

"Make any progress?" I asked, scanning the puzzle, noticing he had added in quite a few pieces.

"A little," he stood from his chair. "Are you ready?"

"Yep."

He took my hand and we phased into a hallway inside a rather nondescript building. The half-glass, half-wood door in front of us had, 'Larry Goodwill, Private Investigator', painted in black on the glass portion. Brand opened the door and let me go in first.

"Howdy," a young, attractive, curly-haired blonde woman sitting behind an old wooden desk greeted us. She was dressed in a tight-fitting dark blue knit dress, which accentuated her azure blue eyes.

There wasn't much else in the room besides the woman and the desk cluttered with various items, including an out-of-date computer system. The only other things in the room were two uncomfortable-looking wooden chairs and a water cooler propped up against the wall closest to the door. The woman, who I assumed to be Larry's secretary, was smacking so hard on the piece of gum in her mouth I was amazed she was able to keep all her teeth attached to her gums.

"Can I help ya?" she asked.

"Brandon Cole," Brand said, holding his hand out to her in greeting.

"Oh, hiya hon," she beamed at him. "I still haven't heard from Larry to give him your message."

"Is it strange to not hear from him for so long?" Brand asked.

"Well, now that you mention it, it is sort of unusual for him to not at least check in with me. Let me call him at home and see if I can find out what's going on."

She delicately picked up her cell phone with her freshly-manicured French nails and dialed Larry's number. After a minute of letting the phone ring, she shook her head.

"He's not home either."

"Has he told you anything about our case?" Brand inquired.

"Oh, no," she said, shaking her curly blonde locks. "He doesn't like to talk to me about the cases. I just answer the phones and type up stuff he needs typed. That's about it."

"Has he had you type up anything about my case?"

"You know, I think he did," the secretary turned to her computer and clicked her mouse around the screen. "He did ask me type up a few of his notes. I could print them out for ya, if you want, hon. But there's not much there."

"Anything is better than nothing," Brand told her, dazzling the poor woman with his smile.

Even though I wasn't affected by the toxic dose of pheromones Brand gave off, which enraptured most females, I wasn't any less affected by him, especially when he smiled.

Only one page came out of the printer. The secretary handed it to Brand.

"It's not much, hon, but you're welcome to it."

"Thank you," Brand said, scanning the piece of paper quickly before folding it and putting in the back pocket of his jeans. "Tell Larry to give me a call when you see him, please. It's pretty important."

"Sure thing, hon."

When we left the office, I asked Brand, "What does the paper say?"

"Not much. There's a name listed as someone to contact about your mother's true identity."

"True identity? You mean she might not be who she says she is?"

"Looks like that's what Larry was trying to find out." Brand took one of my hands. "I know where Larry lives. Would you mind if we went there to check his apartment?"

"No, I don't mind."

We were standing outside an apartment the next instant. The door was ajar.

"Stand behind me," Brand said, instantly on alert. Something was definitely wrong. Even I could feel it.

Brand nudged the door open with his foot. Lying on the living room floor was a white-haired man of average build and height, face-down in a pool of blood. There was a large red stain on the back of his shirt. I couldn't take my eyes off him. I had never seen a dead body before. Brand quickly took my hand and phased us back to his living room.

"Why did we leave?" I asked. "Shouldn't we have called the police?"

"It's not something we need to get involved in, Lilly. We have enough problems to deal with without being entangled in a police investigation. With the door completely open, one of his neighbors is bound to find him soon."

"Who do you think killed him?"

"I'm not sure. From the way the room looked, Larry put up a good struggle with whoever it was before they shot him in the back."

"Ok, so it was most likely a human who killed him, right, since they used a gun? Maybe his death doesn't have anything to do with my case." I knew it was wishful thinking, but it was certainly plausible. He probably investigated a lot of cases which would make him the target for such a violent death.

"I think we should try to find the person he listed in his notes." Brand pulled out the paper from his back pocket. "According to this, Larry was planning to question someone named Nick

Landry. There's a New York address listed. We could go check him out ourselves."

"Let's go."

Since Brand had never been to the address listed in Larry's notes, we ended up phasing to a street corner in New York and hailing a taxicab. It only took about ten minutes to get to the apartment building. There was an intercom system on the outside of the building used to control who was allowed inside. Luckily, the janitor came out to dispose of some trash while we were debating whether we should buzz this Nick Landry's apartment. Brand held the door open for the janitor, and we quietly slipped inside.

When we stood outside the door to his apartment, Brand turned to me and said, "Promise me you'll phase back home at the first sign of trouble. We don't know anything about this person. He could be dangerous, for all we know. "

"I promise," I said, feeling like Brand was just being overly-cautious.

Brand knocked on the door.

"Who is it?" We heard a man say behind the door. I felt certain Mr. Landry was observing us through the peephole.

"My name is Brandon Cole," Brand answered. "We were hoping we could ask you a few questions, Mr. Landry."

"What about?" Mr. Landry asked gruffly.

"We got your name from a private investigator named Larry Goodwill. He was looking into the background of Cora Nightingale for us, and he listed you as someone who might have some information about her."

We heard the rattle of a door chain and the unlocking of a dead bolt. The door opened and Mr. Landry stood in the doorway, looking us up and down. He was an older man of about fifty-five, with balding white hair that he combed over in a futile attempt to preserve the illusion of having hair. He wore a white shirt, which was straining to keep his large belly from spilling completely over the top of the brown wool waistband of his pants, which were being held up by a pair of red suspenders. His sunken brown eyes lingered on me for a while before he spoke again.

"You look a lot like she did when she was your age," he commented before waving his hand, inviting us into his apartment.

Mr. Landry's apartment was rather old-fashioned and distinctly feminine. There were little touches of Victorian style here and there. An antique grandfather clock stood in the far corner, chiming a reminder that another hour in the day had passed us by.

Mr. Landry closed the door, and invited us to sit on the floral settee resting against the wall by the door, between two antique rosewood end tables.

"Has Mr. Goodwill tried to contact you yet?" Brand asked, taking a seat beside me on the settee.

"Yeah, he called me." Mr. Landry said as he walked into the kitchen area attached to the living room. I assumed he was going to offer us something to drink.

"How did you know my mother?" I asked.

Mr. Landry opened a drawer by the refrigerator. "A man came to see me about eighteen years ago, and said she was in trouble and needed a new identity."

"Do you know what kind of trouble?" I asked.

"I'm not sure," Mr. Landry said, keeping his back to us, fiddling with something inside the drawer. "He just asked me to help her out." Mr. Landry laughed harshly, as if he'd said something that wasn't very funny. "He didn't really ask. He ordered me to help her."

"Who was he?" Brand asked.

Mr. Landry turned around then. He was pointing a gun straight at us, his hand shaky.

"I don't think he would want me to talk about him with the two of you," the scared look on Mr. Landry's face told me he didn't really want to kill us, but couldn't see any other way out.

Brand stood and positioned his body between me and the gun in Mr. Landry's hand.

"Leave, Lilly," Brand ordered.

I knew I should but I couldn't. I had to know what Mr. Landry knew. I wasn't about to leave our one and only lead to the location of my grandparents.

Brand grabbed my hand and tried to phase me back home, but I cancelled his attempt with my own, phasing me back to right where I was sitting.

"What the hell are you people?" Mr. Landry asked. I could only imagine he was seeing us blink in and out of existence in front of him.

"Lilly, you promised," Brand said, getting aggravated by my stubbornness.

"We can't leave," I said. "He's our only lead. Please, we have to try to get the information we need."

I leaned around Brand, and looked Mr. Landry in the eyes, trying to act braver than I was really feeling.

"What was her real name? Can you at least tell me that much about my mother before you kill me?"

"I don't want to kill you, either of you," he said, his gun hand still shaking. "But he told me if anyone ever came around asking about her, I should take care of them myself or he would..."

I could see that Mr. Landry was on the verge of crying, and the hand he held the gun in was shaking even more uncontrollably.

"He would what?" I asked gently, hoping to coax the information we needed out of him before we really did have to phase out of harm's way.

"He would kill whoever was closest to me, just like he did my Ella."

"Who was Ella?"

"My wife," Mr. Landry's voice cracked. "I can't lose my grandbaby like that. I refuse to." He held the gun higher, as if he were preparing to shoot.

"Listen," I tried to reason. "At least tell me what I want to know before you kill us. We'll be dead anyway, right? It's not going to hurt anything to give us the information."

Mr. Landry thought about my request, and apparently didn't see any harm in telling me what I wanted to know. I suppose he thought of it as my last request.

"Your mother's name was Anna Miller."

"Do you know anything else about her?"

"I know she was born in Indiana, but that's about all I was told. He wasn't much on sharing information."

"Why did he come to you? How were you able to help them?"

"I used to be an FBI agent," Mr. Landry said with a note of regret. "I was good at my job. We hid people in the witness protection program all the time. Somehow, he knew what I did and made me give her a new life, without telling anyone I worked with about it. They found out, though, and fired me. I lost my job and my wife all in the same month."

"Why did he kill your wife?"

"To prove that he could." The gun in Mr. Landry's hand dipped down to the floor as he told us what he knew. "He told me if I didn't do what he said, the same thing would happen to my daughter, Melody. I couldn't let that happen. And I won't let that happen to her little girl."

"Who was he?"

There was a vacant, dead look in Mr. Landry's eyes as he lifted the gun and pointed it at us, like he was about to shoot.

"I can't live like this anymore. May God forgive me for what I've done." He quickly turned the gun on himself, jamming the barrel into his mouth and pulling the trigger before either Brand or I could stop him. I heard the gun go off just as Brand phased us back home, saving me from seeing the gory details of Mr. Landry's suicide.

The experience left me shaking in my shoes.

"Why would he do that?" I asked. I couldn't help but feel directly responsible for Mr. Landry's death.

If we hadn't been prying into his life, he would probably be alive right now. And if we hadn't hired Larry Goodwill to look into my mother's past, he would still be alive, too. Death seemed to be following me around like a shadow. How many more people would die because of me?

"I know what you're thinking," Brand said, taking me into his arms to help stop my trembling. "There wasn't any way we could have known that would happen. It's not your fault."

I understood what he was saying, but it didn't detract from the guilt I felt. It didn't change the fact that I was the reason two men I didn't even know were dead.

CHAPTER 14

Brand called Larry's secretary later that afternoon for a couple of reasons. He wanted to make sure someone did, in fact, find Larry's body, and he wanted to see if she could recommend a private investigator in Indiana who could help us find out more information about my mother's family. I told Brand I didn't want to involve another innocent bystander in our mess, but he assured me the investigator we hired wouldn't be hurt.

"I'll just ask the person to find out as much information as they can without getting too involved. Since we have your mother's real name and know where she was born, it should be easy to locate your grandparents."

I relented. If I wanted to find my mother's parents, I didn't have much of a choice.

From the conversation Brand had with Larry's secretary, it was obvious she still had no idea her boss was dead. Brand suggested she call his landlord or one of his neighbors to check up on him.

"He's getting older," Brand told her. "Heart attacks aren't uncommon in men his age."

When he got off the phone, he told me she was going to call Larry's apartment manager to check in on him. It was a relief to know the poor man wouldn't be left lying on his apartment floor, forgotten in a world too busy to worry about one person. The secretary also gave Brand contact information for a P.I. friend of Larry's in Indiana.

I really didn't feel like listening to Brand discussing everything about our case with someone new to the situation. So, I grabbed a soda from the fridge and went outside. I left the French doors open, so Brand wouldn't worry too much about me being alone. I walked down to the lakeshore and watched a group of mallard ducks play in the water near the boat dock.

"I'm surprised he lets you out of his sight."

I closed my eyes and tried to stop the sudden acceleration of my heart at the sound of Robert's mocking statement. When I looked to my right, I saw him standing beside me, leering at me with a grin that didn't quite make it to his eyes. He was wearing a stylishly-tailored red jacket with black collar and lining, canary-yellow dress shirt with a maroon tie with white and black stripes, and a pair of khaki pants. His short-styled jet-black hair was feathered toward his face, making his features stand out even more. He still reminded me of a cross between a cobra and a hawk, preparing to strike at its prey.

"What do you want?" I asked, trying to maintain a facade of calm. If Robert were, indeed, stalking me to finish the job Justin had failed to accomplish, I needed to know what his plans were. I tried to remain confident in the knowledge that I could always phase to safety if the situation called for it.

"Why, you, of course. What a stupid question, Lilly," he chuckled in disdain. "Can't you think of something a bit more imaginative to ask me?"

"Whose orders are you following? Who wants you to kill me?"

"Ahh, well, at least that's a better question, though, I'm afraid I can't answer it."

"Why aren't you just taking me back to my cell then?" I asked, confused as to why he was wasting time with this conversation. "What's stopping you?"

Robert grinned smugly. "Where's the fun in winning like that? I would much rather watch you beg me to take you back there to finish what I started."

"You don't honestly think I would ever beg you for anything, do you?"

"Oh, I don't know," Robert shrugged, as if he thought it was only a matter of time before I did. "I don't think I'll have to wait too much longer. After I set a few more pieces into place, we'll see how long you last in my little game before you start begging. I promise you, Lilly," he said, walking so close to me that I could feel his warm breath on my face, "you'll be pleading with me, on your hands and knees, to do whatever it is I want by the end of it all."

He disappeared as quickly as he had appeared.

I took a few deep breaths before I went back into the house. If Robert was still watching me, I didn't want him to know the effect his presence had on my state of mind.

When I stepped back into the house and closed the doors behind me, Brand was just getting off the phone.

"She said it might take a while to track down your mom's parents," Brand said, laying his phone down on the kitchen island. "I guess Anna Miller was a popular name in Indiana when your mom was born. There were at least a hundred of them born the same year. She'll have to check them all out to see which one was actually your mother." When I didn't reply to what he said, Brand narrowed his eyes at me, sensing something was wrong. "Are you all right?"

I didn't want to upset him, but there was no other choice left open to me. "Robert was here."

Brand quickly strode toward me, with a dangerous look on his face. "Where?"

"By the lake."

Brand grabbed me and, before I knew it, we were standing inside Malcolm's house.

"Malcolm!" Brand yelled.

Malcolm was immediately by my side.

"What's wrong?" he asked, looking down at me quickly to make sure I was ok.

"Robert was at my house. I need you to look after Lilly while I follow his trail."

Before either of us could voice our opinion of his plan, Brand disappeared.

"Well, I hope he leaves a piece for me to tear apart," Malcolm said, sounding completely unconcerned about Brand's safety.

"You need to follow him!" I said, clutching desperately at Malcolm's arm. "He might need help!"

"Oh, dearest," he said, waving my concerns away, "you have nothing to worry about. Brand can handle a piece of slime like Robert by himself. You really do worry too much about him."

"That's easy for you to say. You're not in love with him," I said, completely frustrated by his nonchalance.

"Yes, well, that's certainly true. But you need to trust me when I tell you Brand can take care of himself."

"Why are you so confident he won't get hurt?"

"Well, I've fought the man, and I would wager every penny I

have that you have never seen him fight. So take my word and trust me when I say he'll be fine."

"Are you ever going to tell me what happened that night?" I asked, assuming Malcolm was referring to the night Brand reprimanded him for seeing me naked.

"Not unless you torture the information out of me. It's something I would rather just forget about, dearest. Hurt pride and all, you understand. Enough worrying," he said, holding his arm out for me to take. "Come with me; we're making ice cream sundaes in the kitchen."

"Who's we?" I asked as he escorted me toward the back of his house, where the kitchen was.

Malcolm just grinned at me and seemed content to allow me to see for myself.

Abby was giggling at the kitchen table, trying her best to balance a long stemmed cherry on the tip of Sebastian's nose. She wasn't wearing a wig or colored contacts today. Her long white hair glistened in the sunlight, and when she looked at me, there was no doubt which parent she'd inherited her eyes from.

"Lilly!" Abby soon forgot about her playful game with Sebastian and ran over to give me a hug.

"I haven't had a chance to thank you for what you did for us," she said, giving me a kiss on the cheek.

Sebastian stood from the table and came to kiss me on the opposite cheek.

"Thanks a lot, Lilly. I'm not sure how you talked our dads into letting us be together, but we really appreciate it. A lot more than just saying 'thank you' can cover."

"I'm just glad you guys are happy," I told them.

"Tell us what's been going on," Abby took my hand and led me to the table.

It gave me a chance to tell Malcolm what Brand and I had been through that day.

"He shouldn't have taken you," Malcolm said, not holding back his disapproval. "That man could have killed you quite easily with a gun. You need to remember you're human, dearest. Bullets *can* kill you."

"I can take care of myself. Besides, Brand trusts me to use my good judgment," I defended.

"Well, I wouldn't call it good judgment to badger a man holding a gun on you with a million questions."

I could tell Malcolm was frustrated with me for what I had done, and knew it stemmed from how much he cared about me. I put my hand on his arm in an attempt to soothe away his worry.

"Don't be mad at me," I said softly. "I had to do everything I could to get the answers we needed. I'm running out of time."

Malcolm put his hand over mine. "We won't let anything happen to you, dearest. You need to believe that."

"I know you won't," I told him, surprised at how confident I sounded to my own ears.

I tried my best to hide my worry about Brand while Malcolm made me an ice cream sundae. Even with Malcolm's reassurance that Brand was more than capable of handling Robert by himself, I knew I wouldn't feel better until I saw him whole and unharmed with my own two eyes.

I was glad to find that the relationship between Abby and Sebastian had progressed so far in such a short amount of time. They acted like a couple of teenagers in love. I was happy they had found each other, and realized I was the reason for that. It made me feel good to know that at least one good thing had come from the situation I found myself in.

I made a valiant attempt to eat the ice cream sundae Malcolm made me. At any other time, I would have been on my way to a sugar coma, gulping down the two scoops of Neapolitan ice cream, smothered in strawberry and chocolate sauces, topped with a fluffy layer of cool whip with its sprinkling of nuts and maraschino cherries. Unfortunately, after a couple of spoonsful, I gave up trying to pretend it held my interest.

After the others finished their ice cream, Abby and Sebastian tried to talk Malcolm and me into playing a game of croquet in the backyard. I declined, partly because I had no idea how to play croquet, but mostly because my thoughts were still on Brand. Where was he? Shouldn't he have come back by now?

"Why don't you two go on outside?" Malcolm told Abby and Sebastian, placing our dirty bowls in the kitchen sink. "I have something I want to show Lilly."

"Just as well," Abby said, walking to the doorway of the kitchen, which led out to the veranda and backyard. "I'm sure Sebastian wouldn't want you to see him get trounced by a woman," she taunted, turning around, smiling coyly at Sebastian.

"Oh, you think you'll beat me, do you?" Sebastian said, standing from his chair.

"Of course I will," Abby teased. "You have no chance of winning against my superior skill with a mallet."

"We'll see about that!" Sebastian ran toward Abby, causing her to turn and run for the backyard in a fit of giggles.

Malcolm came to me and took my hands, coaxing me out of my chair.

"What did you want to show me?" I asked.

"I made you something," he said, staring down at my hands, lightly rubbing the tops of them with his thumbs in a circular motion. He looked almost embarrassed to tell me anything further.

"What did you make?"

"It's not really something I can describe. I need to show it to you."

When Malcolm's eyes met mine, I could see how worried he was about my reaction to his gift.

"Where is it?" I asked, intrigued by his behavior.

"I'll have to phase us there."

"Ok." I wasn't sure why this seemed to be such a big deal to Malcolm, but my curiosity was definitely piqued.

Almost instantly, we were standing on a cobblestone walkway in front of a house that was a mix of Victorian and country influences. It was a two-story home made of redwood, with an octagonal corner on the right side, banked with windows.

"Do you like it?" Malcolm asked.

"It's beautiful. Is it one of your homes?"

Instead of answering my question, he held onto one of my hands and escorted me up the steps leading to the redwood, glass-cut front doors. He reached on top of the doorframe and pulled down a key.

"That doesn't seem like a safe place to hide a key," I admonished.

"We're so far out in the woods, that it's doubtful anyone would bother us here."

Malcolm unlocked the door and stuffed the key into his pants pocket. He opened the door and motioned for me to go in first.

The interior floors were made of the same wood as the outside of the house. There was a staircase across from the front doors in the foyer, leading to the second floor. To the right was a living room area with a stone fireplace. To the left were a hallway that led to the back of the house, and a door I assumed must lead to the garage. When I stepped into the living room, my eyes were immediately drawn to the windows. Framed, like a painting were a snow-capped mountain and crystal-blue lake.

"Where are we?" I asked.

"Colorado. Do you like the view?" Malcolm walked over to me and admired the scenery with me.

"It's gorgeous."

After taking in the beauty of the natural setting for a couple of minutes, I turned to Malcolm and asked, "So where is this surprise you made me?"

He looked down at me. "You're standing in it."

I wasn't quite sure what he was talking about, so I looked down at my feet to see if I was standing in something. Not seeing anything but wood flooring, it dawned on me what he was saying.

"You built me a house?"

"You like it, don't you?" Malcolm's brow creased in worry. "I tried to design something I thought you would want, something that fit your personality."

"You built me a house?" I asked again, completely stunned and unable to think of anything else to say.

"Come on," he said, taking my hand again, grinning at how flabbergasted he had made me. "Let me show you the rest of it."

On the first floor of the unfurnished home, there was a dining room connected to the living room, and a family room beside a fully-equipped kitchen. The second floor had three regular bedrooms and a master suite, which was directly above the first-floor living room. The same picture windows were up here, allowing you to take in an unobstructed mountain view. I stood by the windows, unable to process everything at once.

"You built me a house," I said, still trying to wrap my mind around the concept.

"Yes," he said, coming to stand beside me. "I built you a house. Do you like it?"

"I can't accept this," I said, shaking my head. "It's too much, Malcolm."

"Nonsense. You have no choice. I'm giving it to you."

"No," I said firmly. "I can't take it."

"Why not?" Malcolm sounded offended. It was the last thing I wanted.

"It's a house!" I said, thinking that was enough of a reason.

"Lilly," it was one of the few times Malcolm called me by name, "please, take the house. I want you to have it."

"But, why would you build me a house?"

"It's what I do," he shrugged. "I build things."

"You could have just built me a doll house, not a real house."

Malcolm chuckled. "I don't do small, dearest. You should know that by now."

"But it's a house, Malcolm."

"Then just think of it as a large doll house, and consider yourself the doll who gets to live in it."

I couldn't help but blush as his statement.

"I thought it would be nice if you had somewhere all your own to go to," he told me, caressing my face with his hand. "You deserve this and so much more, dearest. I could give you the world if you would just let me."

If I wasn't so in love with Brand, I could easily see myself falling for Malcolm. Who wouldn't be seduced by his model-perfect good looks and gentle nature, at least with me? He had always treated me like I was dear to him, and never shied away from letting me know how much he adored me. But, I was hopelessly in love with Brand, and not even Malcolm's charms could change that fact.

"Malcolm, I ..."

"No, don't say it," he said, as if he knew I was going to remind him that I loved Brand. "I know." His hand left my face and returned to his side. "Just let me fantasize for a moment that this is our house, and that you love me more than you do him."

I didn't know what to say. My heart ached for my friend. I wanted to comfort him with words, but knew there weren't any that would erase his yearning for me to return his affections. I put my arms around his waist and laid my head against his chest. It was all I could give him.

He held me close for a long while, not saying a word, before finally letting me go.

When we returned to Malcolm's house, he talked me into playing a game of chess on the veranda. Abby and Sebastian were still playing croquet in the backyard. Though, from what I gathered from their banter, it was their second game. Apparently, Abby was true to her word and had won the first game without much effort.

Almost an hour after he'd left, Brand strolled out the backdoor and onto the veranda. I immediately jumped out of my seat, quickly forgetting about the move I was about to make against Malcolm, which would put me within three moves of winning the game, and threw myself into Brand's arms.

"I really wish you wouldn't do things like that to me," I admonished, hugging him so tight I felt sure I was cutting off the circulation below his waist.

"I'm sorry," he said, hugging me back.

"Did you find the slimy bastard?" Malcolm asked, coming to stand beside me.

"No," Brand replied, clearly disappointed and frustrated. "He had someone helping him hide his trail. I guess he learned a few tricks from Justin."

Brand looked down at me. "What exactly did Robert say to you?"

I told Brand what I could remember about my conversation with Robert.

"What do you think he meant?" I asked. "What could he be planning that makes him think I would beg him to kill me?"

"I don't know, but I wouldn't put anything past Robert." Brand looked to Malcolm. "Do you have any idea what he could be orchestrating?"

Malcolm shrugged. "It's hard to know. Robert's a sadist. I wouldn't put anything past him."

Brand looked back down at me with a grave expression on his face. "Promise me the next time you even think you see someone who looks like Robert, you'll phase somewhere safe. It was foolish of you to stay there and talk with him."

I pulled away from Brand. If there was one thing I hated, it was being talked down to.

"If I hadn't, we wouldn't know he was planning something," I pointed out, trying to keep my temper in check.

"You put yourself in danger unnecessarily, Lilly," Brand said, not trying to hide his frustration with me. "Nothing is more important than your safety. It was stupid to stand there and have a conversation with someone who'd tried to rape you the last time you saw him!"

Out of the corner of my eye, I could see Malcolm staring hard at Brand, shaking his head.

"Well if I'm so *stupid*, maybe you should stay away from me. I would hate for it to rub off on your genius!"

I was standing at the foot of my bed in my own apartment before I knew it. Had he actually had the audacity to stand there and call me foolish and stupid in the same conversation?

Brand phased in almost on top of me, causing me to fall back onto my bed with him falling beside me. He rolled over and pinned me to the bed. I guess he thought that would make me stay put.

"Lilly, I..."

I phased to his bed back home and quickly stood up before he could follow. I ran to his paint studio, and immediately phased to the street in New York we'd gone to earlier in the day. I hoped he would spend some time trying to find me in his house before figuring out I had simply gone to another room to phase from. I put my arm out and hailed a taxi. A cab instantly came to my rescue, and whisked me away before Brand could follow, leaving a cold trail for him to find.

"Where to, miss?" the cab driver asked.

I had no idea where I would go in New York, but it really didn't matter. I just needed to go somewhere and phase so Brand couldn't simply follow me. I knew where I wanted to end up, but I didn't want Brand tracking me there.

"Just take me another three blocks," I told the cab driver. Since I only had a twenty-dollar bill in my back pocket, I didn't want to spend it all on a cab ride to nowhere.

When I got out of the cab, I phased to Utha Mae's trailer. I knocked on the door and called to her. She immediately opened it.

"Well, this is a pleasant surprise," she said, holding the door open for me.

I walked into her trailer.

"I needed to see you," I told her, trying to keep myself from crying.

"Come and sit with me, child. Tell me what's wrong."

We sat down on her brown suede sofa, and I couldn't prevent the tears that began to flow of their own accord.

"Brand and I had a fight," I said, wiping the tears from my eyes, refusing to get too upset in front of her.

"What about, baby?"

I regretted not being able to tell Utha Mae everything. I said as much as I could without bringing her into my troubles.

"He's upset with me because I talked with someone dangerous to get some information we needed. He called me foolish and stupid. Can you believe that?" I snorted.

"Well," Utha Mae sat back on the sofa, watching me, "was he right?"

"What? That I was foolish and stupid?" Was she actually going to take his side?

"Was the person you talked with a danger to you?"

I shrugged. "I suppose he was, but that doesn't give Brand the right to call me those things."

"I'm not saying he was right, baby, but you need to consider his feelings. I'm sure he doesn't really believe you're either of those things. He wouldn't want to marry you if he did. You probably just scared him silly, and he was lashing out in the wrong way, and to the wrong person."

"Well, he needs to learn I won't just stand around and be talked to like that."

"Which is why you're here?"

"Yes," I said, feeling a little guilty for using Utha Mae's home as a safe haven. "I'm not sure he'd think to look for me here."

"Well, it's always good to let a man know where you stand. Since you're here, why don't you help me make us some supper? I think your mom went out with someone, or I'd tell you to go get her, too."

I was at Utha Mae's for almost two hours before the phone rang. When she answered it, I knew it was Brand on the other end of the line.

"Yes, she's here, hon. Do you want to talk with her?"

Utha Mae handed me the phone, forcing me to stop hiding and handle the situation like an adult.

"Hello," I said.

"Come home," he begged. "I'm so sorry, Lilly. *Please*, come home."

The heartbroken way he made his request tore down my resolve to stay mad at him. It seemed like love made you strong against certain situations, but completely weak when it came to the one you were in love with.

"Can you come get me?" I asked. "I don't have my car here."

Utha Mae had already asked me how I got to her house, since she didn't see my car parked outside. I had to concoct a lie and told her I hired a taxi service in Lakewood to get to her home, because I didn't have my car with me at the time of my fight with Brand.

"You know I'll have to actually drive there," Brand said, slightly frustrated that our reconciliation would not be happening immediately. If he just showed up at Utha Mae's, it would cause her to ask too many questions.

"I'm not going anywhere," I promised him. "I'll be here waiting."

"Ok, I'll be there as soon as I can."

I hung up the phone.

"So, are you going to forgive him?" Utha Mae asked me.

"I already have," I sighed. "I love him too much to stay mad at him, especially when he sounds so pitiful."

"Good. I like knowing you're in love with a good man. I just wish Tara would find someone I felt comfortable leaving her with."

"Leaving?" I asked, taken completely off guard. "Are you going somewhere?"

"We're all going somewhere eventually, baby. My time is coming," Utha Mae said, putting a hand to her chest. "I would feel better if I knew Tara had someone to share her life with, who loved her as much as Brand loves you."

"Don't talk like that," I told her. "You're going to be with us for a long time."

The sad smile on Utha Mae's face worried me. "Only the good Lord knows when He'll be calling me home. None of us can predict when our time will come, baby, but I do know that I'm getting old. I don't feel like I have much longer to wait."

I didn't push the issue and attempt to convince Utha Mae she had to live at least another twenty years. But who knew what would happen? For all I knew, I might only have two more months to live.

"Utha Mae," I sat down with her at the kitchen table. "Can I ask you something?"

"You know you can ask me anything, baby."

"Would you think less of me if I married Brand now, instead of waiting until I got out of college?"

Utha Mae looked confused. "What difference would it make when you married him?"

"It doesn't, I guess." I desperately wanted to tell her why I was thinking about moving up the wedding, but knew I couldn't. "It's just that I never wanted to end up like my mom. The only thing most people know about her is that she dates a lot of men. I don't want to be known just for being married to Brand."

"Child, you'll be known for the deeds you do in your life. Whether you marry him now or in four more years doesn't really make a difference in the scheme of things. But, I will say that I probably wouldn't be so willing to let you marry him if he wasn't able to provide for you so well. He can take care of you, and he seems mature enough to be someone you can lean on. He'll support you in more ways than just with his money. He loves you more than I've ever seen a man love a woman. Well, at least as much as my Harry loved me anyway. You know," Utha Mae had a wistful expression on her face, "we married when we were eighteen."

Harry had been Utha Mae's husband. He died from a stroke when Tara and I were only two years old, so we had no memory of him, but Utha Mae had stayed true to him all these years. She never even looked at another man. Many of the single men from her church had tried to take her out, but she always refused their attention, saying her heart would always belong to Harry. Even though he was in Heaven, Utha Mae didn't feel any less married to him. She was just waiting for her time to join him in paradise.

"He's willing to wait until I graduate," I told her, "but the more we're together, the less I want to wait that long."

"Well, baby, only the two of you can make that decision, but you have my blessing to marry him whenever you want. As long as you don't have any doubts about spending the rest of your life with him, I don't see any reason for you to wait. You let me know when you want to have that wedding, though," Utha Mae said. "I'd like to help with the expenses."

"It'll just be something small. I don't have many people to invite."

"Just let me know, baby," she said, patting my hands resting on the table. "I wouldn't mind having a few of my friends there to watch you walk down the aisle in a pretty white dress."

"I'll let you know what I decide. I'm still thinking about it."

Brand drove up to Utha Mae's trailer almost thirty-five minutes later. I knew he must have cheated a little, since it normally took an hour to drive from Lakewood to Dalton. Utha Mae didn't comment on his fast arrival. She probably assumed he sped all the way from Lakewood in his eagerness to see me.

"Now, you take it slow going back," she said to Brand, wagging a finger at him.

"Yes, ma'am," Brand replied, opening the passenger door for me. After he closed the door, I waved goodbye to Utha Mae.

We didn't say anything to each other. When we got on the highway heading toward Lakewood, Brand phased us to his driveway and parked in front of his house within a few seconds.

He took one of my hands into his own and phased us to his living room couch.

"Can you forgive me?" he asked, squeezing my hand gently.

"I already have," I reassured him. "But you have to promise

that you'll never call me foolish or stupid again. I won't put up with that sort of abuse."

Brand winced at my use of the word. I was sure even he knew you could abuse a person just as much with words as you could with actual physical harm.

"I promise to never let those words pass my lips again when referring to you. I was just mad about letting Robert get away from me and took it out on you. I know it was wrong of me, and you have to know I didn't really mean what I said. I can only beg you to forgive me for acting like a complete idiot. I let my worry for you overshadow everything sometimes, including my common sense. When you do things that put your life in danger, like talk to Robert, or even what you did this morning with Mr. Landry, it makes me crazy, Lilly. I don't want you to take unnecessary chances with your life."

"But if I hadn't taken those chances, we wouldn't have the new information about my mother, or know that Robert is conjuring up some convoluted plan. I know you worry about me, but you need to trust me. I don't plan to die anytime soon. If you haven't noticed, I'm fighting for my life as hard as you're fighting to keep me alive."

"I know."

Brand looked so remorseful for what he had done. I couldn't stand to see him continue to punish himself for something he'd already been forgiven for.

"Why don't we just forget about everything for now and try to enjoy the rest of the night?" I suggested, pulling him to me.

Brand held me to him. I could feel him start to relax, finally realizing that I had, indeed, forgiven his transgressions.

CHAPTER 15

I think Brand was still feeling guilty the next morning, because he brought me breakfast in bed when I woke up. Carefully arranged on a beautiful wood-carved serving tray was a crystal bowl filled with some of the largest and reddest strawberries I have ever seen, with a smaller bowl of whipped cream beside it. There was a plate full of freshly-baked croissants on a crystal plate, with a single red rose in full bloom lying across it. It occurred to me that it was the first flower Brand had ever given me. I picked it up and held it to my nose, breathing in its sweet aroma.

"Where did you get it?" I asked, letting the silky petals tickle the tip of my nose.

"It's not fall everywhere in the world," he reminded me with a crooked smile as he leaned down and gave me a kiss. "Now sit back," he half-ordered, half-teased, sitting on the side of the bed.

When he picked up one of the strawberries and dipped it into the whip cream, I realized he intended to feed it to me. As he brought the strawberry to my lips, I opened my mouth and bit down through the middle of it, feeling the sweet juices of the firm, ripe fruit and smooth texture of the cream mix in my mouth.

Some of the cream and juice clung to my lips. I was about to wipe my mouth with the napkin on the tray when Brand said, "You won't need that."

He leaned in towards me, bringing his lips down to mine, and slowly kissed away all traces of the cream and juice from my mouth. It was then that strawberries and fresh whipped cream became my favorite things to eat, forever replacing pizza at the top of my list. I moved the tray down a little from over my lap and sat with my legs folded underneath me.

"Is something wrong?" Brand asked, not understanding what I was doing.

"No," I said, picking up a strawberry and dipping it in the cream. "You need to eat breakfast, too."

A pleased grin spread across his face as I brought the strawberry to his lips.

I'm not sure how long we sat there feeding each other strawberries, but I do know it was one of the most romantic and intimate moments of my life.

After breakfast, I phased back to my apartment to shower and change clothes. Tara was sitting in the living room, watching a movie on TV.

"Hey, girl," she said as I sat down beside her. "How did things go yesterday?"

I filled Tara in on everything that had happened the previous day. She seemed to agree with Brand in thinking I was foolish to put my life in danger twice in one day.

"You need to be more careful," she scolded. "You're half-human, you know. You ain't immortal just because you got some angel blood running through your veins."

"I know that, but you can't argue that what I did wasn't useful."

"I don't care, Lilly Rayne Nightingale. You let the angels take the chances. They can survive flying bullets, but you can't. And what the heck were you thinking, talking to that Robert? You need to keep away from him. He ain't nothing but a bag full of trouble."

I didn't want to talk about it anymore, so I changed the subject.

"How did your day with Malik go?"

"We had fun."

I waited for her to say more, but she didn't. "That's all I get? No details?"

Tara shrugged. "We rode around and I showed him where things were. He took me to lunch at Chili's, and we went and saw a movie. That's about all there is to tell. We had fun, though. I liked talking to him. We're going out again today. He said he wanted to see the college, so I thought I'd take him around campus and show him where I work and stuff, nothing major."

"Well, I'm glad you get along with him. From what I know, Malik's going to be in our lives for a very long time."

"Oh, yeah, we're fine. I like him good enough."

Seeing that I wasn't going to be getting much else out of Tara, I left her to watch the rest of her movie and took a shower to get ready.

Brand and I didn't really have anything in particular planned for the day. We had to wait on the private investigator to wade through the one hundred Anna Millers she found born in Indiana the same year as my mother. I hoped it wouldn't take her long to discover which one had been my mom and where my grandparents were, if they were even still alive. That thought hadn't occurred to me until now. What if they were dead? People died in accidents and from diseases all the time.

No, I wouldn't let myself entertain a negative thought like that again. Brand said we would find the answers we needed, and I trusted his judgment.

After I got ready, Tara was in the kitchen, making some tea.

"I have a question for you," I said, standing against the kitchen counter, uncertain to how she would react to my query. "What would you think about me marrying Brand now?"

"What, like today?"

"No," I said, smiling and shaking my head, "but soon."

"This got anything to do with what Faust told you about having two months?"

"Sort of," I admitted. "I just don't want to waste any time with Brand, no matter how much time that might be, whether it's a hundred years or just two months."

"You might as well marry the boy," Tara said. "You're practically married as it is. You spend all your time with him day *and* night."

"Would you think any less of me if I did it now?"

"Girl, you worry too much about what other people think. You need to make that decision for yourself. Don't worry about me or anybody else. But, if you gotta know what I think, I don't see any reason why you shouldn't do it."

"Thanks," I told her, giving her a hug. "I don't know what I would do without you."

"Die an old maid," she said, sticking her tongue out at me. "Just don't forget who your best friend is after you marry Mr. Wonderful."

"Like you would let me," I replied, rolling my eyes.

"That's true enough. Someone has to keep your feet on the ground."

Now that I had the blessing of the two people whose opinion

meant the most to me, I was having a hard time seeing any reason not to marry Brand as soon as possible. What I told Tara was true. Whether I only had two more months or a hundred years of life left, I knew I wanted to spend my remaining days with Brand, as his wife.

Tara and I received an unexpected guest soon after our talk. Will stopped by to see how things were going. I filled him in on what had happened since I last saw him, after our encounter with Faust. He seemed to be in league with everyone else, and told me I needed to be more careful.

"Let Brand do the dirty work," he said. "You don't need to put yourself in danger like that, especially with Robert. You know a little bit about how cruel he can be, but you don't know the whole story."

"Then why don't you tell me? Malcolm called him a sadist, and Brand acted as if he hated him even before I told him what he'd done to me. What exactly has he done in the past?"

"He likes to watch people suffer, Lilly. It's what he gets off on. He doesn't just hunt down his prey, like most of the Watchers who gave into their bloodlust. He hunts them down then plays with them. He likes to torture people as much as he likes sucking the life out of them. Robert isn't someone you want to mess with. He'll find your weaknesses and use them against you to cause you the most pain."

"Well, we know he's planning something. I guess we'll just have to be as prepared as we can."

"You just stay away from him," Tara told me as she stood up from her chair at the kitchen table. "I need to go get ready. Malik should be here soon. I made some fudge in case you need some. It's in the fridge," she told me as she made her way to her bedroom.

Will and I were alone for the first time since our talk by the lake. Even though he had been totally out of line, he was still my friend. I felt like I owed it to him to tell him I had changed my mind about waiting to marry Brand. I didn't want him to hear it from Tara, and I wasn't sure how often he kept in touch with Utha Mae. I planned to tell Brand my decision that day, and was pretty sure he wouldn't be keeping it a secret from anyone.

"Will, I think we need to talk."

"Have you thought more about what I said?" The look of hopeful expectation on his face was something I wasn't expecting to see. I thought I had made my feelings about his suggestion plain, the last time we discussed the subject.

"Not really," I admitted, and watched his hope visibly fade. "I need to tell you that I plan to marry Brand soon."

"What happened to waiting until you got out of college?" The snide way he made his remark made me wonder if it would be a waste of my time to try to explain my reasoning. Did he even deserve such consideration?

"I don't want to wait," I said, trying not to let his open disdain upset me. "There will never be anyone but Brand for me and, with everything that's going on, I don't want to waste any more time. I want to be his wife for whatever time we might have left together. Can you understand that?"

"You don't have to rush into anything, Lilly," he pleaded. "We're not going to let anything happen to you."

"I know," I tried to put as much confidence into the statement as I could. "But it doesn't matter. Brand's the only one I see myself spending the rest of my life with, no matter how long or short might be. I don't see any point in waiting any longer."

"Why don't you at least wait until we figure everything out

and have things settled once and for all? It would give you more time to be with him and know for sure he's the one you want. It just seems like you're rushing things, Lilly. How do you know you're not just making this decision because of the stress you're under? Maybe you should wait and make sure it's really what you want."

"You're just not getting it, Will." Why was he making this so hard? "I want to marry him. I would want to marry him, even if things were perfect and we had all the time in the world to be together. Everything inside me tells me this is the right thing to do and the right time to do it. All of you keep telling me to trust you to save me from what might happen. Now you need to listen to me and trust that I know what I'm doing. Marrying Brand is what I'm meant to do. I know it. I have no doubts about my decision."

Will let out a heavy, defeated sigh, his shoulders sagging.

"I always thought we'd be together, Lilly," he murmured so low I had to strain to hear him.

"I'm sorry, Will."

Even though he had tried his best to cast doubt in my mind about Brand's true feelings for me, I couldn't help but feel sorry for Will. He was still one of my best friends, and I didn't like to see him in pain. Nevertheless, I knew it was the right decision to let him know where things stood between us. Maybe now he could put his fantasies about us having a future together behind him. It was better to have him know there wasn't a chance I would change my mind than linger around, hoping I would choose him one day.

"It's my own fault," he said, apparently finding the whole situation ironic. "I'm the one who kept pushing you away after we kissed that night. If I had been stronger and taken a chance on us, things would be different."

I didn't say anything. It was hard to know what would have happened if Will had declared his love to me then. I wondered if what he said was true, though. In my heart, I felt like what Will had done then was the way it was meant to be. It was my destiny to find Brand and fall in love with him. He was my soul mate. He was the one I was meant to share my life with.

"I'm not sure this is the right time to ask you to do this," I said, wondering if I should wait to make my request, but wanting to give Will time to think about it before giving me his final answer. "Since I don't really have a male relative to do the job, I was wondering if you would give me away at the wedding."

"I don't know if I'm strong enough to do that, Lilly Rayne," he shook his head at me, as if I had just asked him to jump the width of the Grand Canyon. "That's a lot to ask."

"Think of it as your wedding gift to me. You're part of my family, Will, and you always will be. I hope you'll still be a part of my life, even though our relationship isn't exactly the way you thought it would end up. It would mean a lot to me if you did it."

"Let me think about it."

"That's all I ask."

At least he hadn't given me an emphatic 'no'.

Will left soon after, coming up with an excuse about schoolwork.

I called Brand and asked him to come over to the apartment. I wanted to wait around until Malik arrived to collect Tara. It was odd. I actually *was* starting to feel a connection with Malik, even though I didn't know him that well.

While we were waiting, I thought I should mention to Brand and Tara the house Malcolm gave me.

"He built you a house?" Brand acted as if he was certain he had heard me wrong.

"What kinda house? Where is it?" Tara asked, excited by the idea of me owning my own home.

I described the house as best I could, and told them it was somewhere in Colorado. I hadn't even thought to ask where it was exactly.

"How did he design and build a house in such a short amount of time?" Brand asked.

"Well, I suppose it's like you always say; people will do anything if you wave enough money in their faces," I replied.

"They do it all the time on TV," Tara chimed in. "Ain't you ever seen that show where they build these 4,000-square-foot houses in less than a week? Did he get you any furniture?"

"No," I said, remembering how empty it had felt without anything in it.

Brand looked troubled.

"I told him I couldn't take it, but he wouldn't take no for an answer," I told him.

"No, you should accept it," Brand said, completely stunning me with his easy acceptance of Malcolm's gift. "He obviously went to a lot of trouble to do it for you. It would be rude to refuse it."

"Does this mean I get to try skiing?" Tara asked. "You know, I would look hot in one of those ski suits."

"It might be tempting fate to put skis on either one of us," I told her. "Remember how we used to trip over each other in those ballet classes Utha Mae put us in? I don't think we need a replay of what we did to the Swan Lake recital, on the side of a mountain."

"Yeah, you might be right about that," Tara said, rethinking her earlier enthusiasm. "Maybe we could get a couple of them snow mobiles, though. I bet that'd be fun."

There was a knock on the door.

Tara didn't even bother to get out of her chair to make sure it was Malik. She just yelled, "Come in!" at the door.

Malik walked in and smiled when he saw I was present.

"I was hoping you might be here," he told me. "I wanted to know how yesterday went. Did you two find out anything?"

Brand and I told Malik what we had discovered. He, too, chastised me for not being more careful. At least he was the last person I had to tell. I wouldn't have to hear 'you shouldn't have done that' from anyone else.

"So, now we're just waiting to hear back from this P.I. you hired?" he asked Brand.

"Yes. Hopefully she'll have the information we need soon."

"Well, keep me informed and let me know if I can be of any help."

"Thanks," I told Malik. "We'll let you know."

"Come on," Tara said, grabbing her purse. "Let me give you a tour of the campus. Then you can take me out to eat somewhere."

Malik chuckled at Tara's brashness.

"At least I don't have to worry about knowing what you're thinking," he told her.

"No, I pretty much say what's on my mind," she agreed. "See y'all later!"

After Tara and Malik left, I turned to Brand and made him stand up with me.

"Where are we going?" he asked.

"Home."

I phased us inside his paint studio.

Brand looked around. "Why this room?"

"It's where I first told you I love you," I said, holding his hands in mine and gazing up at him to watch his reaction to my next words. "There's something just as important that I want to say to you now."

That statement definitely captured his attention. "And what would that be?"

"I want to marry you."

Brand smiled, looking completely confused. "I know that, my love."

"No," I said, wanting to make sure he fully understood what I was saying. "I mean I want to marry you as soon as possible. I don't want to wait four years."

He looked almost afraid that he might have heard me wrong. "Do you mean it?"

"Yes, I don't want to wait. I love you, and, honestly, I don't really see the point in waiting four years. It would just be a waste of time." Time I might not have, I thought, but didn't say. "I want to be your wife as soon as possible."

Brand put his hands on both sides of my face and kissed me long and hard. When he finally forced himself to pull away, he looked down at me with an expression of complete bliss.

"I will love you every day of your life as much as I do this very moment. I promise to make you as happy as I can, and I want you to know that you will always be the center of my world. Everything I am, or ever will be, revolves around only you, Lilly. I am completely yours in this life and the next."

"Those sound a lot like vows," I said, unable to hold back my tears of happiness as I stared at his earnest and joyful face.

"They're my vows to you, and I will always keep them."

Brand and I decided to spend a quiet day at home together. It was rare that we actually had time to just enjoy each other's company, and not have to worry about things for a while. We pushed our problems out of our minds as far as we could and spent the day as any other normal couple would.

Brand finally showed me the painting he did of me on our perfect day together, when I'd wrapped myself in one of his paint cloths and sat on a wicker chair framed by the lake behind me. You would have thought I was draped in expensive silk the way Brand painted me. I still couldn't get over how beautiful I looked in his paintings. When I mentioned it again, he still professed it was the way I looked to him. I wasn't going to argue. Who minded if their fiancé had a completely distorted view of them, as long as it was a positive one?

In fact, the next three days made me feel like I was any normal girl going to school and arranging a wedding with the man she loved. I went to Malcolm's house to tell him my decision about marrying Brand early. He didn't seem surprised, and told me to let him know if there was anything he could do to help with the arrangements. I was glad to see him take my decision so well.

When I called my mom to tell her the news, she was over the moon. She started talking so fast about dresses and flowers, that I had to ask her to slow down. I had never heard her so excited before. After talking with her about everything we would have to arrange, I had a sinking feeling that I wouldn't be able to marry Brand as quickly as I had hoped.

After looking at the calendar, keeping in mind everything that had to be done, I decided to set the wedding date for November 17. It would give us plenty of time to do things right. Plus, it was the start of our Thanksgiving break. I had missed so much school as it was this semester that I didn't want to miss any more than I had to. It was still my goal to have my degree in as little time as possible. The sooner I earned that small piece of my life's puzzle for myself, the better.

I wanted to have the wedding in Utha Mae's church, but I was hesitant to ask Brand if he could even step foot inside one. I remembered how he answered Utha Mae's question about attending church, and I wasn't sure if it was a decision he made for himself or if it was something his kind just wasn't allowed to do. There really wasn't any getting around the issue. So, I just asked him one day, while we were walking along the lakeshore after supper one evening.

"There is one detail of the wedding arrangements I need to ask you about," I started, hoping my question wouldn't hurt his feelings if he were, indeed, forbidden to walk on holy ground.

"You know you can ask me anything."

I guess I wasn't hiding my nervousness very well from him.

"I want to have the wedding in Utha Mae's church. Can we do that?"

"Of course, if that's where you want to have it."

"Then... you can go into a church?"

"Oh," he said, with an understanding smile, realizing what I was really asking. "You know all those myths about vampires aren't true. The only reason I don't go to church is because it reminds me of what I lost. It's hard to worship and not actually be in His presence. It would be like loving you, but never being able to see you again."

I'd never thought of it that way, but it made perfect sense to me now.

"Speaking of the wedding," he said. "Why don't you let me

give you the money for the expenses? I'm sure we could hire someone to arrange everything for us."

"It's traditionally the bride's family who pays for the wedding," I told him.

"But I have plenty of money, Lilly. We could pay to have things done much faster and not have to wait."

"Are you in a rush?" I asked. "I did move the day up by almost four years, you know."

"I know," Brand groaned, taking me into his arms. "But now that it's so close, it's complete torture to have to wait a minute longer."

"It'll be worth it. I promise. Plus, just think about how happy you'll make your future mother-in-law by letting her arrange everything for us."

"She does seem happy about it," Brand agreed.

"I've never seen her so excited. She's planning a trip to Jackson for us this Saturday, so we can find dresses for me and Tara."

"This Saturday?" Brand asked in surprise. "Will you be back early?"

"I don't know. Why? Did we have something else planned?" I couldn't remember planning anything for that day.

"Well, I have something I want to do that night. Do you think you can make it back by suppertime?"

"I'll make sure we're back before then," I promised him. "Dress or not, I'll be here."

CHAPTER 16

When Saturday came, Tara and I drove to Dalton to pick up my mom and Utha Mae. As far as the financial arrangements for the wedding went, I told my mom I had some money in the bank from a gambling excursion with Malcolm to help out. The $5000 I won at his casino on that Sunday we spent together would definitely come in handy now. I had been saving it, not knowing when I would need such a large sum of cash.

My mom informed me that she had been saving some money up since I was a little girl, to pay for my wedding. I was stunned she had planned for something so far ahead of time, and wondered why she hadn't planned as diligently for my college education. It made me realize how important my getting married really was to her.

Utha Mae told me she would be paying for the dresses Tara and I would wear. I wanted to argue that I could buy my dress with my own money, but she wouldn't even let me get the words out of my mouth.

Since I wanted to have the wedding in Utha Mae's church, we ended up only having to worry about the expenses for the reception and a few flowers. Having the wedding scheduled so close to

Christmas was actually perfect timing. Utha Mae was in charge of the decorating committee at her church, and told me I had nothing to worry about as far as the church interior went. She planned to have two Christmas trees, large red poinsettias, and white roses festooning the interior. Her church already had candelabras, so all we would have to buy to make the picture complete would be candles, ribbon, and decorative gauze fabric. At least I didn't have to agonize over what the colors for the wedding would be.

Utha Mae warned us that she planned to invite her whole congregation to the wedding. I wasn't exactly sure how many people that would end up being, but I knew it would be close to at least a hundred, depending on how many showed up. Since we would be inviting many more people than I had expected, Utha Mae requested that we let her and the ladies from her church handle preparing most of the food. I had no doubt that they would make food far superior to anything a hired caterer could prepare.

There was one more thing I needed, though; a ring for Brand. I had no idea where I was going to find something that represented how much I loved and adored him. How do you buy the perfect man the perfect ring? I planned to drag Tara ring- shopping some-time during the next week. Maybe with both of us, we could figure something out.

I drove us all to Jackson in my Mustang, but Tara directed from the backseat, telling me exactly where to go. She said Abby had asked her to take me to one particular store in Jackson, and that she planned to meet us there to help me choose a dress. I wasn't sure how long it was going to take to find dresses for Tara and me, but I made sure everyone knew we might have to come back the following weekend, if we didn't find what we wanted that day. I needed to leave by at least 3:30, so I could keep my promise to Brand and have supper with him that evening. It seemed important to him, and I did not intend to break my word.

The wedding dress store was called Couture Collections, and looked a bit expensive for our pocketbooks.

"Are you sure this is where she said to meet her?" I asked, eyeing the store dubiously as we all got out of the car.

"Yep," Tara said, coming to stand beside me as Utha Mae and my mom started walking toward the entrance to the store.

"Give me your phone," Tara whispered to me.

I pulled my cell phone out of my purse and handed it to her.

"Who are you calling?"

Without answering me, she fished a piece of paper out of her back pocket and dialed a number.

"Hey," she said into the phone, "we're here." There was a short pause. "Ok."

She ended the call and handed me the phone.

"Are you going to tell me who you called?"

"Them," Tara said, nodding to the front of the store.

Standing on the front steps of the boutique were Abby and Malcolm.

"They wanted to help. Said they saw a dress here for you that would be perfect," Tara told me as we walked over to our friends.

I gave both of them a hug. "I didn't expect to see you guys here."

Abby's presence didn't surprise me that much, but Malcolm's did.

"We thought you might like our company, dearest. It's not every day you get to help a friend pick out her wedding dress."

I couldn't say anything. I knew if I tried, I would get too

emotional and start to cry. Instead, I took Malcolm's hand and brought him inside the store with me.

Every woman in the establishment immediately looked Malcolm's way when we entered. Malcolm had met my mother and Utha Mae while I was in a coma in the hospital, so I didn't have to make any introductions. I could tell my mother was interested in Malcolm, because of how flustered she looked being so close to him. When we went to the private viewing room, I made sure to sit Malcolm on the opposite side of the mirrored room from my mother. All I needed was for her to become obsessed with my friend.

The lady who was to help me pick a dress took me to a back changing room, and asked me questions to help me narrow down what style of gown I wanted. I had a vision of the dress I wanted in my head, but I just couldn't seem to find the words I needed in order to describe it.

"I think I know the perfect one for you," she said, and went to find the dress.

When she brought it back in, I marveled at how well the woman had deciphered my mangled description of my dream dress. It was a strapless, pristine white satin gown with a thin layer of veil-like material on top, which had been hand stitched with a multitude of pearls, crystals and off-white embroidery. It had a full skirt and mid-length train.

The saleslady helped me put it on so I could get the opinion of my family and friends, even though I knew in my heart it was the dress I'd always imagined wearing on my wedding day. I was hesitant to ask how much the dress cost. I braced myself for the real possibility that we wouldn't be able to afford my dream dress.

Even if we couldn't buy it, at least I would have the chance to wear it this one time.

"It's a perfect fit," she said, adjusting the full skirt and train around me. "Why don't you go show your family? I'm sure they'll love it, sweetie."

When I walked out of the dressing room and down the short hall to the mirrored viewing room, I could hear everyone talking and laughing as if they were having a good time together. As soon as I stepped into view, they all became quiet.

"Well?" I said, standing in front of the mirrors, looking at how well the dress fit. It was as if it had been made for me. "What do you guys think?"

When I didn't get an answer, I looked away from my reflection to Utha Mae first, and saw she had tears in her eyes. When I looked at everyone else in the room, they all had the same expression, except for Malcolm. He just had a rakish grin on his face and winked at me.

"Girl," Tara sniffed, wiping at her eyes as she came to stand beside me, "I don't care how much that dress cost. You're getting it."

Utha Mae wiped away the tears from her cheeks with a handkerchief she'd pulled from her purse.

"How much is it, hon?" she asked the saleswoman, who was standing a little behind me.

"Well, you're in luck," she told Utha Mae. "That dress was marked down to $500 this week."

My mother gasped in surprise.

"We're taking it!" she said, almost as if she was afraid the saleswoman had made a mistake, and didn't want to give her a moment longer to figure it out. I think my mother was more excited than I was about the deal we had just gotten.

As everyone was crowding around me, looking at the detailed embroidery and crystal beading, I noticed Malcolm get out of his chair and go over to the saleswoman. I watched him in the mirrors as he leaned down and whispered something to her while shaking her hand. She looked down at the hand he shook and discretely put something in the pocket of her dress, all the while nodding to him, quietly saying, "You're welcome".

"Excuse me," I said to everyone around me. "I should probably take it off before we get it dirty." After I carefully rotated the full skirt and train so I wouldn't knock anyone down, I walked over to Malcolm and yanked on the sleeve of his shirt, making him follow me down to the end of the hallway.

"What was that all about?" I asked him quietly, not wanting anyone else to hear.

"What was all what about, dearest?" Malcolm asked innocently.

"What did you hand that woman just now?"

"Just a tip for her help today," he shrugged.

It took me a second to put the pieces together. It made sense, though. The fact that Abby told Tara where to go to find the perfect dress, the cheap price of the dress, and Malcolm's involvement could only mean one thing.

"How much does this dress actually cost?" I asked him.

"Dearest," he said, taking one of my hands into his. "Why do you insist on worrying about things which mean nothing? Just enjoy the dress. It looks wonderful on you."

"Did you pick it out?"

"Would it matter?"

"It matters to me," I said. I could be just as stubborn as he could.

He sighed, realizing he had been caught in his little scheme. "Abby and I saw it in Paris and thought it looked like you. Don't ruin what's supposed to be a happy time, dearest; just consider it an early wedding present."

"And the $500?"

"Commission for the saleswoman. It's what she would have earned for selling a dress in a store like this. She was more than willing to help me with my little ruse."

"How much does this dress actually cost?" I pressed.

"It doesn't matter," he said. "It's a gift."

I didn't want to argue with him. He was just trying to make me happy, and he and Abby had done a perfect job picking out the dress of my dreams. I rose up on the tips of my toes and kissed him on the cheek.

"Thank you," I whispered, so only he could hear. "I don't know what I did to deserve a friend like you."

"You're more than welcome." He cocked an eyebrow at me and grinned. "Now, do you think you need my help getting out of it?"

I just shook my head in exasperation and turned towards the dressing room, leaving him chuckling behind me. I supposed some things would never change, whether I was getting married or not.

We ended up buying some shoes and hair accessories at the store to complete the ensemble. I bought a simple veil and some thick-heeled satin pumps.

Finding Tara a dress took a bit more time and ended up costing about half as much as my dress did. Nevertheless, it fit her personality and the theme of the wedding perfectly. It was a red, mermaid style-dress with half-capped sleeves and a shimmering crystal brooch in the shape of a leaf attached to the left side of the bodice.

It wasn't until we made our purchases that I worried about stuffing my dress inside the trunk of my car.

"We can take it home with us, love," Abby offered, knowing I would much prefer them just phasing it back home, and not having it cramped up in the back of my car for two hours.

"We can just keep it at my house," Malcolm said. "I seriously doubt Brand will see it there."

I thanked them both before they left.

The drive back home was filled with chatter about the wedding. It was one of the few times Tara and my mom actually got along. Tara was usually so overprotective of me whenever my mother was around. She always had her guard up, ready to defend my honor at a moment's notice if my mother said anything negative about me in her presence. Nevertheless, with the conversation dedicated to the wedding, I didn't have to worry about my mother saying anything that would ruin what had been a great day of shopping.

After we dropped Utha Mae and my mom home, I didn't even bother wasting time driving all the way back to Lakewood. I simply phased Tara and me, car, packages, and all, to our apartment.

"I just don't know if I like that," Tara said. "Seems like cheating."

"It is cheating," I laughed. "But I told Brand I would be back in time for this special supper he has planned. It's already 4:30. I'm barely going to have time to get ready for our date, as it is."

No matter how much I hounded him that week, Brand refused

to tell me what was so special about having dinner together that evening. He simply said it was important to him and, to be honest, that was all I needed to know. When we got our packages unloaded, I took a quick shower and changed into a pair of black slacks and a maroon two-piece sweater set before phasing home to Brand.

He was sitting in the living room, watching a football game on the new TV mounted above the fireplace. We had just bought the TV a couple of days before, since I liked to watch television on occasion and he didn't have one in his house. I hadn't expected him to splurge on a 65" plasma screen, but it was the best he could find in town.

"I'm home," I announced, walking to stand in front of him.

He quickly turned off the TV and stood up, pulling me into his arms, kissing me as if he hadn't seen me in a year.

"I missed you today," he whispered, trailing kisses from my forehead to the side of my neck, unwilling to let me go. "I think I've gotten spoiled having you so close all the time these past couple of weeks."

"I missed you, too," I told him, "though we did have fun shopping for dresses today."

"Did you find what you were looking for?"

"Yes." I didn't feel like telling him Malcolm had been involved in finding the dress for me. It just didn't seem like the right moment.

"Are you ready for our night together?" he asked, forcing himself to stop kissing my neck.

"What are we doing? You've been so secretive about it."

"I just wanted to surprise you, since you seemed to have no clue what today is."

I wracked my brain, trying to figure out what he was talking about.

"Should I know what today is? Am I going to feel stupid for not knowing?"

"No," he laughed. "You won't feel stupid. And today is actually two things."

Before I knew it, we were standing inside a room I had never been in before. It was a sunroom with paned-glass walls and white painted joints. I felt like I had stepped into a confectionary menagerie, filled with boxes of chocolates, cakes, cookies, almost anything sweet you could think of, surrounded by crystal vases filled with red roses and white lilies carefully arranged on tables draped with white silk fabric. White and red pillar candles were scattered around the room, making everything glow in the romantic warmth of their candlelight.

"What's all this for?" I asked, completely confused, but loving the intoxicating aroma of flowers and chocolate that permeated the air around us.

"It's Sweetest Day," he said, holding me close.

"Sweetest Day?"

"I'm surprised you've never heard of it," he replied, looking down at me in surprise. "It's a day to tell the people you love most in your life how much they mean to you. It's a little different from Valentine's Day, because it's not just for lovers. In our case, it gave me an excuse to buy you flowers and chocolates."

I smiled at him, wondering what our first Valentine's Day would be like together. If he went to this much trouble for an obscure holiday I had never heard of, what would a night as his wife on the most romantic day of the year be like?

"So what's the second thing? You said today was two things."

"On this day, two months ago, my life changed forever. It was the first day we met."

"Has it really only been two months?" I asked, marveling at how little time had actually passed. "I feel like I've known you so much longer than that."

"I know what you mean. It's almost like we've known each other for years." He held me close and looked deeply into my eyes. "I promise, from this moment on, you will hear me tell you I love you at least once a day, for the rest of your life."

I laid my head down on his chest and hugged him to me. "That's better than any chocolate or flower you could have bought me."

I looked out the windows and saw the moonlight reflecting off the Thames River. It was then that I realized we were in Brand's house in London.

"Why are we in London?" I asked.

"I have one more surprise for you." He went to a chair in the room and picked up a large wool blanket before taking my hand. "Come on, we need to go out by the river to see it."

We walked out the back door of the sunroom, down the steps, and across the lush green lawn leading to a dock on the river, and sat down on a wrought-iron bench there. Brand draped the blanket over us and reached for a flashlight sitting on his side of the seat. He flashed it towards the woods on the other side of the river twice before putting it down.

"What was that for?" I asked, wondering about his odd behavior.

"I was signaling to Jack that we're ready. Just sit back, my love," he said, putting his arms around me to pull me closer to share his warmth. "Look up at the moon."

A minute later, I heard a whining noise and started to laugh as firecrackers of all different colors burst across the night sky, illuminating everything around us. I'm not sure how long the show lasted, but I do know my toes were starting to feel numb from the cold by the end of it. After the last firecracker popped, we hurried back inside the house, grabbed some of the sweets from the sunroom, and made our way down to the kitchen to make some hot chocolate to help warm us up.

As we sat across from each other at the table, drinking our cocoa, I couldn't keep from smiling.

"Have I made you happy?" Brand asked, reaching for my hands across the table.

"You always make me happy," I told him as our fingers touched and we held fast to one another. "Mostly because I can't believe how thoughtful you are most of the time. Even I didn't remember it was our two month anniversary."

"When you've lived as long as me, certain things stand out in your memory more than others. Seeing you sitting at that desk in Physics class is a day I will never forget."

"Even when I'm old and grey, will you promise to remember me like that?"

I could tell what I said disturbed him. I didn't mean to remind him of my mortality, but I knew that was where I had led his thoughts.

"No matter how old you are, you will always be beautiful to me, Lilly."

"We'll see if you still think that when I'm ninety and some young college girl catches your eye," I tried to joke, in a failed attempt to lighten the mood.

"No one will ever replace you in my life," he said so seriously that it caught me off guard. "I'll be yours forever, even after you've left me."

A selfish part of me hoped he was right. I didn't even want to think of him sharing himself with anyone but me. Yet, another part of me didn't want to imagine him pining away, living through a lonely existence, with no one to share his wonderfulness with. It would be such a waste.

I didn't feel like dwelling on such a morbid topic after the beautiful night he'd planned for us. I felt certain that each day of my life would be filled with his thoughtfulness. If anyone understood how short a time each person actually had to enjoy life, it was Brand. I knew he would do his best to make every day we spent together as unforgettable as he could, because those memories would be all he had after I was gone.

I stood from my chair, leaving my hot chocolate forgotten on the table, and made him stand up in front of me.

"I seem to recall a very comfortable couch in this house of yours," I murmured next to his ear. "Care to show me where it is again?"

The roguish smile I loved so much appeared on his face, and we spent the rest of the evening much like we did the first night we'd spent in his London home.

It wasn't until the following Monday that we received the call we had been waiting for, from the private investigator in Indiana. She'd found my grandparents. Brand asked her to email the details to him as soon as she could, and promised to send her a hefty bonus for tracking them down so quickly.

After the email came, I stood over Brand's shoulder and read what it said. I had to read it a second time just to make sure I hadn't misread it the first time.

"It says what I think it says, right?" I asked, not quite believing my eyes. How did my mother end up completely on the other side of the lifestyle spectrum from my grandparents?

"Yes. Are you all right?" Brand stood from his computer, worried by my reaction.

"I..." I didn't know what to say. To say I didn't expect it would be an understatement. Now I understood why my mother didn't want me to contact her parents.

"They're Amish?" I asked, sure I'd read the letter wrong. It had to be a mistake.

"It appears they are," Brand put his hands on my shoulders, forcing me to look at him. "Are you all right, Lilly?"

"Yes, I'm fine," I tried to reassure him. "It's just... they're Amish?"

"You say it like it's a bad thing." He grinned at me, as though he wasn't sure whether I actually did think it was a bad thing.

"No, it's not bad," I assured him, "just unexpected. You *know* my mother. Would you have ever thought she was raised by Amish parents?"

"Well, no," Brand said, understanding why I was having such a hard time connecting my mother with my Amish grandparents. "Would you like to go see them? She gave us instructions on how to find their home."

"Give me a minute." I knew we should probably go to them as soon as possible, but I was still trying to get over the shock of our discovery.

If anyone had ever told me as a kid that my grandparents were Amish, I would have just laughed in their face. As far as I knew, the Amish shunned most everything modern, and liked living a simple lifestyle of hard work, communion with their neighbors, and worship. None of those things even came close to describing my mother. All the times I asked her where they were, she would always tell me we were better off without them. I always wondered why she didn't want to contact them. What had happened in my mother's life to change her so completely?

We got into Brand's car and phased to Interstate 90, heading east out of Chicago,. It was the closest point Brand had been to the town my grandparents lived near, which was called Nappanee. It was going to take us about two hours to reach it by car.

I knew from the P.I.'s letter that my grandparents owned a dairy farm. Their names were Amos and Rebecca Miller. Besides that, I didn't know anything else.

Brand tried to reassure me that everything would be fine and even tried to distract me from my worry with talk about the wedding. I loved him for trying. However, there was really nothing he could do to prevent me from dwelling on the possibility that my mother's family would turn me away, leaving us literally out in the cold. Without their help, I might not find the answers I so desperately needed in order to solve the mystery of my existence.

As we entered the small town in which my mother grew up, I finally took notice of my surroundings. Dotting the landscape were acres of what looked to be farmland. There weren't any crops in the field, just bare, fresh-tilled earth. I supposed it was past harvest time now, since it was late October. The farmers would have gathered all of their crops and were probably resting until the start of the next season. Brand told me on the way over that most Amish people either farmed or owned dairy farms to make their living.

He turned the car off the highway, onto a dirt road. I could see a large red barn in the distance with a plain, white, two-story home not far from it. My stomach felt like it was tied up in knots so intricate there would never be a way to untie them again.

After Brand parked the car in front of the house, he looked over at me and asked, "Are you ready to meet them?"

I took a deep breath to steady my nerves as best I could and nodded my head. We needed answers, and there was only one way to get them.

CHAPTER 17

Brand laced his fingers with mine in an attempt to lend me his strength as we walked up the well-worn wooden steps to the front porch of my grandparents' home. My heart betrayed how nervous I was feeling. I was sure its beating was so loud Brand could hear it easily in the cool stillness of the autumn day. I tried to reason with myself that my nervousness served no purpose. This visit could only have one of two outcomes: either they would turn me away, not wanting to talk to me or acknowledge my existence; or they would welcome my unexpected arrival into their otherwise-tranquil lives with open arms.

Brand knocked on the front door for me. It only took a few seconds before it was answered by a woman dressed in a plain, calf-length, light-blue cotton dress. Her hair was pulled back from her face into a tight bun at the nape of her neck, and covered by a thin white bonnet. She wore no make-up, and looked like she had spent a lot of time in the sun, from the fine lines and occasional sunspots on her face. When her soft brown eyes fell on me, they lit up in hopeful recognition. It left no doubt in my mind that she knew exactly who I was.

She turned her attention back to Brand. "Can I help you?"

"We're looking for Amos and Rebecca Miller. Would you happen to be Rebecca?"

"Yes," she said, looking back at me as if she wanted me to speak and confirm her supposition.

I knew it was now or never. I let go of Brand's hand and took a step closer to my grandmother, fearing to hope that she'd actually want me.

"I'm Anna's daughter," I said, using my mother's true name. "My name is Lilly."

My grandmother no longer fought against her natural instinct, and took me into her arms, hugging me tightly to her as if she was afraid I would disappear if she let go. I could feel her tremble slightly in my arms. Finally, she released her hold on me and stepped back with her hands on my forearms to study my face.

"You look so much like your mother when she was your age," she marveled. "Please, come in." She took one of my hands in hers and led us into a plain, yet normal- looking kitchen with a gas stove and refrigerator. There was a small, round wooden table with four chairs around it in the middle of the room.

"Please, sit down," she said, pointing to the chairs at the table.

She quickly walked over to a cupboard and pulled out a plastic container from one of the shelves. Before I knew it, there were a plate full of cookies and two glasses of milk sitting in front of us.

"Thank you," I told my grandmother, wanting to reach for a cookie, but unable to make my hand move. I was still so nervous.

"Your mother didn't come with you?" my grandmother asked.

"She's back home," I hesitated to say the rest, but knew it would probably come up in the conversation eventually anyway. "She doesn't actually know that I'm here."

"Ah," my grandmother nodded. "I suppose I should have expected as much."

"Why?" I asked immediately, wanting the mystery solved as to how my mother went from being Amish to what she was today. "Every time I've asked about you and my grandfather, all she would say is that we didn't need you. Why would she say that? What happened between you?"

"Your mother was a wonderful child," my grandmother began. A serene smile spread her lips, as she seemed to be remembering my mother in the days of her youth. "We never had any trouble with her, not until she went on her *rumspringa*."

"I'm sorry," I said, with a slight shake of my head. "What's a *rumspringa*?"

"It is when our teenagers are allowed to go into the world of the English and experiment with their ways. Our children aren't considered full members of the church until they declare themselves and choose to be baptized. They are given the chance to see how the outside world is first, in order to make a conscience decision to give up the modern world and continue with our way of life. Your mother wasn't interested in it at all until I told her she should purge herself of any desires she might not even know she had, to make sure our way of life was truly what she wanted for herself." The regret on my grandmother's face was evident. "She went with a few of her friends to Chicago on a weekend trip. It was there she met the man who is your father. At first, we didn't even know she had met someone. She came back, and immediately wanted to join the church. So we baptized her to make her a full member right away. It wasn't until a couple of months later that we found out she was pregnant. Somehow, she contacted your father and he came to get her. She turned her back on us, and said she wanted to live in the outside world with him."

"Did you ever meet my father?" I didn't know anyone else who had ever met him, besides my mother. I was desperate for any information she could give me just to assuage my own curiosity about what type of person he was.

"He was a handsome English man with a fancy car," I saw my grandmother's eyes flash toward Brand as she said this, obviously making a connection. "There was something different about him, though," my grandmother looked troubled as she thought more about the details of how to describe my father to me. "He looked pleasant enough on the outside, but there was something inside him that didn't seem quite right to me, though he did seem to have this overpowering connection with your mother that neither your grandfather nor I could break through. Anna came to us again after you were born. I think she thought it might soften your grandfather's heart to perhaps forgive her for abandoning our way of life if he saw you."

"Did it?" I asked.

"Your grandfather is very true to the old ways. Once your mother chose not to return to us, he followed the Old Order rules and shunned her. When she came with your father, unmarried and with you in her arms, any hope we had of her returning to us was gone. Even after we turned away from her then, she still came back to us one last time."

"Why?"

"Your father passed away, leaving her to raise you on her own. He had left her a little money to live on, but she wanted to come back home and raise you in our community."

"And you turned her away?" I asked incredulously.

"She was the one who left us," my grandmother defended, although half-heartedly. "Your grandfather couldn't allow her to come back."

I finally understood my mother's refusal to allow me to contact her parents. After being shunned by them, I couldn't blame her for not wanting anything else to do with them. But why had she kept this information from me all this time? Was she ashamed of what she had done, or was she ashamed that her parents had turned her away when she'd needed them the most? She was most likely afraid that they would not recognize me as their granddaughter and turn away from me, too, breaking my heart as they had hers.

"Your grandfather never mentions her name, but I can tell he thinks of her often. He is not a bad man, just true to the ways he was taught when he was a boy."

"Will he mind me being here?" I asked, worried that I might be causing trouble for my grandmother.

"He would acknowledge your presence, but he would not acknowledge you as his grandchild. For him, your mother is no longer a part of this family."

"And for you?" I questioned. "Do you still consider her your daughter?"

A melancholy smile spread across my grandmother's face. "I think it's different for a mother. You carry a child for nine months inside you and ultimately the responsibility of raising children falls on the mother's shoulders, no matter how good a man your husband may be. It broke my heart to turn away from her in her time of need. I don't think I have the strength to do that again or to turn you away now. I can't speak for your grandfather. He is a stubborn man. Once he sets his mind to something, it is set."

My visions of a cheerful reunion with my grandfather quickly evaporated.

"Where is he now?" I asked.

"He went into town. I do not expect him to be back for a little while yet."

"Perhaps it would be best if you asked your other questions before he returns, Lilly," Brand quietly suggested.

"Questions about what?" my grandmother asked.

"I recently had a genetic profile done on myself, and I was hoping you could help me understand one of the results it found about my DNA," I said. "It has to do with some genetic information that can only be passed down from mother to child."

"Are you sick?" my grandmother asked, clearly worried about my welfare.

"No," I reassured her. "I'm not sick. But the results showed I have DNA that is completely different from anyone else in the world, except for my mother," I answered, "and more than likely you. We came here to find out more about my mother's family history."

"I would assume it has something to do with Lilith."

"Who's Lilith?" I asked.

"She is your ancestor. She was the first."

I sensed Brand's body fill with tension at my grandmother's words. Apparently, I was the only one who didn't know who Lilith was.

"The first, what?" I asked, still completely at a loss.

"The first woman."

My grandmother said these words so matter-of-factly that I wasn't sure what to make of what she was saying.

"I thought all of Lilith's children had been killed," Brand leaned his elbows on the table, watching my grandmother intently.

"Not the first," my grandmother told him. "Not her child with Adam. She was the only one spared."

"Adam?" I asked. Then her previous statement started to make sense. "Are you talking about Adam, as in Adam and Eve?"

"Yes," she replied.

I looked to Brand. "I still don't understand. Who's Lilith?"

Brand's eyes were troubled. Total and utter disbelief was the only way to describe his expression. He had not been prepared for the information my grandmother provided. "She was the first woman God made. Eve was the second."

"I will tell you the story that has been passed to each generation of Lilith's daughters. I'm surprised your mother hasn't told you this story before now," my grandmother said, clearly disappointed in another failing of my mother's. "Lilith thought herself equal to Adam, since she was made the same way as he was," my grandmother continued. "When she refused to be subservient to him, he asked God to make him another mate, one who would follow his orders without questioning them. So, God made Eve for Adam. Lilith left Adam and bore him a daughter in her home by the Red Sea. She hid the child from the demons who followed her and forced themselves on her because she could bear their children. She was even cunning enough to hide the girl from the angels who came and took away her demon spawn to murder them. The Jewish people still tell the tale of Lilith in their folklore, but she has been demonized by them and many other cultures, just because she refused to follow the orders of a man and be true to herself."

I looked at Brand to see if what she was saying was true. He looked back at me and nodded his head slightly, silently confirming that my grandmother's tale was accurate.

"Since then, each generation of Lilith's progeny has one child, always a girl. We are unable to have any more children than that for some reason. You are the last, sweet child. You will give birth to a daughter, when the time comes for you to carry on the line."

Brand sat back in his chair, trying to absorb my grandmother's words.

"Does that help answer your question?" my grandmother asked.

"Yes," Brand answered for us since I had no idea if the information helped us at all. "It clears some things up for us."

My grandmother eyed Brand warily, and it was then that I realized they hadn't actually been formally introduced.

"Grandma," I said, not really knowing how else to address her. "This is Brandon Cole. We're going to be married next month."

Her eyes lit up at the news. "Married? Oh, how wonderful," she said, clasping her hands together. "Wait one moment." She left us alone in the kitchen and quickly walked out of the room to somewhere at the back of the house.

I looked at Brand. His brow was creased in worry.

"What's wrong?" I asked, not understanding how knowing about Lilith answered our questions concerning Lucifer's plans for me.

"Lilith wasn't just the first woman," he whispered, though I couldn't be sure it was so my grandmother wouldn't hear or if he just couldn't bring himself to say the words. "She was the only human who could phase into Heaven anytime she chose."

"How?"

"We never knew. God never told us how she was able to do it exactly."

The pieces of the puzzle began to fall into place.

"Is that why Lucifer wants me? Does he think he can use me to get back into Heaven?"

"It has to be," Brand said. "But I don't understand why."

"What do you mean?"

"Even if he possessed your body and used you to get into Heaven, why would he do it? He has to know God would just cast him out again. We're missing something." Brand remained quiet, deep in his own thoughts about why Lucifer's plan included using me to get back into Heaven.

When my grandmother came back out, she had a folded quilt in her arms. From what I could see, it was a white hand-stitched quilt with pink material cut out and sewn to resemble the circular pattern of rose petals, with green material cut out in the shape of leaves and pink piping along the edge.

"I want you to take this as a wedding present," my grandmother said. "My mother made it for me when I married Amos. I always hoped to be able to give it to your mother when she married. Did she ever marry?"

"No," I said, shaking my head. I stood from my chair to take the quilt from her arms.

"Then I give it to you. I will pray that your marriage is long, and that you both have a wonderful life together."

"Thank you," I whispered, touched that she seemed to feel enough of a connection with me to pass down such a precious heirloom.

Since the house was so quiet and the walls thin, we could clearly hear the voice of a man saying "Whoa", a horse neighing, and the rattle of a buggy as it came to a stop in front of the house near Brand's car.

"That'll be Amos," my grandmother said, turning toward the sound. "Let me go out and tell him you're here."

She may have been outside, but they might as well have been inside the house. Brand and I could hear their conversation clearly.

When my grandmother explained my presence, I heard my grandfather say, "Since I have no daughter, I do not have a granddaughter. I will be in the barn until they leave."

I could hear the crunching of his footsteps as he walked across the gravel from his buggy to the large red barn beside the house. My grandmother had warned me that this might be his reaction, but I was ill-prepared for it. I couldn't help but feel like someone had just slapped me in the face. Brand came to stand beside me and put a comforting arm around my back.

When my grandmother came back in, I could tell the pleasure of seeing me had been tempered by my grandfather's refusal to even be in the same room as me.

"He has some things to tend to before sunset," she explained. I was sure she knew we had heard his words. She had probably lived in this house most of her life. She would know the walls weren't thick enough to muffle their voices from the outside.

"We should probably be going," I told her, not wanting to cause her any more trouble with my grandfather. "Can I write to you?" I asked, unsure if that would be permitted.

"Please do," my grandmother replied as she walked up to me and placed a loving hand on top of the one I had resting on the quilt. "I want to know all about your wedding and your life. Are you still in school?"

"Yes, I'm in my first semester of college."

"Oh, how wonderful. We don't go to school past the eighth grade, but I always thought it would fun to learn more. Please try to keep in touch, and come see me again when you can. Perhaps your mother would join you. I desperately want to see her."

"I'll try to get her to come," I said, "but I can't promise you she will. I think she's still hurt by what happened before."

Even if my grandfather didn't want to have anything to do with my mother or me, my grandmother did. What I had assumed earlier was true about my visit having one of two outcomes, except I had both of my hypotheses come to fruition.

"There's one other thing," Brand said, pulling out one of Allan's DNA kits from his jacket pocket.

"Would it be all right if we took a DNA sample from you? We only want to compare it to Lilly's."

"What would I have to do?"

It only took a second for Brand to collect the DNA he needed from the inside of my grandmother's cheek. I thanked her once again for her help, and hugged her before I left. I had no way of knowing if it would be the only time I ever saw her or not, so I kissed her gently on the cheek and told her goodbye.

When Brand and I stepped outside to get back into his car, I happened to glance toward the barn, wondering if I might catch a glimpse of my grandfather before I left.

He was standing at the door to the barn, leaning against its opening and watching us with hooded eyes. He stood tall in a plain black suit and white shirt, with a straw hat on his head. His jaw was covered with a mustache-less, long white beard. I couldn't tell what the expression on his face was exactly from the distance between us. I assumed I was probably imagining the yearning I thought I saw in his eyes to come and speak with me. I didn't know what else to do, so I nodded my head to him, curious to know if he would at least acknowledge my existence. After a few seconds, he nodded back.

I got into Brand's car, and we drove back down the gravel driveway. As we left, I wondered if my grandfather would change his mind about meeting me one day. I made a note to myself to put it on my wish list of things to do in the time I had left.

As soon as we left my grandparents' home and made it back onto the highway, Brand phased us to his house. He turned off the engine and we both just sat in the car, each silently contemplating the information we had just received.

"What do you think it all means?" I finally asked, turning to look at him.

"I'm not sure, but I think we need to tell the others what we found out. Maybe they can help us, especially Will. He's been around Lucifer the most. He might have information he doesn't even realize is important, and be able to piece things together."

We went inside the house and Brand made a few phone calls. Malcolm came right over, and Will picked up Tara and Malik on the way. We all sat around the dining room table. Brand and I gave them the information we had gathered from my grandmother. Will and Malcolm were as surprised as Brand had been that Lilith was able to hide her child with Adam so completely.

"Well, He must have known," Malcolm said, sitting back in his chair. "But why would He hide it from us?"

"He, who?" Tara asked. "God?"

"Yes," Malcolm answered.

"He must have had His reasons," Will said. "But He allowed her other children to be killed, the ones she had with my kind." Will sat back in his chair with a heavy sigh. "I guess I should have suspected Lilith's connection before now. It just didn't occur to me that she would have had a child who actually survived."

"Don't beat yourself up too much about it," Malcolm said. "None of us thought of it."

"So you think Lilly has inherited the ability to enter Heaven, like Lilith?" Malik asked.

"It seems like a logical conclusion," Brand answered. "But we still don't understand why Lucifer would want to use her to go back."

"It doesn't make any sense," Malcolm agreed. "Even if he did manage to go there, he would just be kicked out again. Where's the logic in that?"

"Do you have any ideas, Will?" Brand asked.

Will shook his head. "No, I don't know what the purpose would be either. We're still missing something important."

Brand sighed. I knew he'd hoped Will might have insight the rest of us lacked, but it looked like Will was as clueless as we were.

"I have a question," I said. "If Lilith's children with Will's kind were all killed, why let me live for so long?"

"Good question, dearest," Malcolm sat back in his chair, with his arms crossed over his chest. "A few of the angels were ordered to destroy her children almost as soon as they were born. It does seem odd that you would be allowed to live, when they were not."

"It must mean God has a plan for you," Brand said to me. I felt like he was grasping for some sign, to give me hope. "Otherwise, you wouldn't be here."

I wasn't exactly reassured by his statement. We knew someone powerful wanted me dead, at least powerful enough to enlist the help of a group of fallen angels and a jinn. Could it be God? That didn't seem likely. He could probably destroy me without having to use a go-between to get the job done. But if it wasn't Him, then who was it?

"Where do we go from here?" I asked, not seeing any way for us to find out the information we needed to know.

Brand slid his hand across the table and cupped it over mine.

"We concentrate on our lives. We plan the wedding of your dreams, and keep an eye out for other clues. Something else is bound to happen, to show us where we need to look next."

Brand was so sure God had brought us together for a reason, but what if the reason wasn't the idyllic 'love conquers all' scenario we both wanted it to be?

"Well," Tara said, standing from her chair, "I don't know about y'all, but all this talk has made me hungry. Why don't you show me how to make them cookies you made for me the other night, Prince Charming?"

Brand tried to put on a happy front for me. "Sure, I can do that."

"Prince Charming?" Malik asked, standing from his chair.

"Yeah," Tara answered, following Brand into the kitchen. "Lilly got Prince Charming, and I always end up with the toads."

"Hmm," Malik said, following them to the kitchen. "Maybe you're just looking in the wrong places. You need a man, not a boy."

Tara laughed. "Well, if you see one who fits the bill, you let me know."

I saw Malik raise an eyebrow at her, but he didn't say anything else on the matter.

"You know how to play chess?" I heard Malcolm ask Will.

"Of course," Will answered, which was the wrong answer if he intended to leave early. Malcolm quickly had him talked into playing a game. He phased to his house and retrieved his own chessboard and pieces, even though Brand told him he had one stored in the hall closet. I had a feeling Malcolm felt like he held an advantage by using his own set.

As I sat on a stool at the kitchen counter, watching Malik, Tara, and Brand as they made cookies and tried not to get cookie dough everywhere, intentionally or unintentionally, I looked over my shoulder at Malcolm and Will playing chess. Malcolm must have felt me watching them, because he looked up at me and winked as his lips stretched into a contented smile. I smiled back. I was most definitely home.

"Hey," Tara said while she and Malik were spooning the dough onto a cookie sheet. Brand came around the kitchen counter and stood behind me, putting his arms around me, kissing me lightly on the cheek. "Are y'all going to the Halloween Dance?"

"What Halloween Dance?" I asked.

"The one they're having at the school. Ain't you seen the posters up all over campus?"

"No. I guess I've had too much on my mind to pay attention."

"It's Halloween night, at the indoor stadium. Y'all should go."

"Are you going?"

"Yeah, I already got asked out. I'm sure Prince Charming over there would take you."

"Who asked you out? I thought I made it clear I was going to get to interrogate the next person you dated. We don't need another Leroy incident."

"Girl, you let me handle my own love life. You got enough to worry about as it is."

"I'm going to it," Malik announced, surprising us all.

Tara stopped spooning the dough and looked up at him. "With *who?*"

"Your friend, Cheryl, from the library asked me to go with her."

"Cheryl?" Tara asked, putting the hand with the spoon on her cocked hip. "When did she do that?"

"She asked me for my phone number when you went to the bathroom the day you showed me around the library."

I could tell Tara wasn't exactly pleased with this revelation, but she didn't say anything else. She just continued placing the dough onto the cookie sheet.

"Can I come?" Malcolm called from the table, waiting for Will to make his next move. "It sounds like fun."

"You have to come with a student," Tara told him.

"Will can take me then," Malcolm said matter-of-factly.

"How do you know I don't already have a date?" Will questioned, a bit miffed.

"Because I know you. I'm sure you're still pining away for Lilly, hoping she'll come to her senses and leave Brand for you. I think it's time you gave up that particular fantasy. They'll be married soon enough. Besides, maybe we can find a couple of unattached females at the party. With me as your wing man, you'll have as many women to choose from as you want."

I looked over at Malcolm, worried by his plans. I didn't like the idea of him in a stadium filled with attractive, scantily-clad females all looking for a good time. It was bad enough Malcolm looked the way he did, but with the added benefit of his intoxicating pheromone, I couldn't imagine anything but trouble coming from the combination of the two. However,, it definitely helped me make up my mind.

"So do you want to go to a dance with me?" I asked Brand, turning around on the stool and into his arms.

He leaned down and kissed me chastely on the lips. I could only assume it was because of our houseful of company.

"You know I'll do anything you want," he murmured.

"Cool," Tara said. "We can go costume-shopping together."

I hadn't thought about buying a costume. We would definitely have to go look for some when Tara and I went ring-shopping. I told her as much and we made plans to go that Thursday, since we both got off work early. Halloween was the following Wednesday, so there wasn't time to waste.

CHAPTER 18

That Thursday afternoon, Tara and I went to Clive Jewelers, the best jewelry store Lakewood had to offer. We had an afternoon of shopping planned, between picking out Brand's wedding ring and shopping for costumes for the Halloween dance. Brand didn't seem to care what he wore, so he told me to pick out a costume for him that matched whatever I chose to wear. Tara told me she and her date, a boy named Aaron, from her chemistry class, had already decided to go as a hippie couple from the '60s. I had no idea what I wanted to dress up as, and hoped something would jump out at me when we went to the store.

The jewelry store was empty, with the exception of a blond-haired man dressed in a well-tailored blue suit, browsing at the merchandise when we arrived. After only a few minutes, I could tell Tara was in a bind by the way she kept switching back and forth on her feet.

"Why don't you go to the bathroom," I finally whispered to her, "before you have an accident?"

"Well, I didn't want to leave you alone," she said. "You know you're no good at bargaining. You'll just take the first deal they give you."

"I promise not to buy anything until you get back," I told her.

"Ok, I won't be but a minute." She quickly went out the door to find the public restrooms in the small strip mall.

I had no idea what type of ring to get Brand. Would he want something flashy? No, that didn't seem like him. He would want something sentimental, but how do you buy a piece of metal that has sentiment to it?

"Looking for a ring?"

I looked to my right and saw the other customer I had noticed when first entering the store. He was a handsome man around my mother's age, with wavy dark blond hair and an easy, disarming smile that instantly made me feel like I had met him before. The fine laugh lines at the corners of his eyes gave his face a boyish charm, and the way his shoulders were slightly slouched, and his open stance, gave him the appearance of someone completely nonjudgmental and friendly. I felt inexplicably drawn to him. His soft, light-blue eyes studied my face for a moment, as if he was watching my reaction to him. After a while, he turned his attention back to the glass counter of wedding bands I had been looking at.

"I'm trying to find one for my fiancé," I answered, not quite sure why I felt so comfortable telling a stranger what I was doing.

"Ahh, a hard decision," he said, with an understanding nod. His voice was as comforting as the accompanying smile. "It's usually best if you pick something you like. As long as you like it, he'll like it. Men aren't that fussy when it comes to jewelry for themselves. I'll bet your fiancé doesn't even wear any, does he?"

"Well, now that you mention it, no," I hadn't thought about that. Great, what do you get a man who doesn't really even like to wear jewelry?

"I'd go for something simple and classic," the man said, unintentionally answering my question, "probably just a simple band of some sort without any fancy embellishments."

"Yeah, you're probably right." That certainly narrowed down the choices presented to me in the glass case, not that I could afford anything with a load of diamonds on it anyway.

"He won't care how much you spend on it either. He'll be more interested in knowing you took the time to consider what he would want."

The stranger's words made sense. It would mean more to Brand if I picked out something I thought suited him. Maybe I could even get it engraved to make it more sentimental.

"I just bought something for my girlfriend," the stranger told me. "They're engraving it for me now. You might want to think about doing something like that."

Ok, this was weird. I looked up at the man. How did he seem to know what I was thinking? His last few statements seemed to connect with what I was saying to myself at the time, almost like he was answering the unvoiced commentary in my head.

"Who are you?" I asked.

"Oh, excuse me for forgetting my manners," he held his hand out to me. "I'm Dr. Lucas Hunter."

I shook his hand. The moment my hand touched his, I felt a tingling sensation travel from his hand to mine, up my arm and shoulders to my head, making me feel like I was about to faint. I felt him put his arm around my waist to prevent my fall.

"Are you all right?" he asked me, making sure I was steady on my own two feet before relinquishing his hold on me.

"Yes," I answered, trying to shake off the effects of his touch.

Who was he? There was definitely something going on with

him that I couldn't quite put my finger on. Was he a Watcher? Could he have been sent by Robert to spy on me?

"Here is your item, Dr. Hunter," a saleswoman behind the counter handed Lucas a shopping bag with a small box inside.

He took the bag from the woman and thanked her for being so fast with his purchase.

He turned to me. "I hope you find what you're looking for, Lilly. I'm sure your fiancé will like whatever you choose. Good luck to you."

Before I knew it, he was out the door.

How had he known my name?

When Tara finally came back into the store, I took her aside and told her what had happened.

"Who do you think he was?" she asked.

I shrugged helplessly. "I don't know."

"But he didn't seem dangerous?"

"No, the complete opposite, I felt really comfortable with him."

"Well, we'll need to tell the others later. There ain't much we can do about it now. We'll just have to keep an eye out. You find a ring yet?"

Tara and I spent a good thirty minutes trying to decide on a ring. Luckily, when I told the woman behind the counter my description of the perfect ring, she told me they had just received a shipment that day, and that it might contain what I was looking for. When she brought it out, I knew it was the perfect one for Brand.

It was a grey and gold band that split into three individual bands connected by an invisible hinge design. When put together, the ring was concave in shape, with two grooves in the middle where the ring split. If you didn't know the ring could come apart, you wouldn't think it should. The woman said I could put a hidden inscription inside the band of rings. She gave me a book of inscriptions to help give me some ideas. I already knew of one thing I wanted to inscribe in the ring, and it didn't take me long to find another inscription I wanted to put in it.

On the first inner ring, I had them inscribe something simple and from my heart. On the second ring, I had them inscribe something I knew would mean a lot to Brand:

To the love of my life, forever and always.

Deus Nos Iunxit 11-17-2012

"What's that second one mean?" Tara asked, looking over my shoulder as I wrote down my selections on the order form.

"It's Latin," I answered. "It means 'God joined us'."

"Oh yeah, Brand will like that."

The saleslady said it would take a couple of days to have the ring ready, since the engraving on this particular ring would need to be sent out to be done. I assured her that there wasn't a rush.

Tara and I went straight from the jewelry store to the costume store, which was located on the other side of town. Tara doubled over in mirth when we stepped inside.

"Ok, that's what you have to buy Brand," she said, pointing to the display of costumes.

I just shook my head at her. "Are you seriously going to make me dress him up as Prince Charming?"

"Yep, and that means you have to go as Cinderella."

Well, at least I didn't have to spend a lot of time figuring out what it was I wanted to go as. Tara quickly found a pink thigh-high dress with a flower design in gold and lavender, with pink gauzy sleeves. There was also a pair of pink knee-high boots with a flower cut out on the sides and a pink headband that finished her '60s-themed outfit.

We were in high spirits when we stepped out of the store, at least until I saw who was standing across the street from us.

Robert stood on the sidewalk, dressed in a simple white shirt and black suit. He tapped the black leather watch on his wrist and grinned as if he knew something that I didn't before phasing.

"What's wrong?" Tara asked, immediately following my eyes to the empty spot where Robert had been.

"We need to go."

As soon as we got back into my car, I phased us to Brand's house.

Brand was clearly troubled to hear I had seen Robert again, but he was glad that I had taken his advice and come straight to him before Robert had a chance to do anything else.

"I got the feeling he was telling me time was running out," I told Brand and Tara.

"He's playing with you, Lilly. He wants to scare you as much as he can." Brand couldn't hide the worry in his voice. We knew Robert was up to something, but what that something was completely eluded us.

"Oh, hey, don't forget to tell him about that guy in the jewelry store, too," Tara reminded me.

I told Brand everything I could remember about my encounter with the man who called himself Dr. Lucas Hunter.

"And you're sure you've never met him before?" Brand asked.

"No, I've never seen him in my life."

Brand stood, went to the kitchen, and pulled a phonebook out of the drawer. He came and sat back down with me, flipping through the yellow pages in the physician section.

"I don't see him," Brand said, closing the book.

"He might be on the Internet," I suggested.

"Come on," Brand took my hand and we stood up to go to his computer located in the spare bedroom upstairs.

"Hey, could y'all take me home and tell me what you find out later?" Tara asked. "I need to go finish my report for my Biology class."

We phased Tara home and went straight back to Brand's spare bedroom.

Our search for Lucas Hunter didn't take long. He was a doctor of pediatric oncology with a well-established practice in Jackson. He had been there at least ten years. From what we could tell, he was highly-respected in his field for advancements in curing his pediatric patients of cancer.

There was a picture of him on his practice's website. It was definitely the same man I met in the jewelry store.

"So he's not a Watcher, right?" I asked Brand. "You don't seem to recognize him."

Brand shook his head. "No, I don't know who he is. It could be one of Will's kind. He might know."

Brand took out his phone and found Will's number on his contact list. "Hey, could you come over to my house? Lilly and I have a question for you." There was a pause. "We're on the second floor in the spare bedroom."

"I'm here," I heard Will say in the hallway a second later.

I called out to him so he knew which room we were in. When he came in, Brand pointed to the computer screen.

"One of yours?"

Will studied the picture on the screen. "It's hard to tell from just a picture, but I don't recognize him. I would need to get close to him to tell. Why?"

I told Will what I'd told Brand about my encounter with the man.

"Give me the address to his offices in Jackson," Will said. "I'll try to get up there as soon as I can to check him out."

"Is it possible Lucifer has sent someone else to look after Lilly?" Brand asked while writing the address down on a scrap piece of paper and handing it to Will.

Will shrugged, reading the address before putting the paper in his back pocket.

"Anything is possible with him, but he hasn't told me anything about it. I'll let you know what I find out."

"Thanks, Will," I said.

Will looked at me and nodded. He tried to give me a reassuring smile before he disappeared, but I could tell he was worried about this new development.

Brand stood from the chair at the computer and took me into his arms.

"I think we need to stop thinking about things for a while," he announced before kissing me until all I could think about was him.

When he finally pulled away, I heard a low moan escape his lips.

"It gets harder and harder to pull away from you," he sighed, kissing my forehead first and then my cheeks before he returned to my lips.

I understood his torment. It was getting harder for me, too.

"Three more weeks," I said, forcing my lips away from his for a deep breath. "Besides, I still need to go see a doctor for birth control. I think they say you need to be on it for a little while anyway."

With the reminder of the repercussions our lovemaking could have, I felt Brand's arms loosen around my waist.

"I spoke to someone about that," he confided. "We'll need to have you on birth control, and I'll need to use something also, just to be sure we don't have any accidents. Birth control is only 99.9% effective, from what I've read."

"Who did you ask that sort of question?" I was curious to know who Brand would go to for such knowledge.

"Do I have to tell you?" he asked with a lopsided grin, obviously embarrassed.

"Well, no, you don't *have* to do anything you don't want to, but I would like to know."

With a resigned sigh he said, "Malcolm."

I couldn't help the giggle that burst out of my mouth as I tried to imagine Brand going to Malcolm with such a question.

"Why him?" I asked, still chuckling as I tried to imagine that scene between the two of them.

"He's probably the most promiscuous Watcher I know. I figured he would know better than anyone how to not get someone pregnant."

"He didn't give you a hard time about asking, did he?"

Brand lifted an eyebrow at me. "Do you even have to ask?"

Poor Malcolm. I knew how he felt about me and could only imagine how awkward it was to tell Brand what he needed to know before we made love for the first time. However, I also knew him well enough to understand that he wouldn't have been able to control himself and probably tortured Brand as much as he could to garner the information.

"I don't want to use a condom the first time. Ok?" I said.

"Why?" Brand seemed suspicious of my motives.

"Because I don't want my first time to be filled with passion and then you have to stop to put one on. I mean it's not like we don't know each other. Neither of us has a disease. Besides, I'll be on birth control anyway. Please," I begged. "Just not the first time, ok? After that, you can use as many as you want."

A cheeky grin spread across Brand's face. "I'll remember you said that."

Later that evening, Brand got a call from Allan. From what I heard on Brand's end of the conversation, Allan had completed his genetic comparison of my grandmother's DNA and found that the results were similar to my mother's, as we had already thought they would be.

"We'd be delighted to, Allan," I heard Brand say as I was just finishing my Chemistry homework. "Ok, see you then."

"What are we delighted to do?" I asked.

Brand came and sat beside me at the dining room table. "He invited us to eat with him and Angela at their home, tomorrow night."

"From the look on your face, I assume that's unusual."

"I've never seen Allan walk around inside his own home," Brand said, completely astounded. He looked at me from the corner of his eye. "Though, I have my suspicions that he just wants to see you again, and dinner with them seemed to be the most congenial way to request your presence."

"I wish I knew why I affected your kind the way I do."

"It's not just us," Brand said.

"What do you mean?"

"That night your car broke down and you sought help from Abby. Do you remember what she did while you were in there?"

"Do you mean the growling?"

"Yes. She felt your presence in the house."

"What do you mean she felt me?"

"It's the only way she could explain it. She felt you there and had this almost uncontrollable urge to be near you. That's one reason Rose Marie was so upset. She thought Abby was going to break down her cell and attack you."

"You know, Malcolm said something similar happened with Sebastian the first night we met. I do remember feeling like Sebastian wanted to come closer to me then. Why do you think that is?"

"I'm not sure."

"Do you ever think we'll figure out why I'm so strange?"

I didn't mean for the question to come out as a whine, but it did. Why couldn't I just be normal?

"You are *not* strange," Brand said, standing from his chair while taking one of my hands in his, urging me to my feet. "You are the most wonderful person I know. Don't ever think of yourself as anything less."

I leaned my body against his for warmth and comfort. "You're just saying that because you're hopelessly in love with me."

"It's because of who you are that makes me hopelessly and endlessly in love with you," he said, trailing small kisses down my neck.

I completely lost track of time for the rest of the evening, which wasn't a bad thing.

Since there was a six-hour time difference between our time and London, Brand and I ditched Physics class, and I took some time off from work that afternoon, so we could have dinner with Allan and Angela.

We needed to be there before nightfall anyway. Angela called Brand earlier that morning to make sure we came well before she was due to transform. She also asked us to bring Abby, since it had been so long since she last saw her friend. But, wherever Abby went, Sebastian had to go. They had been joined at the hip ever since they'd declared their love for each other. From what I knew, they spent almost all their time at Malcolm's home.

"You know," Brand said to me while we were getting ready to go to Allan's, "why doesn't Tara move into Abby's house? She's not using it anymore, and it would be nice to have Tara closer to us. Do you think she would like it?"

"Why don't you ask her?" I suggested. "I think she would appreciate hearing the invitation come from you."

If the offer came from Brand directly, I was sure Tara would feel like she was going to be a major part of our new family. I had worried about leaving her in the apartment alone, after I married Brand. For one thing, I wasn't sure she could afford to pay for it on her own, and I knew she wouldn't take money from me, even if I tried to help her out. Secondly, if she was just down the road from us, she could come over any time she wanted, and not feel like she was intruding.

I understood the relationship Tara and I had with one another would have to evolve once I was married, but I felt like our friend-ship was strong enough to endure such a drastic change in both our lives. We were sisters by choice, and I always thought that was a stronger bond than simply being born to the same parents.

By the time we all arrived at Allan's, it was 4 o'clock London time. We had at least two hours before we would need to leave to get Abby and Sebastian back to Lakewood. Abby didn't bother with ringing the doorbell to Allan's house, and simply stepped inside like it was a second home to her.

"Angela!" Abby called from the foyer.

Angela came bounding down the stairs from the second floor and flew into Abby's arms, laughing.

"Can you believe it?" she asked Abby, full of joy and excitement. "He's really serious about changing this time. It's totally different than the last few times he's tried."

"Well, I hope it works out, Ang," Abby told her happy friend while kissing her affectionately on the cheek. "I know you try to pretend the way he is doesn't affect you, but I know it does."

Angela looked at Sebastian. "Hiya, you must be Abby's new squeeze."

"Pleased to meet you," Sebastian said with a slight bow in Angela's direction.

Angela looked to me. The unvoiced pleading in her eyes told me she hoped my presence would help her father overcome his fear of the outside world.

"Where is Allan?" Brand asked.

"He's still in his room," Angela answered, tugging her lower lip in worry, with her teeth. "I was hoping you and Lilly could go in there and get him. He might feel braver if she's with him."

We didn't have to be asked twice. Angela opened up the hidden doors leading to Allan's sterile environment. After passing through the decontamination chamber, we stepped in to find Allan sitting on one of the metal stools inside his glass bubble. He was dressed in a nicely-tailored grey pinstriped suit, with a white shirt and grey silk tie. The trepidation on his face had me worried. Angela was so sure her father was finally strong enough to face his fears. I was glad she wasn't with us to see Allan's anxiety. It didn't take long for Allan to realize we were in his space. When his eyes rested on me, they immediately lit up, and his anxiety seemed to fade away a small bit.

He stood from his chair and opened the door to come out and meet us halfway.

"I'm so glad you both could make it," he said, trying to put on a brave face.

I knew he was nervous about leaving his safety net, and venturing out into his house for what would be a prolonged period, at least long enough to eat supper.

I let go of Brand's hand and walked up to Allan. I wasn't sure how he would react, but if he was serious about changing his life and providing his daughter with a better way to live than the care-taker role she had been forced to play all these years, he needed to be nurtured and, at the same time, tested to see how far his limits could be stretched.

I put my hand on Allan's forearm. He didn't flinch away. He even seemed to relax a bit under my touch.

"It's so good to see you again, Allan," I told him. "Thank you for inviting us back to your home. I've been looking forward to it."

A genuine smile graced his face. "I'm glad you're here." He put one of his hands on top of the one I had on his arm. "Shall we go out and join the others?"

I stood by Allan's side, never taking my hand off his arm, and letting him keep his hold over mine as we left his self-imposed prison cell.

When we stepped out of the room and joined the others, who were still standing in the foyer, I thought I saw tears shimmer in Angela's eyes. The pride she felt for her father couldn't have been more evident. I felt a small sense of pride in being able to help give her hope for a brighter future.

From the way Allan looked at things inside his home as we made our way to the dining room, I had to assume it was the first time he had ever seen them himself. He scrutinized every detail, and told Angela where he thought things should be changed. She didn't seem to mind his direction at all. In fact, she more often than not completely agreed with his assessment.

Dinner was an easy, comfortable affair, and everyone had a great time together. I sat beside Allan, so I could touch his arm casually if I saw him slipping away from us and into obsession. He still held onto some old habits, like wiping his utensils ten times each with his napkin before using them for the first time, but it seemed like a small enough indulgence to let slip by. He was making such wonderful progress, and seemed to enjoy our companionship and light conversation.

By the end of the meal, it was time for us to go back home. The sun was just setting and the moon was sure to follow in its wake.

"Perhaps," Allan said as we were getting ready to make our departure, "you could show me where your home is one day soon. I think it might be too much for me this evening, but I would like to give Angela the opportunity to visit Abby on occasion."

"Of course, Allan," Brand said with a smile, showing how extremely pleased he was with Allan's simple request. "Any time you're ready."

We made our goodbyes and promised to come back for another visit soon. When we phased Abby and Sebastian back to Malcolm's house, Abby said, "Well, I think that went better than Angela could have hoped for. And she owes it all to you, love." Abby gave me a hug and a kiss on the cheek.

"I'm glad I could help," I answered. "I just wish I knew why I can."

CHAPTER 19

Will called Saturday morning to inform us that he had gone to Jackson on Friday, but wasn't able to find Dr. Lucas Hunter. Apparently, the doctor was on an unexpected vacation. The nurse Will talked to was quite flustered about it, saying she had never known Dr. Hunter to go on vacation in the ten years she'd worked for him. It was uncharacteristic of him to dump all of his patients onto another doctor, while he took time off. He didn't even leave a way for them to contact him. Will was able to get the address of Dr. Hunter's home, but found the place empty. From the information gathered, we were all sure Lucas Hunter was no longer himself, but a body possessed by one of Will's kind.

The rest of my week was normal, by my standards. I met all my classes, went to work, and came home to Brand in the evenings. I tried to enjoy the lull of normalcy in my life while I could. I was sure it wouldn't last for long. I also found time to go to the gynecologist my mother recommended, in order to get my first prescription of birth control.

On the night of the Halloween dance, Tara and I got ready in our apartment. I wanted to be there when Tara's date came to pick her up. I still hadn't met him, and wanted to at least check him out before she left with a complete stranger. Tara just rolled her eyes at me when I told her why I wanted to meet Aaron.

"Girl, he's just taking me to this dance. I don't plan on marrying the boy."

"But is he someone you might end up dating? If he is, I'd like to get to know him."

Tara shrugged. "Can't say for sure. I don't know him all that well. I just wanted to go to this dance, and he offered to take me."

Seeing that I wasn't going to get a lot of cooperation from Tara, I decided to bide my time and make my own decision about Aaron.

I told Brand I would phase to his house after I met Tara's date.

When I showed him the costume he would be wearing to the dance, the first thing he said was, "I assume Tara picked this out?"

"Of course she did," I told him. "You *are* Prince Charming, after all."

"You won't disappear on me at midnight, will you?" he teased.

"I'll try not to," I told him.

Tara's date picked her up at a quarter to eight. He was dressed as what I could only categorize as a pimp. He was wearing a black velvet-looking long coat, trimmed with fake tiger fur at the collar, with an oversized matching pimp hat and tiger-skin platform boots. He wore a pair of black slacks, but no shirt. There was a large gold chain around his neck with a dollar sign medallion. To top off the costume, he wore a pair of red-tinted sunglasses trimmed in gold, with dollar signs at the corners that covered almost half of his face.

I wasn't sure I cared for Tara going out with someone dressed in such a getup. I mean, seriously, if he was the pimp, what was she supposed to be?

After making pleasant conversation with him for a few

minutes while Tara finished getting ready, I decided the costume was just a costume. Aaron was definitely not a Leroy. Whether he was a Simon was hard to say, since the former didn't show his true colors until well into their relationship. But Aaron seemed a decent enough guy. He even took off his hat and glasses while he talked with me, which definitely earned him some brownie points for politeness.

"I'll be staying here tonight," I told Tara. I didn't want her out with a stranger and not have someone waiting at the apartment for her. It also gave me a chance to make sure Aaron knew that someone would be expecting her back home safe and sound, and at a decent hour.

"Ok, girl," Tara winked at me, understanding my motives for saying what I did in front of Aaron. "I'll see you and Brand at the dance."

After they left, I went to my room to put on my Cinderella costume. It was a lot larger and more cumbersome than I had origi-nally thought when I first saw it in the store display. It was about a third of the size of my wedding dress but, still, for a dance, it might give me problems. The dress was made of light blue satin with white satin brocade peplums on either side of the waistline. The costume came with a multilayered petticoat, long white gloves, jeweled choker, and rhinestone tiara. The low-cut top half of the dress had me worried at first. I was showing a lot more cleavage than I had intended to. Nevertheless, Tara assured me it wasn't so low that it made me look indecent.

Tara helped me put my hair up earlier that evening in the same up-do Malcolm had designed for me the night Brand proposed. My hair bore no resemblance to Cinderella's, since it was the complete opposite of blonde, but it did look elegant enough to belong to a princess. When I studied my reflection in the mirror, I really did almost feel like I belonged in a fairy tale. It made me think about what would be happening in only three more weeks. I would be at my wedding, walking down the aisle to marry my Prince Charming, for better or for worse. I was praying we would have more 'better' than 'worse', though.

I quickly put on a pair of ballet-style slippers on my feet. I knew if I had to deal with the petticoat all night, I didn't need to add high heels to an already-precarious equation, or I might end up looking more like Alice in Wonderland, falling down rabbit holes all evening long.

When I phased to Brand's house, he was adjusting the gold sash that crossed from his left shoulder to his right hip. The costume was simple, but the way he filled it out made my heart miss a beat. The white jacket was trimmed with gold satin fabric at the cuffs and neckline. On each shoulder was a black epaulette trimmed with gold fringe. It even had a couple of fake medals pinned to the left side of the gold sash. There was a narrow maroon leather belt around the waist, which matched his pants in color.

"You really do look like Prince Charming," I told him, unable to move for fear that my legs would betray the effect he was having on me.

He grinned at me, and I watched as his eyes traveled over the length of my costume only to come back up and openly stare at the cleavage the dress so brazenly displayed.

"I definitely like your costume," he said, coming to stand in front of me with an appreciative grin on his face. "I like it a lot."

I felt my cheeks flush as I looked down at the tops of my breasts. "Do you think it's too much?"

"No, my love. You look lovely," he told me, leaning down to kiss my perfect red- stained lips lightly. "Shall we go, my princess?" he asked, offering me his arm to take, as any prince would do.

We drove Brand's car to the dance. I almost wished we had just phased there. The parking lot outside the indoor stadium was so full we ended up parking almost a quarter of a mile away from the entrance. Luckily, Brand had been there before to watch an exhibition basketball game before school started and was able to phase us to the entrance, so I wouldn't have to walk so far in my cumbersome dress.

The inside of the stadium was decorated with a plethora of orange, gold, and black Mylar balloons, streamers, and fake head- stones. There must have been at least one or two smoke machines in operation, because the floor was covered with a thin layer of wispy white smoke, to give the dance an added feel of graveyard spookiness. The spotlights were covered with red and blue filters, casting an eerie glow across the room. There was a band playing on an elevated stage underneath the scoreboard.

I immediately searched through the sizable crowd to locate our friends. It didn't take me long to find Tara and Aaron. They were boogying on the dance floor, keeping in character, gyrating as if they were at a disco party. Tara waved at me when she saw me looking at her, and pointed over to one of the tables set up with refreshments.

I'm not sure what I expected Malcolm to show up as. To be honest, I guess I thought he would wear a black cape and come as a vampire. The ironic statement of wearing such a costume would have fit his personality. But, as usual, he surprised me.

Malcolm and Will were standing beside the refreshment table Tara had pointed to, talking to a couple of girls I didn't recognize; not that I knew many people on campus anyway. Will was dressed like Lancelot, resplendent in a costume of chainmail and black tunic with a gold griffin embroidered across the front. Malcolm was dressed like an Egyptian pharaoh. Dressed is a loose term for how he was clothed. All his costume consisted of was a knee-length hieroglyphic print skirt, large leather collar with gold-colored trim, and matching armbands and headscarf. It looked like he was carrying a riding crop of some sort in his hands. I understood why he had picked the costume. It displayed his muscular upper torso and legs, since there wasn't any cloth to get in the way, but I instantly noticed there was something different about Malcolm. His skin color was darker than it should have been. I remembered him telling me that one of the ways I could tell if he had broken our bargain and consumed human blood was a change in his skin color. I was instantly worried he had done something very bad.

The blonde and brunette Malcolm and Will were talking to were dressed a bit trampy for my taste. The blonde had on a naughty nurse's outfit that looked more like a corseted white teddy with red piping and three-inch lace trimmed skirt. She wore white fishnet stockings and red stiletto heels to complete the look. The brunette was dressed in a slim-fitting black faux-leather mini-dress, which zipped up in the front and a pair of knee-high boots. I assumed her outfit was supposed to resemble a police uniform, since she also wore a cop hat and had a pair of silver handcuffs dangling from her hands.

Malcolm must have felt me looking at him, because his eyes soon met mine. He said something to the girl in the police costume and handed her his riding crop before making his way towards us through the crowd.

"We wondered if you were going to show up," he said as he approached us. "Will and I have been perusing the delicate young flowers here for almost half an hour."

"She doesn't look all that delicate," I said, nodding toward Malcolm's admirer, who was openly staring at us, apparently offended by being left alone holding something for Malcolm like a servant. "You'd better watch out. She might use those cuffs on you if you misbehave."

"Well, I certainly hope so," Malcolm's cheeky grin irritated me for some reason. He held out his hand to me as the band began to play a slow song. "Could I have the first dance, fair princess?" he asked.

I looked at Brand to make sure he was ok with it.

"Go ahead," he told me. "I need to speak with Will anyway to see if he's been able to find out more about Lucas Hunter." Brand looked at Malcolm with a silent warning in his eyes.

"I promise to be on my best behavior," Malcolm held his hands up as if to prove he had nothing up his sleeves, if he had been wearing sleeves that is.

Malcolm took my hand and led me onto the dance floor.

"You look lovely this evening, dearest," he said, holding me as close to him as my bulky dress would allow.

"And you look a bit too tan," I quipped. "You haven't been doing anything you shouldn't, have you?"

Malcolm actually looked hurt by my accusation. "I promised you I wouldn't do that anymore, Lilly. Why would you think to even ask me such a question?"

I immediately regretted having jumped to the wrong conclusion. But how else had he developed such dark skin in such a short amount of time?

"Then how do you explain why your skin is so dark?"

"Have you ever seen a pale pharaoh?" he asked. "I couldn't come without a tan. There's a salon in town that sprays them on."

"It's fake?"

"Yes, completely fake."

I felt bad now. "I'm sorry. I shouldn't have jumped to conclusions. Will you forgive me?"

From the lopsided grin on Malcolm's face, I knew forgiveness wouldn't come cheap.

"I might if you do something for me."

"What?" I asked, completely suspicious.

"I want to spend a day with you alone before you marry. Could we do that?"

"Why before I'm married? It's not like Brand has me on a leash, Malcolm. He's not going to make me stop being friends with you just because I'm his wife."

"I'd rather not think about Brand when we're together on that day, and if we waited until you were married, that's all I would think about. Please, dearest. Just one day?"

I didn't see why it was so important to him, but I also didn't see what it could hurt to spend a day with my friend before I became a married woman.

"All right, if that's what you want. Now, do you forgive me?"

"Yes." Malcolm grinned in satisfaction and his eyes twinkled as if he'd just won the lottery.

When the song was over, he dutifully walked me over to Brand. I saw that the girl cop was eyeing my fiancé with more interest than she should have been. Not that I could blame her for practically salivating over him. He was the most handsome man at the party, though I guess I could have been a little prejudice in my opinion.

"Hey, Lilly!" I turned around and saw Malik walking toward me with a pretty black girl on his arm. I assumed she must be Cheryl.

Malik was dressed as Jack Sparrow, and Cheryl seemed to be dressed as a bar wench.

"You look great," he said as they came to stand beside us.

"You too," I told him, taking in the braided wig, tri-corn hat, and brown leather duster he wore.

"Y'all need to come on and dance," Tara called from the dance floor. She and Aaron had danced their way over to us. I saw her give a sideways glance at Malik and Cheryl, but her attention was soon diverted by Aaron as he swooped her up into his arms and twirled her around, causing her to giggle.

We all had a good time dancing and laughing together for most of the night, at least until I found out Malik and Tara were missing.

It first came to my attention when I was making my way back to the dance from a short trip to the ladies' room. Cheryl approached me and asked if I had seen Malik. It was getting close to midnight and she wanted to go home.

"I've been looking for him for like thirty minutes," she complained. "You have any idea where he might be?"

"No," I told her, completely confused by Malik's unexpected absence. "I haven't seen him."

"Hey, Lilly, you seen Tara?" Aaron came to join Cheryl and me.

"No," I told him.

"You think you could go in the ladies' restroom and see if she's in there?"

"I was just in there. I didn't see her."

"She's been gone for like half an hour."

"I should have known," Cheryl said, crossing her arms in front of her ample bosom. "All Malik talked about was Tara tonight. They're probably off together somewhere."

"You think?" Aaron asked, not completely sure he agreed with Cheryl's assessment.

"Yeah, that's what I think," she replied, completely miffed. "Hey, you mind taking me home, since our dates are off together doing who knows what? I need a ride."

"Well, I hate to leave without knowing Tara's ok. I just don't see her as the type to ditch one guy for another one at a party."

"She's not," I defended, giving Cheryl a withering gaze for talking about Tara in such a defamatory way. "But, you should go ahead and take Cheryl home," I suggested. "It is getting late. I'll look for them while you're gone. I can probably find Tara before you get back."

"Ok."

Aaron earned a few more brownie points then as he took care of Cheryl for me.

I was about to search out the guys to help me find Tara and Malik when I felt someone touch my shoulder. I turned to see who it was hoping it was either Tara or Malik. Unfortunately, it wasn't either of them.

"Hello, Lilly," Robert said, grabbing me by the arm and phasing us outside the building before I could call for help.

"Don't even think about phasing back inside," he hissed, gripping my arm so tight I thought I could actually feel my hand go numb from the loss of blood.

I was surprised he knew I could phase. As far as I could remember, he had never seen me do it.

"Yes, I know about your powers," he said, after seeing my reaction. "He told me all about them. But if you want to save your friends, you need to do exactly what I tell you to do."

"What are you talking about?" I asked, already fearing his next words.

"I have that fairy and your other friend, the human. I have to admit fairy blood does have a certain unique quality to it." He licked his lips with his tongue, as if removing the last traces of Malik from his lips.

My own blood ran cold. "You didn't..." I literally couldn't make the words come out of my mouth to finish the question.

"Not yet," he grinned, relishing my response to what he was implying. "I've only tasted a bit of what they have to offer. Whether or not I go back and finish what I started is completely up to you."

If I could just get him to show me where they were, I could phase them to safety.

"I know what you're thinking," he said. "And no, I'm not going to make it that easy for you. I told you we were going to play a little game, and I meant it. You don't honestly think I would make it that easy for you to get your friends back, do you?"

"What do you want?"

"I want to see you grovel at my feet," he said, savoring the power he knew he held over me. "I want to watch you suffer just for the right to beg me for your friends' lives. I have a few more of your friends with the fairy and human, a few of your werewolf friends. Now, let's see, there's Abby, of course; I couldn't very well not bring your future stepdaughter. Then there's Sebastian. I've always wanted to see him play in one of my games, but Malcolm's never wanted to bring him. And, of course, poor little Angela. She just can't seem to catch a break. Her father saw me take her, you know, but he's too completely paralyzed by his own fears to do anything to help her," Robert chuckled.

"What sort of game are you talking about?"

"We like to call it Bait. You see, some of my Watcher compatriots and I like to pit our children against each other to see who is the fastest, the most agile. We set up a couple of humans as bait somewhere in a secluded area, and let our children loose to see who can reach them first. There's usually a bit of fighting between them in the beginning, but as soon as they catch the scent of fresh blood from the victims, they forget all about each other and let their bloodlust take over completely."

"No," I covered my mouth with a shaking hand. Not only were Malik and Tara in danger of losing their lives, but Abby, Sebastian, and Angela were in jeopardy of losing their souls if they were allowed to drink human blood. It was the one thing all of my Watcher friends had been protecting their children from all these years. I couldn't let it happen.

"What do you want me to do?" I asked, determined to find a way to stop what Robert had set in motion.

"Oh, I don't know, Lilly. Why don't we start with something simple? Why don't you start by bowing down to me?"

I knew he wasn't going to make this easy for me. He would try to humiliate me as much as he could.

I did what he asked and got on my knees. At least the petticoat under the dress came in handy and provided a cushion for my knees and legs against the cold concrete.

"See? That wasn't so hard, now was it?" he asked, knowing I resented the hold he had on me in that moment.

"Will you take me to them?"

"I might, but first I think I need to hear a little more pleading in your voice. You don't seem completely convinced that I'll let your friends die so gruesomely. Maybe you've never seen a pack of werewolves tear into a human body before. I can assure you, there won't be anything left when they get through."

I tried to fight against letting my anger show. "Please take me to them, Robert."

"There's just something about the way you're saying it," he said, sounding disappointed. "It just doesn't sound like it's coming from your heart, Lilly."

"*Please*, I'm begging you," I bowed my head to him in a gesture of complete supplication. "Take me to them."

"Well, now," he said, sounding genuinely pleased for the first time. "That's more like it. I hoped it would just take a little persuasion on my part to bring you in line."

He placed his hand on top of my head, and I was suddenly kneeling on a dirt- packed forest floor. I looked up to see the moon in the sky directly overhead. High- pitched howls of excitement and urgency from the wolf pack could be heard in the distance.

Robert tilted his head toward the sound, as if the howls were beautiful music playing. "Ahh, the children are searching for your friends."

"Please," I begged. "Where are they?"

"I'll give you a hint," he said, turning around and pointing straight ahead. "There's a clearing about a hundred yards that way somewhere. Your fairy friend has transformed into his animal, but it won't do him any good. I think he feels like he can protect the girl in that form better."

I sprang to my feet, intent on running as fast as I could to the spot Robert had pointed to. Before I could start running, I felt him grab and yank on my arm.

"Wait," he said, pulling me to him, forcing his mouth down onto mine. His warm, slimy tongue pushed its way between my lips. The thought of biting down on it occurred to me. But I knew if I did that, he wouldn't let me go without suffering some sort of repercussions, and that was time I couldn't afford to waste; not with so much at stake.

"Kiss me back," he ordered, cupping his hands on the sides of my face, forcing me to look into his lust-crazed eyes. "Or do you think your friends can survive without you for much longer?" he sneered.

I felt nauseated at the thought of having to pretend I enjoyed kissing a loathsome creature such as Robert. I shut my eyes so I wouldn't have to look at him and followed his lead in the kiss, trying to imagine that I was somewhere else, anywhere else. Every fiber in my body rebelled against complying with his wishes, and I had to quell my urge to shiver in revulsion for fear he would get mad and never let me go in time to save my friends.

I felt his hands leave my face and cup my breasts, fondling them roughly through the silk of my dress, tearing the material. A small whimper escaped my lips, which seemed to make him even more excited. I tried not to think about anything except finding Tara and Malik, and getting them to safety before the wolf pack hunted them down.

Robert finally released me, stumbling back like the kiss had affected him more than he had intended it to.

"Go," he whispered with a small jerk of his head in the direction I needed to run. I felt his eyes follow me as I sprinted away from him.

It was so dark I could barely make out where I was going. My dress wasn't helping matters, since it seemed to get caught on every branch I passed. Finally, I took a few precious seconds to pull down the petticoat and leave it on the forest floor. I hiked up the blue silk and ran as fast as I could, hoping I wouldn't be too late. Branches lashed at my body, but I didn't have time to care. I had to save them.

But which direction were they? I could barely see in the pitch black. I feared I wouldn't be able to find them in time. Suddenly, I saw a soft blue light appear about twenty feet in front of me. It was the ghostly shape of the eight-year-old Will.

"Follow me!" he shouted, and started to run ahead of me, leading me to where I needed to go.

"Lilly!"

I heard the cry come from somewhere beside me. I slowed down long enough to see that it was Allan.

"Follow me," I yelled to him, not wanting to lose sight of my guide. I could tell Allan was having trouble being outside in the strange environment of the forest, but I didn't have time to deal with his peculiar idiosyncrasies. I had to find Tara and Malik before it was too late.

Allan did as I told him and ran along beside me.

After a few minutes, my ghostly guide disappeared as we came to the clearing Robert said I would find.

"Tara!" I screamed so loud, the sound of my hysterical voice bounced off the trees around us in a shrill cacophony.

The only answer was the growl of a cat. I ran toward the noise, hoping what I heard was Malik. Robert had said he'd transformed into his animal form.

When I found them, Tara was lying on the ground, unconscious, with a black panther licking the wound at her neck. I could hear the wolf pack crashing through the brush at the edge of the clearing. They would be on us at any moment.

"Allan, you need to phase them somewhere safe!"

"But, Angela..."

"Listen to me," I yelled. "If you want to protect Angela, you need to get these two away now! Then come back here to get the others. Now go! They're almost here!"

It didn't take Allan long to come to his senses and phase Tara and Malik to safety.

Before I knew it, I was surrounded by at least twenty werewolves, preparing to launch themselves on the spot where Tara and Malik's blood still stained the ground at my feet.

"Stop!" I ordered.

Amazingly enough they all stopped dead in their tracks, as if I had put up some sort of barrier around myself. In the dark, I could make out their eyes all staring down at me, watching me.

"Kneel!" I ordered again, not sure if it would work, but not seeing how it could hurt to try.

In unison, they all knelt as best they could on their backward-looking legs.

"Well," Robert appeared beside me. "I didn't see this coming." He studied the wolf pack in wonder. "You're full of surprises, Lilly."

"Abby! Sebastian! Angela!" I called, ignoring Robert. "Come forward!"

Three of the wolves stood and came closer to me. Allan quickly reappeared beside me, apparently having found a safe place to deposit Malik and Tara.

"Take them home," I told Allan, having already resigned myself to the fate I knew I would have to endure. "Tell Brand I love him," I couldn't help the crack in my voice as I tried to rein in my emotions, "and that I'm sorry. I don't have any choice."

"Just leave, Lilly," Allan implored.

"I can't," I told him. "It won't matter. Robert will just do this again if I don't go with him now. Don't you see that? They'll never be safe."

"I'll bring back help," Allan said, thinking a fight was what was called for in this situation.

"Oh, I don't think that would make a difference." Robert snapped his fingers. Almost immediately, there were at least thirty Watchers surrounding us, all dressed in their black feathered cloaks, a sign that they were ready for a hunt. "I doubt you and your friends could take all of them."

I turned to Robert. I knew it was finally time to meet the person who had been so determined to end my life over the past ten years. If I had to face death, I wanted to do it on my own terms, without regret. My sacrifice would protect the lives of those I loved. As long as I kept that thought in my mind, my fear of dying would have to take a backseat. At least I would finally understand why my death seemed so important to the person who had been trying to kill me since I was child.

"I'm ready," I told Robert. He grabbed me by the shoulder and walked us deeper into the forest, while the other Watchers phased out of the clearing with their children in tow.

"Just in case your friends decide to come back," he explained. "I doubt they will look for my trail here. They'll have quite a few false trails to follow first. By the time they figure things out, it'll be over."

I was actually thankful for Robert's thoroughness. I didn't want Brand, Malcolm, or Will to try to rescue me. It would be futile at this point.

I took a deep breath, steeling myself to meet death as Robert phased us out of the forest.

CHAPTER 20

We appeared on a beach under a 'J'-shaped palm tree. The sun was just rising over the watery horizon, casting an orange glow against the pale blue sky. The lapping of the water against the sand at my feet did little to help calm my aching heart. Would this be the last sunrise I ever saw?

"Enjoy it while you can," Robert snorted, as if reading my thoughts. "He's been waiting a long time to get rid of you. I doubt I'll have very long to wait before he tells me to finish you off for him. You'd be dead by now if he didn't have this absurd notion that you deserve to know the truth before you die."

"What do you get out of killing me for him?" I asked. If I understood anything, I knew Robert wouldn't be doing someone else's dirty work for nothing.

"I get to stay alive," he told me, obviously not liking the fact that his life had been on the line with my capture.

"I didn't think your kind could die."

"Not by a human's hand or even our own," he smirked. "But there are special circumstances when we can be killed like anyone else."

It made me think of what Will had once said about Lucifer.

One of the reasons he followed Lucifer's orders so explicitly was because he could destroy him. I knew it wasn't Lucifer who had been trying to kill me all these years. He was trying to save me for plans of his own. So who was threatening Robert?

It wasn't long before I felt him getting closer. It was just like the time I was in Justin's prison cell, waiting for him, before I knew I could phase to safety. I could go again if I wanted to but didn't have the heart. I knew if I didn't stay to face my executioner, Robert would hurt my family just to get to me again. Things had to end now, one way or another. There wasn't any point in running away. There was nowhere to hide. I would have to sacrifice myself in order to keep the ones I loved safe. I only hoped Brand could forgive me for my decision. His heartache would run deeper and last longer than anyone else's.

I could feel the heat of my executioner's aura surrounding me. It was stifling, like being too close to the sun. However, I couldn't hear his thoughts this time. I got the impression he was shielding them from me, knowing I could read his mind as easily as I knew what *I* was thinking.

I couldn't see him at first. I just felt his presence beside me. When I looked at where I knew he was, all I could see was a slight shimmer against the white sand, like a mirage. He had no true form that I could make out.

"You've done your job," he said to Robert. "Now go and leave us."

"How long should I wait until I can come back to finish her off?" Robert asked, bowing to the entity beside me.

"Your assistance is no longer required. I will not need for you to come back."

"But... you promised I could have her!"

The heat of Robert's little tantrum shocked me. Even I had the presence of mind to know talking to the entity beside me like that was a bad idea.

"You will not address me like that, you filthy mongrel!" The entity beside me roared with absolute authority. "I did not give you permission to put innocent lives in danger just for your own amusement. You will not get what you were promised, and I order you not to bother Lilly's friends again. Is that understood?"

"Yes," Robert reluctantly whispered, glancing up at me. I could tell he hated being dressed-down in front of me. "But I thought the whole point of my capturing her was so I could kill her for you."

"I will handle things from here. You need to leave now. She and I have much to discuss with one another."

Robert looked at me. I could see the longing in his eyes to finish what he had started in the forest. He certainly hadn't planned to kill me before he was able to satisfy his urges.

"Maybe I'll see you again one day, Lilly, if you survive."

Then he was gone, leaving me alone with the being that had been trying to kill me for so many years.

I turned toward the shimmering apparition beside me, feeling a lot calmer now that Robert was gone.

"Why can't I see you?" I asked.

"You are seeing me," he answered. "At least as well as your half-angel eyes can see me."

"Who are you?"

"My name is Uriel."

"What are you?"

"I'm an archangel."

"Did God send you to kill me, like He did to Lilith's children?"

"Do you really think He would order the slaying of the innocent?"

"That's what the angels I know told me. What are you saying? They weren't killed?"

"I'm not allowed to tell you what happened to them. However, I can tell you He was never behind the previous attempts on your life. And, before now, He never ordered me to stop trying to eliminate you and the threat you pose."

I grasped onto the hope his statement provided. "What do you mean, before now?"

"He's ordered me to stand down and let things run their natural course. I'm not allowed to interfere anymore."

"Why have you been trying to kill me?"

"I felt it was necessary in order to fulfill my duty."

"What duty?"

"To protect Heaven."

"Why am I such a danger?"

Uriel was silent. I knew he was still there, because I could still feel the heat of his presence and see his shimmering form. I tried to listen to his thoughts, but he was hiding them too well from me.

"I can't tell you that, Lilly. I wish I could, so you could decide for yourself whether your life is worth the chaos to come."

"Can't you tell me more than that? Anything?" I pleaded.

"The fallen should be able to figure it out. They just haven't thought of it yet. Look to yourself, Lilly. You have the potential to become even more powerful than all the angels in Heaven and on Earth. You are the key to everything."

"The first time, when Justin had me and you were coming to speak with me, you know I heard your thoughts and felt your feelings then. You kept thinking one life was worth sacrificing to save so many. Please, tell me why I'm a danger so I can understand what needs to be done."

"I have given you the only clues I'm allowed to give. You need to discover the answers on your own. I am forbidden to interfere any further."

"Can you at least tell me if we're on the right track? We think Lucifer wants to use me to get back into Heaven for some reason. Am I special because I contain Lilith's power to enter Heaven?"

"It is not the only reason. But, I think you have already figured that out. You need to search deeper."

"Please," I begged. "You know what I need to do! Just tell me!"

"I have done everything within my power to eliminate you as a threat," Uriel said. It was a little disconcerting to hear the regret in his voice at not being able to accomplish his mission. "Trying to kill you was not pleasurable for me, but I saw no other alternative."

"Are you saying I have to die in order to stop what's going to happen?"

"Once you learn the true treachery of Lucifer's plans, I hope you will be strong enough to choose the right path." He paused for a few seconds before saying, "There is no sin in a martyr's death."

"Are you implying that I should kill myself in order to stop what's going to happen?"

"That is not for me to say," he said cryptically.

"Has God told you anything? Does He know what will happen?"

"He has not shared His thoughts with me but, obviously, He has hope you will do what is right."

"Why has He ordered you to stop trying to kill me now? Has something changed?"

"I have no idea why He has chosen to step in now. I can only assume you have chosen to do something which will stop Lucifer's plans for the future."

"Then we shouldn't have anything to worry about."

"Perhaps. But you humans are fickle creatures. You may have chosen the right path for now, but what happens if you stray from it? Are we all to be doomed because of one wrong decision?"

"I won't stray," I promised him. "If He believes in me, then I have to believe in myself."

"I hope you are right, Lilly, for all our sakes."

In an instant, Uriel was gone. I felt him leave before I actually noticed that the shimmering of his presence was no longer in front of me.

I was filled with a new sense of hope for the future. Maybe Brand had been right all this time. Perhaps God actually did have a plan for us.

I quickly phased back home, desperate to see my family again.

When I got home, I was surprised to see only Will in the living room. He was pacing in front of the fireplace. As soon as he saw me, the worry in his eyes disappeared. He rushed towards me, taking me in his arms and holding me tightly.

"Where have you been?" he demanded, almost harshly, though the tone in his voice was filled with worry so I knew it wasn't intentional.

"I'd rather wait until we're all together so I only have to explain things once," I told him. "Where are they? Are Tara and Malik ok?"

"They're at Allan's house. Allan took Brand and Malcolm back to the forest to search for you."

"And Abby, Sebastian, and Angela?"

"They're at Allan's, too, in the room he has for Angela."

I took Will's hand and phased us to Allan's home. I knew Allan might not appreciate me bringing Will along, because of his prejudice against the fallen angels, but I really didn't care. Will was part of my family, and I wasn't about to leave him behind.

We were standing in the foyer when we heard the shuffling of feet and the sound of hushed voices emanating from the sitting room to our right. When we stepped inside the room, I saw Tara lying on the formal couch with Malik kneeling beside her. He was only wearing a black and white plaid blanket tied around his waist and a thick gauze bandage taped over his left shoulder. I assumed his state of undress was because he'd lost his clothes when he transformed into the black panther I had seen in the forest.

There was a tall, lanky man of about sixty, with grey hair and a mustache, dressed in a maroon velvet housecoat, at the foot of the couch, talking to Allan.

"I've stopped the bleeding, but she's lost a lot of blood," he was saying to Allan. "She should be all right after she gets some rest. I'm afraid the bite mark will leave a nasty scar, though. There isn't much I can do for that."

Allan looked up as we came further into the room to stand beside Malik.

He walked to me and gave me a hug. "I thought..." He couldn't make himself finish the sentence.

"I thought so, too," I replied, looking down at Tara. Guilt wracked my body. She looked like a corpse. Her ebony skin was ashen in color. If I hadn't heard the man say she would be all right, when I came into the room, I would have thought she was already dead.

"Malik," I touched his naked shoulder and felt him jump. He hadn't even realized I was standing in the room.

"Lilly?" His eyes slowly left Tara's face as he looked up at me. He stood, letting go of Tara's hand and hugged me. "I tried to protect her," he said to me, more in an attempt to convince himself that he had done all he could to keep Tara from being harmed than convince me of his efforts. "I tried..."

I pulled away from Malik and saw the distress and guilt in his watery eyes.

"There wasn't anything more you could have done. If this is anyone's fault, it's mine. Don't blame yourself. You did the best you could under the circumstances."

Malik nodded his head like he understood what I was saying, but the haunted look in his eyes told me Robert had done his best to make Malik suffer while playing his sadistic games with Tara.

"He didn't do anything else to her, did he?" I asked, knowing Robert's predilections ran toward the sexual spectrum.

"No," Malik said, seeming to understand the meaning behind my question.

"She'll be fine after some rest," the stranger in the room said to me.

"Who are you?" I asked, trying to remember if I had seen him in Allan's house before.

"This is Elliot," Allan answered. "He helps us with certain things around the house."

"Shouldn't we get a doctor?" I asked, not understanding why a servant had been put in charge of taking care of my best friend's medical needs.

"He's a licensed doctor, among other things," Allan explained. "You can trust him."

Brand and Malcolm phased in behind the couch Tara laid on. Both of their faces were absent of hope until they saw I was standing in the room. Brand had me in his arms, kissing me like he had completely lost all control over what he was doing, not caring that we were in a room full of people watching us.

"Where have you been?" he asked me, pulling away to search my face for any damage or signs that I had been hurt.

"I finally met the person who's been trying to kill me," I told him.

I told them all what I had learned from Uriel.

"*We* know the answer?" Will asked. "You're sure he said that?"

"Trust me. I have every word he said etched in my memory."

"What could we be forgetting?" Malcolm pondered. "It's obviously something we should know about."

I saw Tara stir on the couch. Malik hadn't left his position on the floor beside her, and immediately sat up on his knees, hovering over her slightly as she opened her eyes.

"Where am I?" she asked him weakly.

"You're safe," he told her, caressing her cheek gently with the back of his hand, unable to hold back his tears of relief.

I went to her, kneeling beside Malik.

"How do you feel?" I asked.

"Tired. My neck hurts," she cried.

"Here," Elliot said, handing me a glass of water and a couple of pills. "Have her take these for the pain before she goes back to sleep."

Without asking him to, Malik gently lifted Tara in his arms and sat back down on the couch with her in his lap, to make it easier for her to drink the water and take the pills. Once she was done, she rested her head against his shoulder and quickly fell back to sleep.

I got instructions on how to care for Tara's pain and wound

from Elliot. I also arranged to bring him to our home the next day to check on her.

"I want to keep her close," I told Brand.

"We can make up the spare bedroom for her," he replied.

It didn't take us long to make sure we had everything we needed to bring Tara home with us. Malcolm took Abby and Sebastian back to his house and asked us to call him if we needed anything else.

Will and Malik refused to leave Tara's side, even after we brought her home and had her resting in the spare bedroom. We brought in chairs for them to sit in to make their vigil more comfortable. Will quickly turned on Brand's computer in the room, determined to start his own research into Uriel's cryptic statements.

Brand made me change clothes and lie down on our bed with him.

"You have to be exhausted from what you've been through tonight," he argued. "You're probably just running on adrenaline right now. Lie down for a little while, and if you aren't asleep within a few minutes, I won't badger you anymore."

I cuddled up next to him and tried to relax. If only I knew what had caused God to order Uriel to cease his attempts on my life. What had changed? The warmth of Brand's body against mine helped lull my tired mind and body. He was right, as usual. I was a lot more tired than I'd thought and quickly found myself drifting off to sleep.

CHAPTER 21

I was standing inside the house Malcolm built for me, looking out the picture window at the snowcapped mountain and lake in the distance. My eyes fell on the table in front of me and I saw the beautiful mango-wood bowl we had received as a wedding gift. It was filled with large red apples, because those were what I had been craving the past few months. My hands cradled the large bump of my belly as the child inside me kicked. I knew it had to be a boy. Only a man could kick so hard.

"Give me your hands," I told Brand as he came to stand behind me. I put his palms on top of my belly just as our son kicked again.

"He'll probably be a kicker for the NFL one day," Brand said, kissing me on the side of the neck, making my flesh break out in involuntary goose bumps like his touch so often did.

"Mommy!"

We turned at the sound of our daughter's excited voice as she ran down the stairs from the second floor of the house. She was almost three years old now, with a head full of chestnut hair like mine and beautiful grey eyes like her father. How quickly time passed when you were enjoying life. Brand bent down as she got closer and picked her up, holding her against his side.

"Mommy, will you come play princess with me?"

"Oh, not again," I said, pretending I wasn't interested in playing her favorite game. "Do I have to be the evil witch again, or can I be the beautiful, courageous princess this time?"

"I'm the princess," she said, as if not understanding how I could even conceive of asking such a question.

"Well, while you girls play princess, Daddy's going to go make you both some supper."

Brand kissed our daughter on the cheek, setting her back down on the floor.

"Ok, Daddy."

Brand kissed me on the lips before leaving us and heading to the kitchen at the back of the house.

"Can we play, Mommy, please?" Our daughter had the cutest look of pleading in her eyes. I wasn't sure who she had learned that from, probably her Uncle Malcolm teaching her bad habits again.

"Lilly."

I heard Brand call to me, and turned to see him standing only a couple of feet away from us.

"Aren't you supposed to be cooking us some fabulous gourmet meal for supper?" I asked. "I'm eating for two, you know, and we're both hungry."

"What is this place?" Brand asked, looking around him as if he'd never seen our house before.

"What are you talking about? It's our home in Colorado," I replied, wondering why he was acting as if he didn't know where he was. "We've lived here for a while now, Brand. Are you all right? Are you coming down with something?"

"Who is that?" he asked, nodding to our daughter. "And..." he stared at my protruding belly like he'd never seen a woman with child before, "are you pregnant, Lilly?"

"Go up and change into your princess costume, sweetie," I told our daughter, not wanting Brand's odd behavior to frighten her unnecessarily. "Mommy and Daddy need to talk for a minute. I'll be right up."

"Why's Daddy acting so funny?" she asked.

"Just go up to your room, please. I'll be there in a bit."

Without any more protest, she went back up the stairs.

"You act like you've never seen our daughter before, when you just saw her a minute ago," I said, coming to stand in front of Brand, who seemed unable to move on his own. I picked up one of his hands and laid it on my belly as our son began to kick again. "I swear he's going to kick his way out one of these days," I laughed.

"Lilly," Brand said, taking his hand away from my stomach like what he felt was unnatural. "This isn't real."

"What are you talking about?" I was getting worried about him now. "What isn't real?"

"My love, you're dreaming."

"Dreaming?"

"Yes, this is a dream. And somehow, you've brought me into it. I thought I would give you a nice dream tonight after everything you just went through with Robert and Uriel, but when I fell asleep, I found myself here, in your fantasy world."

"But," I could feel the sting of tears well in my eyes, "*this* is real. Our daughter..."

"Just a dream," he said gently, seeing how distraught I was becoming.

"No," I said firmly, determined to make him understand. "She's *real*. I can remember everything about her. I know her favorite color, what she likes to eat, her favorite games to play. My God, I know what she smells like! I remember giving birth to her and holding her in my arms for the first time. You saw her. She's real! And this baby," I said, touching my stomach. "He's real! I can feel him moving, living inside me."

"Lilly, it's just a dream. You need to wake up before you get more upset."

"No," I said stubbornly. "I'm not leaving our children."

I turned away from Brand and hurriedly made my way up the stairs to our daughter's room. I found her standing in front of a child-sized vanity, dressed in one of her frilly pink princess dresses, putting on the tiara I had bought for her the previous Christmas. I stood there staring at her, marveling at how perfect she was. It was then that I realized I had no idea what her name was.

She turned to me and smiled before slowly fading away.

I could feel things around me slowly being pulled away from me. I tried to hold on to the image of our daughter's smiling face and will her back into existence, but nothing seemed to work.

I opened my eyes. Brand was shaking my shoulders.

"Wake up," he kept saying.

I burst into tears, unable to control the sense of immense loss I felt. My chest felt empty, like the part of my heart where my children lived had been unceremoniously ripped out and thrown down a bottomless pit, forever out of my reach. Brand held me close to him, trying to soothe me as I cried uncontrollably over their absence.

"It all felt so real," I finally said between sobs. "I had memories of her. I had memories of us in that house. How could that be?"

"I'm not sure," Brand said, cradling me to him. "I've never been able to make a dream like that; not one where everything had a history and felt so real."

"It did feel real, didn't it?" I asked, concerned that maybe I was losing my mind.

"Yes, my love. It felt very real."

I sat there silently trying to etch everything I could remember from the dream into a lasting memory, before it had the chance to fade away as most dreams have a tendency to do over time. I didn't want to lose the feeling of joy and contentment I had felt seeing Brand with our daughter, and feeling the powerful movements of our son inside me. It was a future I desperately wanted, even if the dream had just been fabricated by some unknown longing I had buried deep inside my subconscious.

The future was uncertain and free-flowing. That was what Uriel had been trying to tell me. I knew the future for everyone I cared about would hinge on the decisions I made from this moment on. Maybe my dream was a sign, showing me a possible future for Brand and me. I held on to that thought, desperately clinging to the hope it gave me. I let myself be comforted in Brand's arms as he softly sang me a lullaby in a language I didn't understand. Exhaustion from crying finally made me drift off to sleep. I hoped to meet my daughter again someday, even if it were only in a dream.

The End

AUTHOR'S NOTE

Thank you so much for reading **Blessed**, book 2 in **The Watchers Trilogy**. If you have enjoyed this book please take a moment to leave a review. To leave a review please visit:

Blessed mybook.to/Blessed2

Thank you in advance for leaving a review for the book. I hope you have loved it as much as I do.

Sincerely,

S.J. West.

THE NEXT IN THE WATCHERS TRILOGY

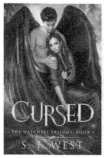

***Forgiven**, **The Watchers Trilogy**,* book 3
Get the last book in the trilogy today, and continue Lily & Brand's
the beautiful story.

In the finale to The Watchers Trilogy, Lilly and Brand prepare for
their wedding and search for more clues to uncover Lucifer's plans
for her. With the help of her fallen angel friends, Lilly must face
the ultimate battle between good and evil to decide the fate of both
Heaven and Earth.

Exclusively on Amazon, Free on KU!
http://mybook.to/Forgiven3

ABOUT THE AUTHOR

Once upon a time, a little girl was born on a cold winter morning in the heart of Seoul, Korea. She was brought to America by her parents and raised in the Deep South where the words ma'am and y'all became an integrated part of her lexicon. She wrote her first novel at the age of eight and continued writing on and off during her teenage years. In college she studied biology and chemistry and finally combined the two by earning a master's degree in biochemistry.

After that she moved to Yankee land where she lived for four years working in a laboratory at Cornell University. Homesickness and snow aversion forced her back South where she lives in the land, which spawned Jim Henson, Elvis Presley, Oprah Winfrey, John Grisham and B.B. King.

After finding her Prince Charming, she gave birth to a wondrous baby girl and they all lived happily ever after.

As always, you can learn about the progress on my books, get news about new releases, new projects and participate on amazing give-aways by signing up for my newsletter:

FB Book Page: www.facebook.com/SJWestBooks/

FB Author Page:

https://www.facebook.com/sandra.west.585112

Website: www.sjwest.com

Amazon: author.to/SJWest-Amazon

Goodreads:

https://www.goodreads.com/author/show/6561395.S_J_West

Bookbub: https://www.bookbub.com/authors/s-j-west

Newsletter Sign-up: http://eepurl.com/bQsosX

Instagram: @authorsjwest

Twitter: @SJWest2013

If you'd like to contact the author, you can email her to:
sandrawest481@gmail.com

Made in the USA
Coppell, TX
20 March 2020